This book is dedicated to survivors and families of drug addiction. A special thank you to the storytellers, friends, & artists that challenge the shame and lack of self-worth at the core of so much substance abuse.

Thank you Carmel. Thank you Rajiv. Thank you Arron.

MARK JAMES BIRKETT

WHAT ABOUT NICK?

MJ Birkett Publishing: Salisbury, UK
mark@mjbirkett.com

Illustrations & Cover by MJ Birkett Publishing

Mark@mjbirkett.com

Contents

PART I

LIVING WITH THE MONSTER

Chapter 1 – Remembering the backdoor

"She sat on the step by the back door. Her back leant against the grey, crumbly wall, and although her neck bent downward, her eyes stared up. The need in her eyes sprayed out into the back-porch like a gas that suffocated me. That stare taught me what true helplessness feels like. Proper teaching. I felt the entrapment she felt; like a fish caught on the end of a rod, it was a question of when not if I was pulled into her world; her emotions. Her addiction."

Nick paused. His stomach ached as if he had been fasting. He hadn't. It was the topic. Talking about his sister triggered his insides to knot, to tighten into clustered bundles of stressed tissue. Heeta stared at him deadpan. She was still too annoyed at what he had done to convey any compassion, but she at least stopped feeling like throwing a knife at him. Her silence encouraged him to continue.

"It couldn't have been more than a few minutes, but time stuck to us in that porch like a nasty sap. Neither of us wanted to be there. She wanted a tenner from mum so that she could escape – get another hit – and I have no idea what I wanted. I didn't want mum to give her any money. I didn't want her to do it anymore. But I didn't want her to stay on that step, in that much pain, either." Nick searched for words, but the truth was hollow. Empty. He had stopped wanting on that step.

"I suppose I became numb. It was too hard to want, so I didn't. I sloped and leant against the porch-wall; the backdoor was open between us. Her eyes rested on mine. And I guess I stared back and slowly…" He could not finish.

Heeta by this point, had not only stopped feeling like throwing the knife at him, she had metaphorically put it down on the coffee table. Nick's honesty disarmed her. She sat on the couch beside him and stretched out her hand to his knee. She brushed her delicate brown fingertips as a gesture of compassion, a truce.

"I'm sorry, Nick." She had a million questions but didn't ask. She waited. Somebody doesn't start telling such a personal story and want to be interrogated before they've barely begun. To an outsider, their silence would be mistaken for awkwardness. But neither of them felt awkward. Heeta was seeing Nick and he was allowing her to. She was seeing him properly for the first time in all the years that she had known him. He wasn't the perfect, stoic, mature guy. He was a traumatised man who had turned an important part of himself off – his way of dealing with his sister's heroin addiction; his way of dealing with his mother's subsequent switching off; his way of dealing with a childhood infected by pain and suffering.

"I didn't think about it… I mean, I didn't go out of my way to not think about it. It just disappeared, apart from when she turned-up and was physically there." Nick scratched the top of his nose. "Sorry I'm not making any sense."

Heeta did not affirm or contradict him. She just sat and continued to listen. After another lengthy pause, he did. "It wasn't that I told myself I wasn't going to think about it… Her." He replaced the pronoun to reference his sister directly.

"I wasn't some self-help disciple trying to control my feelings… they just weren't there. I had no feelings, no thoughts to control. I genuinely didn't even think about it – her. It doesn't really make sense…" That silence emerged again. It gave Nick the space to think, to consider his own experience. "I suppose it was too much… too much to properly process, or whatever…" He laughed at his own vocabulary. He hated when colleagues at work used phrases like 'processing', as if they were experts in the workings of the human brain. Heeta smiled. She understood and felt the same. They both knew that the human condition was far more complex than any teacher could understand, let alone explain. But she didn't say anything. She just smiled, conveyed that the vocabulary was a bit cringe to her too. But that it didn't matter; that it was better to experience a bit of a cringe if it meant he was dealing with whatever this was.

Nick continued. "I guess she sort of died. I mean psychologically. Like my mind erased … deleted her." He felt a little sick saying this aloud. Nick loved his sister and felt no hostility or anger toward her, not even when she was at her most selfish and destructive, not even when he saw her spaced out, lying half-dead in some waster's dump of a bedsit. His words were not hateful. They were factual, and this charged them with shame. He rubbed his fingers across the sides of his forehead and allowed the shame to ride through his stomach on an upward wave to his mouth. He could taste a little bit of sick. *How could I do that to my own sister?*

"You didn't do it." Heeta broke role sensing the dark place that Nick was plunging himself. She slid her fingers into his and clutched his hand. "You did not inject her with heroin, Nick. She did that." Heeta's words were not said in anger or judgment. They were factual, from a place of compassion, not self-righteousness. There was no morality in her declaration. And this enabled Nick to listen. He listened because he knew she spoke out of love for him, not condemnation for his sister. His head twisted slightly beneath his hands and his hazel eyes connected for a brief moment with Heeta's. She continued. "She will have had her reasons, but this isn't about her … for now." She paused to check that she hadn't lost him. "It's about you, Nick. You need to say this. You cannot pretend it isn't a part of who you are; pretend it didn't happen; pretend that her loss wasn't real."

"But it wasn't. She didn't actually die, not then."

"She did to you."

It felt like a steel bar swept down from the ceiling and slammed through his chest, leaving a hole larger than the rest of his body. Her words didn't go to the bone, they took his diaphragm out. He hurt. A lot. So much that he needed the cartoonish imagery to take him away from it.

"Sorry." She clutched his hand tighter and brought him back. With a tear in his eye, she continued. "But she did, and you need to accept that. You need to let go of the grief and the shame."

Nick nodded. He knew she was right. He needed to let go of the ghost of the sister so that he could acknowledge and mourn the death of his actual sister. A small tear slid slowly down his cheek.

Heeta moved along the sofa to be closer. She released her hand from his so that she could wrap her arm around his back. She leant her head and rested it on his shoulder. "I'm so sorry, Nick." She rubbed his waist. More tears trickled down his cheeks as he allowed a grief buried long ago to surface.

Chapter 2 – Four years earlier, rejecting untruth

Nick liked Mondays. They promised fresh opportunities and deep down, Nick wanted his life to change. He had built himself a safe provincial existence, but he wanted more than that. He wanted more than Sasha and a clean, compartmentalised flat. He wanted more than weekend hook-ups.

He did not bring men home often, but he had indulged himself. A colleague from work tiptoed out of his flat in the early hours of Sunday. Nick kept his eyelids closed in mock sleep and focused on the ringing of the church bells echoing over Nuneaton.

The click of his bedroom door fixed into place. The guy had gone. Nick was safe. He opened his eyes and blew a large sigh of relief. *Hopefully, Sasha didn't see him leaving.* Nick thought. Sasha knew Nick was gay- he wasn't worried about that. It was the thought of her knowing that he had slept with an egotistical, melodramatic mess: Fred Baker. The thought embarrassed him. Sure, Fred was attractive, but he was selfish, overly dramatic, and impulsive. How would he justify his decision? *What does it suggest about me?*

The white Egyptian sheets folded away from his athletic body. His legs pivoted out of bed onto the wooden floor. A glass of tap-water levitated into the air and made its way down Nick's throat. He placed the glass back onto the bedside table only when it was empty. A stale smell of smoke lingered in the room. Nick did not smoke, but Fred did. Nick's head lowered onto the sheets. He sniffed them and they stank. He stripped the bed immediately, and after putting-on some clothes, he took the clumped sheets bundled in his hands and face, to the washing machine. The door clipped shut. The lights flashed and some device bleeped an irritating melody. The sheets began twirling inside the circular plastic window of the machine. He would wash away Fred and his stale cigarettes.

In the orange light of the next morning's sunrise, Nick peeled back his fresh sheets. The warm air beneath his duvet released into the room. Nick stretched his arms into Monday. He drank his water from the bedside table as usual and got ready for school.

He looked sharp in his suit. Unlike half of the other male teachers, his shirts were ironed. Eliot High with its 1960s windowed walls, became one giant greenhouse in the summer, yet tatty jumpers (hiding creases) jumbled around the place no matter how hot it became. Nick removed his layers and kept cool. He was not aware of how cool he was.

He stood at the back of the staffroom during the morning briefing. The senior leadership team attempted to energise the staff with a mixture of rhetoric, threatening glances, and gruesome smiles. The Deputy Head, the least worst to stomach, announced the upcoming Head of Year interviews and Nick caught her glance. She wanted him to get the job.

And he got it. He prepared thoroughly and survived the litter of informal hurdles: Sasha asked him practise questions at home; his classes excelled in their mid-term assessments; and the leadership team were impressed with his teaching during sporadic informal observations. His interview was a technicality by the time it came. Although the Headmaster did not formally offer Nick the job, after the interview he gave Nick a creepy wink and pout of the lips. His body language conveyed that Nick either had the job or was a fresh victim of an unwanted infatuation. The Head wasn't gay, so Nick assumed the former. He left the lofty boardroom filled with pseudo-trophies and self-certifications, and the butterflies flew free from his stomach. Once the door shut, he stood still, closed his eyes, and squeezed-out an earnest hearty smile. Warm air sucked into his nostrils and fell down his spine like a fresh waterfall. He was proud of himself.

He entered the staffroom and tried to contain the smile. He wanted official confirmation before sharing his news. Sunshine poured through the smeared, dusty panes of glass along the staffroom wall. It was freakishly warm for the end of February. His skin welcomed the heat.

The staffroom was almost empty: Nick went to sit in one of the comfy chairs before he realised that he wasn't alone. It was Fred. Nick had managed to avoid the awkward post-hook-up conversation all week. He felt rotten. It wasn't that he didn't find Fred attractive – he did. And it wasn't that he wasn't intrigued – he was. It was rather that Fred wasn't appropriate. Nick had no intention of pursuing a relationship with him. They were too different.

The bell would announce the end of the school day in a few minutes. Nick thought as he walked toward Fred. *Might as well get it out of the way.* Nick swallowed and slid his tongue beneath his pressed teeth as he ran a few lines through his head in preparation for the conversation.

"Hey Fred."

Fred's eyebrows raised a little as his pupils glanced upward to meet Nick's. He appeared equally uncomfortable, and it became obvious that his greeting was limited to that movement of the eye. Nick continued. "I'm sorry about…"

"Please!" Fred interrupted. "Do not feel sorry for me. I am not interested."

Those butterflies flew further from Nick's heart. Today was good. Fred hadn't fallen in love with him after their hook-up. Warm hair exhaled from his gut. "Sorry… I thought that it had been a bit weird and that…"

"You're the one that's been making it weird."

Nick considered Fred's words before replying. They seemed fair. Accurate. "You're right. I'm sorry. I have been weird. It has been me, not you… I'm not great at this sort of stuff. I'm not ready for a relationship or anything like that, and I was worried that I'd…"

"You don't need to be." Fred said.

"I'm really sorry for avoiding you." Nick meant what he said. Embarrassment flushed across his face. He hated thinking that he had been responsible for unfairly depicting Fred in such a needy light. "I should have come and spoken to you – not just assumed… well, you know."

Fred was silent, and Nick took it as a positive sign. Fred was rarely silent. It must have meant that he accepted his apology. A sincere smile radiated from Nick. He locked eye contact with Fred and filled his apology with sentiment. Fred continued to not bite and Nick assumed all was well. "Ok. I'm really glad we cleared this up." Nick said. "I'll see you down the pub."

Nick waved, turned away and left. The bell rang shortly after and the school began its weekend shutdown. Hordes of children ran along the corridors like salmon and Nick waded through them. He was on his way to meet Sasha. He promised to let her know how the interview went.

Her classroom was immaculate: the desks aligned with one another better than a piece of German engineering. The walls were fitted with angular display boards. Emboldened key words in font sizes for the partially blind glared out of them. Nothing was out of place. Nick thought of their flat.

"Hey there." She said. Her mouth hung open and her eyes conveyed expectation.

Nick smiled and nodded back, an open mouthed, teeth clenched nodding smile. "I think I got it."

Sasha put the lid on her red pen, rested it on a pile of marking, and then pulled her hands together to clap. "Oh my god – congratulations!" She sprang from her chair and rushed over. Nick remained in the doorway. Her arms wrapped around his shoulders and without thinking she pressed her lips onto his. Nick was stunned. His soul buried deeper into himself, and his body thinned. *What was she doing?*

The kiss lasted a long time. The clock-hand measuring seconds flickered from quarter-past to twenty-past. Nick felt each flick of the machinery.

Sasha lost herself in the ecstasy of his warm lips. They transported her to a place beyond; to a place unrecognisable; to a place she had never been before. Her controlled classroom melted away. She let go of everything in those five seconds. She slowed herself and connected with the world; with Nick's warm lips; with Nick's buried soul. She unbound her restraint and allowed her heart to move into his body. She allowed it to burrow into his internal caverns; to settle down beside him. To snuggle and spoon in an ephemeral realm of divinity. She was changed. Courage and strength; optimism, hope and passion flowed together like an alcoholic punch for the Gods.

Nick watched the clock-hand pass onward. He detached his lips from hers and stared at her closed eyelids. He wanted them never to open. He wanted this more than he had ever wanted anything in his life. He could not bear the reality of her delicate blue irises opening; of their being cast adrift by his unreciprocating hazel orbs. He did not feel anything for Sasha; anything other than pity, and he knew that this pity would inflict a blow harder on her, than any physical slap across the cheek, punch in the gut, or kick in the teeth. He hated how much he was going to hurt her, yet it was an undeniable certainty. He could never feel what she felt for him.

Sasha opened her eyes and a gentle space breathed between their faces. Nick's brown, sultry orbs poured into hers. At first, it was pleasant. Her lips curled mirroring the foetal position of her soul. His stare was like a warm wave rushing over her bare legs at the beach. Warming. Welcome. But it became faster and deeper: it ran over her entire body. Pulse racing. Dynamic. And finally, it turned deadly, trapping her beneath the waves – suffocating and choking her. She yearned for it to get off. She was drowning. She wanted dry land. She wanted to be away from Nick's eyes, Nick's stare, Nick's pity. But it was in her. She knew it. She knew what he felt. Knew he could not love her in the way she loved him.

"I'm sorry." he said.

Like a fortress gate in an ambushed siege, her eyelids slammed closed. Tears spewed out like dust kicked up from the ground beneath the crashing gate. She sobbed loudly. She tried to contain the volume, but this only made her sobbing more deeply loud. Agonisingly loud. Appallingly loud.

Nick felt appalled. He pulled back so they were no longer connected. Sasha pulled her hands into her chest. She stood alone crying into them. Nick covered his forehead with his own hand, his palm rested over his nose and his wedding-ring finger stretched across his eyes. His other hand covered his mouth, his fingers rested across his warm lips and his palm cupped his chin. He felt sick, a motion sickness, as if the classroom had become a ship that rocked them further apart from one another.

Pam the cleaner knocked the door. Her gap teeth offered compassion. She knew both Nick and Sasha were good people. Something terrible must have happened. Nick moved to the side and lifted his hand so that it remained on his forehead but liberated his sight. He made eye contact with Pam and swallowed, thinking about what he was going to say.

"What's up love?" Pam said. Sasha was too adrift in her own ocean of tears to notice. Nick did not know what to say. He swallowed again, and shook his head while looking at Pam. "It's alright dear." She said to him, parking the hoover and popping the bottle of cleaning fluid onto one of the student-desks. She rubbed Nick's arm in a motherly manner and moved over to Sasha.

"There, there love." Pam said rubbing her arms. It made no difference. She continued to sob, an emotional equivalent of the forty-day flood. Pam hugged her. Nick watched. But Sasha continued to cry, and cry and cry. He couldn't handle it any longer. Pam released her grip, just enough to twist and glance at Nick. She wanted to see whether he could shed any light on the situation. Nick looked away. He couldn't articulate what had happened. It felt too cruel to say it aloud. He avoided eye contact with Pam, who returned her full attention to Sasha. She encouraged her into one of the student chairs.

Nick seized the opportunity to leave. He caught Pam's eye, and pointed to the doorway, indicating that he was going. She nodded compassionately and gave him a little wave. He wanted to stay and sooth Sasha; to tell her how sorry he was, but he knew it was better to give her space. There was nothing he could say that would make her feel better right now. He pulled the door closed, pressing, and releasing the handle so that its click was inaudible.

He rubbed his forehead with all his fingers, except his pinkies which prodded over one another, and then breathed out a long gush of trapped air. He needed to get out of the school. He walked along empty corridors and left.

Chapter 3 – You don't love anybody

The receptionist waved Nick a hearty, *it's-the-weekend* goodbye as he left school. He thought about how joyful Fridays were to everybody except himself. Sure, he liked the lie-ins and leisurely breakfasts – but he felt pressurised by weekends. He had purpose and a schedule throughout the week, while weekends imposed an aimless, openness on him. It made him need to want to do things. Work did not demand that. He got on with his duties because he had to; because it was expected – work did not feel like a choice, and that made it easy: choices were difficult for Nick.

The orange glow of the sun warmed his neck. It was freakishly warm for the time of year. He planned to get a lift with Sasha to the pub, but the intensity of her emotion made him appreciate the walk. He needed the air. The peace. Space.

Rows of terrace houses passed either side of him. His school shoes tapped along the cobbled pavements and kids kicked balls to each other in the middle of roads, diving out of the way when a sporadic car sped past. A text message informed him that the staff had chosen another pub for the evening.

At the end of the street, Nick joined the busier road leading into town. He waited at the pelican crossing for the cars to stop – one didn't. Its burnt-out sagging tires charged across the black and white strips of paint like a dystopian war chariot on its way to collect a weekend bag of weed. Nick glanced toward the car coming along next to see whether it was more likely to stop... it was a red Toyota with an elderly couple whose spectacles were uncomfortably close to their window screen. They sped over the pelican crossing faster than the previous car. A larger gap emerged after though, and Nick began his crossing – the next car would have to stop. He waved to thank the young woman sitting in the car on the other side of the road that had been waiting the entire time. She smiled back at him.

Nick decided to cut through the rec – it would be quicker to get to the pub. The wind whipped his cheeks in the wider open spaces. His phone vibrated in his suit-trouser pocket. Sasha's name appeared on the screen. He had started to relax and loosen from the incident, but those few letters on a cheap electronic screen brought it all back as if it were a needle injecting his bloodstream with something strong. He wasn't sure whether he would answer but between glances of the football pitch, the rec fields, and his phone, he knew that he would. It was the right thing, and Nick did the right thing.

The seconds between clicking accept and lifting his phone to his ear reminded him of that long moment her lips pressed to his, the flicking of the clock-hand. "Hey." Nick said.

"Hey." Sasha replied.

A silence rested between them like a romantic no-mans-land. They both wanted a peace treaty. Sasha of course, wanted more, but neither of them wanted to ruin the relationship. "I'm sorry." She said.

Nick felt more wretched. He had caused this and now she was apologising. "I'm sorry, Sash. It's just…"

"Please Nick. Don't apologise."

He could hear her voice faltering. She had started strong, but fake-strong, as if she knew it was only a matter of time before she depleted her stock of strength, a battery bar dropping percentages by the second. "Look. I'm really sorry. I should never have…" She paused to muster energy, reversing her depleting stock by a couple of percentage points. "I never should have kissed you. It was wrong." The charge ended and depletion resumed. "Foolish. I know you won't…"

Nick hardened at her choice of words – *won't wasn't fair*. He thought.

"… can't…" She amended her word knowing that it wasn't fair. "Can't love me…" She was running low.

"Sash…"

"I know." She said, and a tender silence emerged for the first time. Her battery was low, but it felt like it was stabilising. "I know, Nick. I'm sorry. I didn't mean to, you know, make it awkward…"

"Sash…" Nick said again. He was saying her name only to convey empathy.

"I don't want to ruin what we have."

Nick nodded on the other side of the phone and he knew Sasha could feel it, but he also knew that it was too late, and that she did not yet know this.

"Can we talk, please?" She asked.

Nick hesitated. He did not want to go through a lengthy emotional binge. It was why he liked Sasha. Their relationship was clean. Tidy. But he knew it was right. She needed to see him. "Of course."

"Where are you? I'll drive over."

"I'm in the rec."

"Wait there – I'm leaving now." She said it before he could suggest a more adult meeting point.

"If it's easier, I could…"

"No. Please, Nick. Just wait in the rec. I'll be less than five minutes."

"Ok."

"Ok…" Sasha wanted to say 'I love you'. "See you in five minutes." She ended the conversation by repeating her previous comment rather than what she felt.

She hung-up. Nick looped around the football pitch and realised that if he continued walking, he would he would be out of the rec before she arrived. He glanced at his watch and knew that it would take her ten minutes, not five.

Waist-high metal railings fenced a crappy playground. It was empty – the younger kids had already been and gone: despite the clear blue sky, the late February weather was too cold for them to linger, and it was too early for the older kids to hangout. The rusty gate squawked its oil-deficient hinges as Nick passed through. He sat on the carousel and pushed his foot on the squeezy tarmac to make it move slowly. The rec span. The football pitch, the back gardens of a fancier row of terraces, the graffitied bridge, the even more graffitied playframe supporting the little slide, connected into a circular scene. Nuneaton span around Nick while he sat on that carousel in his dapper work suit.

He lifted himself off and moved over to sit on the swing. He launched his legs backward and forward, willing himself higher. He tried to remember the last time he had been on a swing. He couldn't, but he liked it and so he decided to stop trying. He enjoyed the moment.

Sasha parked in the cul-de-sac adjacent to one of the rec entrances. Nick watched her lock the door and walk into the park. Her antish appearance swelled and padded-out as she trod the path between the playground and the goal posts. Her face thickened, and Nick could make-out her features. Her eyes acquired colour and she came more to life the closer she got.

The squawk of the gate made another appearance. Sasha passed through and walked over to sit on the empty swing beside Nick. "God, I can't remember the last time I sat on a swing." She had not started moving yet. Nick was swooshing back and forth through the air.

"You should try it." Nick said expressing more joy than he usually did.

Sasha smiled. It was more comfortable than she had expected. She pushed the spongy ground with her fancy work shoes and her tights began to scissor through the air as the swing kicked into motion. "You're right – it's fun." She said.

"Told you."

They both cut into the air. Nick in his suit and Sasha with her hair blowing free. They began to laugh. Silly, irrational laughs. Laughs that beget laughing. Guttural laughs that spilled unselfconsciously into the air. Sasha shouted. Not words exactly. Sounds. Emotion. The sound and emotion of letting go.

Her swing began to slow, and Nick's imitated. Their speed decreased slowly, and their intersecting criss-crossing narrowed until they became one. Still, feet back on the ground.

"I love you Nick." Sasha said. Her voice was stronger. "I love you, and I know you can't love me back, not in the way I love you, but I do, and as I can't do anything about it, I'm just telling you."

"I know, and I'm sorry, Sash. I love you to…"

"Thank you." She said. Nick's face puzzled. For the first time, he turned to look at her. Their eyes connected.

"You don't love me. But thanks for saying it."

Nick didn't argue with her. The truth was that he wasn't sure if he loved her or not. He didn't really understand love. He wanted to love her.

"It means a lot that you'd say it." She continued, "but I realised that you don't love anybody – not yet…"

Nick felt like she had just attacked him. A passive-aggressive stab in the back, but from the front. He did not understand.

"I don't mean that nastily. I love you Nick."

Nobody had told Nick that they love him, not even his mother. She did. But she never said it. His father was the same. They weren't the 'I love you' family.

He sat on the swing in the middle of the rec hearing it over and over.

"I love you, but you don't even love yourself yet." She said. Her voice was declarative, truthful. It wasn't mean, but it still hurt. Nick had nothing to say. He had never really thought about it and couldn't say either way. He didn't know if he loved himself; whether that phrase even meant anything – *what did it mean to love yourself?*

"But it's ok…" She said. She started swinging again, but only softly. Nick sensed that it wasn't completely *ok*.

"I'm sorry Sash – I thought I was clear the whole time."

"You were." There was no delay in her response. Now she turned to look at him. Her head rested on the metal links that held the swing in place. "Can we carry-on as normal, just for a while?"

Nick nodded. He did not want to move out of the flat. Sasha was the most responsible person he knew, and he determined that there were worse things than living with somebody that loved him. "Yeah, of course." He said in earnest before leaving a slight pause. "But I'll never be able to, you know…"

"Love me?"

Nick nodded.

"I know." She said.

"So, we're ok?"

"Sure." She swung a little higher, but not as high as earlier.

"You can be happy knowing that I can't be with you that way?" Nick pushed a little harder wanting more certainty. He disliked the thought of instability. He needed to know she'd be fine.

"Definitely. Let's just see how things go… but can you promise me one thing?"

Nick's skin tightened. What was her condition? What did she want, and could he meet it? "Yeah?" He said askingly.

"Promise me that we can leave this conversation – everything that's happened today – leave it all aside for a while?"

Nick breathed-out his inner smile. He rested his head on the metal links and relaxed properly. "Deal." he said back to her.

They smiled genuinely at one another for a few long, meaningful seconds. Then Sasha kicked herself higher in the swing and jumped off from ahigh. "Come-on then!" She called back from the ground. "We've got to go and celebrate your promotion."

Nick smiled and imitated her jump. He landed beside her, and together they left the playground and the rec.

Chapter 4 – Punctured

The evening played out unexpectantly. Relieved at Sasha's handling of their incident and overjoyed at his promotion, Nick suggested a proper night-out in London with his teacher friends. They ditched the stale pub after a few pints and headed for the train station. It was sporadic in the best way.

They agreed to share a taxi home and sold themselves the necessary lie that it would not cost as much as it did. In the spare 30 minutes before the train left, they pillaged the already pillaged booze aisle of the Asda beside the station. A bottle of unbranded vodka left its sisters to join the mesh basket. Several six packs of lager joined, and pre-made, tinned gin and tonics too – they were a bit pricier, but Fred added them to the basket once he realised that they were splitting the bill evenly. Fred was tight.

The nasty vodka bottle shifted from hand to hand as they walked back. Heeta nudged the bottle a little higher with her formidable little brown fingers as each of the teachers lifted it for a swig. "Keep going." She'd add encouraging a little more of the legalised poison into their suckered mouths. Between them, they hoovered most of the bottle before they reached the platform. Bea – the wiser matriarch of the group – handed out can after can of lager. She had been the Head of RE at Eliot High for longer than anybody could remember, and her strongest belief was drinking. She practised and preached it. Everyday.

In their professional work attire, they swigged vodka from the bottle and necked cans of lager. The only member of the group that did not look out of place was PE teacher Tom. He already looked like a feral youth, grown big. Even Sasha let down her guard. Her work tights mirrored the glitter of the Gin & Tonic tin that spun around as she twirled and twirled beside the platform edge to the clapping and encouragement of the others. Everybody – Nick, Sasha, Fred, Heeta, Bea and Tom – were on top form. Ecstatic energy radiated among them. That energy people crave; that they live for. It replicated itself over and over. Joy begot joy.

The joyful binge drinking continued in the carriage. Most of the seats were taken with business people being shipped home, so the group set-up camp in one of the little junctions where the carriages adjoin and people nip to the loo. The alcohol dried-up thirty minutes into the journey, but nobody – except Bea – minded. They needed the break if they were going to last the rest of the night, especially Fred – he couldn't handle drink as much as he thought, and he became more of a mess than usual if he drank too much.

"Just nipping to the loo." Sasha said as she lifted herself from the filthy lino-floor.

Bea who leaned against the bit of wall beside the loo, stretched her hand upward to press the button to open the door. It expressed that swoosh-like noise, as if the impressive sound compensated for the skanky condition; whereas in reality, it only raised expectations and caused customers to feel even more disappointment as they attempted to pee and wash their hands without touching any surfaces. Sasha squeezed through intersecting legs sprawled out on the floor to enter the smelly toilet. She pressed the button and the automatic door swooshed closed.

"She's in an unusually good mood." Tom said, between guzzling the last can of Fosters. The others looked to Nick for an explanation.

He evaded their stares to avoid providing one.

"I'm not complaining. She's pretty cool when she lets go." Tom added.

Bea's face recoiled as if a wasp had just stung her lips. Her tongue darted out to lick the imagined wound, and her horse-like teeth glinted momentarily. She wasn't particularly interested in Tom – she told herself. Yet she became jealous if he showed interest in anybody else. He noticed he had prickled her.

"Don't worry Bea – your tits will always be my favourite."

Bea's lips now opened into a wide oval smile, and her teeth bobbed as she chuckled to herself in pleasure. She gave a little look into her own cleavage and bathed in the satisfying self-approval she had of her breasts. They were good.

"She didn't mind you and Freddie fucking last weekend then?" Tom said, jibing at Fred and Nick.

"Fuck off." Fred said marginally before Nick. The others laughed. Desperate to change the conversation, Nick became more willing to engage in the banter; primarily so that he could steer the topic away from him and Fred. He had not told Sasha that it was Fred he had brought home last weekend. She knew somebody had stopped over. Nick didn't want her to know it was him for another reason other than Fred's general capacity to embarrass; it was more serious now. He didn't want to risk hurting her. She loved him, wanted him more than anything, and even though he wanted to give himself to her, he couldn't. He would never feel that way. Yet, Fred, a narcissist that Nick didn't even like that much, had gotten closer to him than she could. That reality would hurt her. Nick didn't want her to know for her sake, not his. It would feel too cruel.

"Did you get the skid marks out of Tom's pants?" Nick asked Bea. It was a high-risk strategy: Tom would likely assume Fred had told him about seeing Tom in his skid-marked underpants, whilst lying hungover on Bea's bed last Friday. This would provide an opportunity for them to re-focus the conversation back on Fred and Nick, but it was all he could think of. The flush of the toilet announced that the train was moving Sasha's waste into the train's bowels. The door would make its swooshing opening noise, and she would be out.

The group laughed at Nick's comment. "Oh, gross!" Heeta said. "Bea you better not have washed his dirty underpants." She gave Tom a stern look, conveying that there would be consequences if he took advantage of Bea's generosity; if he allowed her to touch and wash his skid marked pants.

Nick's decoy worked. Tom laughed, but in a different mode: he laughed from a position of defence not offence, and not being overly bright, it would take him a while to get back on form.

"They weren't that bad." Bea galloped to Tom's protection, entrenching his weakened position. Nick was relieved. Sasha's face emerged as the toilet door opened.

"What isn't?" She said hopscotching between the plethora of limbs back to her original space.

"Tom's skiddy underpants." Nick said.

"Gross."

"I know right." Heeta added.

"Leave him alone." Bea leant over Tom and smacked her bulbous lips onto his. Her cleavage hovered over his body while her breasts bobbed onto his Rugby shirt.

"Yeah, leave me alone." Tom said playfully after Bea's lips and body gave him space to breathe again. Like a little boy in receipt of unwavering motherly love, he was recharged, and ready to charge back into the offensive. "Stop using my undies as a way of justifying your perverted thoughts about my gorgeous bottom. I've told you boys before you can't have me. I don't swing your way."

Nick and Fred rolled their eyes at the same time. Tom was, objectively speaking, very attractive: muscular, hairy (without being a jungle), rugby-player stocky, an all-round stud. But they knew him, and sometimes knowing a person blunts attraction…

"No matter how 'objectively' good looking somebody is, if they're as dumb as a box of rocks, that attraction goes…" Heeta said.

Tom twisted his head like a dog sniffing the general emotion but missing the precise meaning. Before he could mull on it, Bea saved him – again.

"Come here baby." She said leading with her breasts. And like a dog allured by a good treat, he forgot everything that had gone before. He focused on what mattered in that moment by diving into her cleavage and blowing raspberries between her breasts. Bea screeched aloud as the others laughed. A few members of the corporate cargo twisted their heads from the aisles to disapprove of the human contact, but they returned to their grey newspapers to skim the grey details in their grey suits.

The conductor announced that the train was arriving at Euston Station. He thanked passengers for travelling and hoped they had had a comfortable journey.

Bea crunched herself up from the sticky floor and stretched her back. Nick shook his lanky legs, allowing them to breath properly. Fred flicked his fingertips simultaneously, in a sort of jazz hand motion. Sasha straightened her tights. Tom twisted his torso side to side, his pecs flecking with each twist. Heeta, the smallest but most formidable of the group, stood with ease and hooped her disproportionately large bag onto her arm. "Come-on! Let's get fucked!" She said, her beautiful hazel eyes glinting above her beautifully cheeky white-teethed smile.

They piled out of the train and strutted through the station as a single unit. Their drunkenness expressed itself like the smell of an alcoholic – the suits moved out of their way before territorial skirmishes began. The night belonged to them.

They slid down the escalators and shot through the underground in the same rowdy manner. Closer to Tottenham Court Road, the groups became equally rowdy. The outgoing party-Londoners replaced the head-down, ear-phone-in Londoners as the city warmed itself up for an evening of sin.

Tottenham Court Road spewed them out and Old Compton Street swallowed them in. The bars pumped-out music. Men in leather trousers minced and kissed in public. Hen parties squeezed themselves through unofficially pedestrianised streets.

"Get the drinks in then Freddie, you tight bastard." Tom announced after Nick suggested one of the bars.

"Fuck off – Nick's the one that's just been promoted." Fred said.

"Don't worry, I was going to offer. What do you all want?" Nick said.

"Pint." Tom said.

"Pint." Heeta said.

"Pint." Sasha said – she did not want a pint, but knew they were more economical and made buying rounds easier.

"Gin and Tonic." Fred said.

"I'll come with you – we can split this one." Bea said.

Inside the bar, music washed over hordes of men that danced as if the place were a nightclub. Nick and Bea had to slide against their bodies to get to the bar. The sweat was aromatic. Literally, more than fifty brands of aftershave and deodorant leaked itself down men's perspiring necks and exposed armpits. Bea's horsey nostrils soaked it all in.

The barman-come-bodybuilder served Nick as soon as he reached the counter. "What can I get you, sweetheart?"

In his mild Geordie accent, Nick gave the barman his order.

"I do love a fellow Geordie," the barman said to him. Nick could see veins throbbing in the side of the barman's head and throughout his huge muscles, which bulged the entire way down his unclothed arms. The whiteness of his teeth twinkled, exaggeratingly so against the blackness of his tank top and black skin-head haircut.

Bea twisted to look at Nick as if the barman had just handed her a pair of spectacles to view him afresh. She had grown used to his soft accent, and forgot he was not a native Nuneatoner. In fact, she had never heard him speak about where he came from. People tended to assume he had been there forever like everybody else. They ignored his *off* accent. But more than this quirk of his unknown history, she had not seen Nick as this exotic object of infatuation; this beauty capable of mesmerising men. She stared at him and considered just how attractive he was.

"You're a little stud, you know." She said to him.

"Ain't he just." The barman said placing one of the pints on the counter with his honey-coloured skin.

Nick rolled his eyes. He was used to the complements in gay bars, but he inaccurately assumed that they were merely charms, cast to woo him. He had no idea of just how true they were.

"Seriously Nick." Bea said. "You're a catch."

"Sorry love, I seen him first." The barman said, placing another pint on the counter. "Give me a kiss and I won't charge you for one of those pints." The barman's thick lips puckered, and his gigantic pecs flecked as if he were ready for a photoshoot.

"Thanks, but it's ok." Nick said lifting his debit card into the air.

"Worth a shot…" The barman said.

"How about a round of tequilas?" Bea cheekily added, pimping Nick out. The barman looked along the bar to a fellow meathead, who was busy making a line of Manhattan cocktails for a group of older gays wearing white linen, top to bottom.

"Go on then." He said after calculating the risk of getting caught for giving the shots away. "But I want a good taste – no holding back."

"Seriously?" Nick said to Bea. Then to the barman: "Don't worry, I will pay for the drinks."

"Well now you're just offending the man…" Bea teased.

The barman's face puckered into a wound. It worked. Nick hated the idea of hurting people. It didn't usually stretch him into prostitution, but his experience with Sasha and the promotion had thrown him a little.

"Fuck it." He said more to himself than either the barman or Bea. "You better fill those shot glasses up." He leant across the bar like a tiger that had fooled everyone into thinking it was tame. On the spring, Nick sank his lips into the barman's. They stayed there for a good five seconds and while the five second kiss earlier that day caused his soul to recoil into the depths of his being, this kiss relaxed every muscle in his body as if he had just dosed up on heroin.

The muscles in the beefy barman's face relaxed in the same way. Nick pulled back and he stood in a post-coital smug satisfaction. "Fuck, Geordie, you can kiss too."

Nick took a large sip from the pint of Newkie Brown he had ordered, and from atop of the glass, his gorgeous hazel eyes continued to seduce the man he had just kissed. They captured and controlled his attention like the eyes of an Eastern princess manipulating her predators. The boss – midway through making those Manhattans – stared along the counter, but the barman was too mesmerised with Nick to care. He poured the shots of tequila with pride and grateful servitude.

"Thanks." Bea said taking the tray of drinks as Nick handed his debit card to the man. They kept eye contact as the card slid into the chip and pin machine and Nick's middle finger slid his code into it, authorising the payment, minus a round of tequila.

As the barman went to hand the card back, he leveraged his body across the counter so that he was in range for another kiss. The card stopped mid-air. Nick could easily take it, but his arms remained flat on the counter, leaving the barman with the choice of moving his hand closer to Nick's or lingering in that frozen mid-air position.

Nick smiled at the barman waiting with his debit card. He raised his hand slowly and leant his body forward at the same speed. As his hand reached the barman's hand, his face reached the barman's face. They kissed again. Another long, five-second kiss.

Nick pulled away faster this time. He pocketed his debit card – he would put it back into his wallet later. He took his pint, Fred's Gin & Tonic, and left. The barman watched him slide between the dancing hordes sprawled across the bar, watched him fade into them.

Outside, the drinks disappeared into their cauldron-like kidneys and they took it in turns to re-enter the bar for more. Bea tended to accompany (and split the round) with whoever's turn it was. She took Fred's hand and led him in – he had scared one of the other customers by attempting to slap his arse with far too much force, and the group decided without saying explicitly, that he ought to take a short timeout.

The others laughed about Fred once he was out of earshot, and once they felt comfortable that he wasn't going to get them into trouble.

"He's got the home advantage, hasn't he?" Tom said.

Heeta extended Tom's football metaphor to redirect the attention to his relationship with Bea; his improved odds of going home with her, given the immediate homosexual landscape, which removed the obstacles of competition. "Perhaps there is something for the away team too?" She said with a wink.

Before Tom could say 'I fucking hope so', Sasha said it – although she didn't swear. Nick glanced at her – slightly nervous. Sasha didn't voice an appetite for sexual encounters. She didn't refer to her own sexual needs.

She continued, and Nick continued to be anxious. "It's been way too long." She said elbowing Nick.

What was she doing? He thought. This wasn't her. He didn't disapprove of the action in itself. It was good that she was being more open – camp. But her doing so made him uneasy because it was out of character. Instability made Nick nervous. *Where would it lead?*

"Unlike Nick, I haven't brought a man back in forever." She said and Nick gave an awkward nod to her tagging him. *Why does she have to hook her newfound liberality onto me?* Couldn't she just stand on her own feet – talk about her desire independently. He did not want to be enmeshed. He lacked confidence in her authenticity. Deep down, it was a ploy. She didn't want to bring a man back. She didn't want to meet someone. She wanted him. This was going to end badly.

"Oh yeah – I forgot you two were here last weekend." Tom's hand floated horizontally over the backdrop of Old Compton Street. "This is where the Nick-Fred magic began."

Sasha cricked her neck like a dog affected by a key word that changed her entire disposition. Nick knew it.

"You mean it was Fred?" She twisted to look at Nick squarely. "You slept with Fred last weekend?" It wasn't a question. It was an outlet for her pain. "You've always said that you've never been interested."

Nick contained his frustration. He was too emotionally drained to go through this again in the same day. He deflected and downplayed what had happened, stating that it was a drunken one-time event, that Fred and he were very different people and that nothing else would come of it.

Fortunately, Sasha seemed too emotionally drained to go through it again too. To his surprise, the flickers of pain that he sensed in her, evaporated. She did not push it. She seemed to let the matter go. *Perhaps she was accepting the situation and moving forward.*

Fred and Bea spilled out of the bar with more pints and tequila shots. As it was his round, Fred had switched from Gin & Tonics to pints. They each tossed back the shots, licking the salt and biting the lemon slices to soak up the nasty burn. Tom slapped

Bea on the ass, converting his emotional reaction from the tequila into sexual energy. She neighed in pleasure and grabbed at his crotch. Fred, impressed at their electricity, thought he would try out the same thing. He lent behind Nick and slapped his ass. His palm landed flat on the soft fabric of Nick's work trousers.

Nobody was sure how to react. It was awkward. Beyond awkward. Fred filled the silence with another stinging slap. His arm pivoted backward and like a grandfather clock on speed, slammed its pendulum back onto Nick's ass.

"Don't do that!" Nick shouted at him, causing the other patrons to pause their conversations and look at what was going on. Heeta made a joke by referring to their bedroom activity the week before. The resulting laughter pierced the tension and a buzz returned to the atmosphere; the street was released from its temporary pause.

Sasha enjoyed watching Nick snap at Fred. It reassured her that there was not anything between them; that there was no love in their relationship – they might have slept together, but Nick was prepared to be harsh and stern with Fred; harsh and stern in ways he never was with her. She felt privileged to have Nick's tenderness. She layered that in meaning. Although she had been visibly looser that evening – drinking far more than she normally would – she wasn't properly relaxed – not for her. This, however, changed that. For the first time that evening, she slid back into herself. She stopped pretending to be interested in promiscuity and a wild night out. She became Nuneaton Sasha. Nick noticed immediately. And he relaxed too. He stopped worrying about what she was thinking; feeling; anticipating how he needed to act around her. He smiled – but ensured that it did not extend to Fred. Not because he felt mad at him. In fact, he was quite grateful, Fred's silly slap on the bum had softened the dynamics between him and Sasha. He ensured his smile did not extend to Fred because he did not want Fred to think he was interested.

More drinks vanished. More laughter erupted. More endorphins brewed. The moon had joined the neon signs and magical glow illuminating Old Compton Street. Men wearing hot-pants handed out fliers for Nightclubs and the group decided to advance into the second layer of the night, the layer reserved for those born wild and with a restless energy, an energy that magnetically attracts them to the divine halls of light, sound, sweat and movement: the modern nightclub. They set-off to dance; to be one with their bodies; to synchronise their internal rhythms with the pulses of a sensuous environment; to bathe in life and commune with the essence of the almighty: to become joy itself. Dynamic. Mobile. Energy personified.

"Nick." Sasha reached out her arm and took his wrist. She had said his name quietly indicating that she wanted to speak to him privately. They fell back from the group, which was now moving along to find a club.

"What's wrong, Sash?" Nick had relaxed around her. He was delighted at how normal things were – and he was drunk.

She looked at him, a little pale. "Nick I'm not sure if the club…"

He misread her, assuming that she was sick from the drink. She usually didn't drink anywhere near the amount she had this evening. "Don't worry Sash. You don't need to come." He said, cutting her off. "I'm so happy that you came tonight… you know…" Nick conveyed his happiness about her coming to Old Compton Street. "You know… here, to see the stuff beyond work. I know it's not your thing. But I'm so glad you came to see it." He waved his arm at the street. "This place, where I belong, properly… you know, the real me."

She was crushed; no, she was almost crushed, like an autumnal leaf laying on the floor with its full potential crunch, ready to be destroyed by the lightest footstep. Almost was worse. Nick didn't see it though. He assumed she was just becoming nauseous from the drink. "Thanks, I know it's been a rough day for you, but it means so much to me that you've been so generous by coming to see this place."

His voice was earnest and he had no idea that his words were stabbing her in the back but from the front, just as her words had stabbed him in that way earlier. Their relationship was over. Neither of them knew it, but this was the moment it truly ended. Nick shouted to the others that Sasha was heading back; that she wasn't feeling too good and that she was going to get the last train home. He hailed a taxi and shuffled her into it, making sure she was safe and comfortable. "Thanks Sash." His eyes locked onto hers. The door then closed. He waved through the window, and she was gone.

Nick joined the others. A line of arms interlinked across shoulders, and the bodies beneath them marched forward in euphoric unison. They danced into the early hours of the morning in a nightclub that throbbed music with the intensity of a child's heart on Christmas morning. Nick flowed, twisted, span, spun, and swayed beneath the waves of strobe light.

He loved dancing. It released him from his responsibilities; from his neat, organised life of order and sensibility. It was hard for anything else to matter while he span and spun others. He could not worry about his career, about his finances, about his sister. He could only feel the beat and rhythm of the piece. Dance-music was one of the few things that could override his nature: his impulse to be considerate; his intuitive responsibility; his struggle to ignore consequences; to be reckless; or overtly risky; it all melted as he danced. It was his loophole. One of the few ways, he could experience that sensation of 'switching-off'. He danced; submitted his mind and body to the supreme algorithm: music that pounded not only his ears; music, that pounded and provoked response from his entire body, over and over. Nick switched-off by offering himself to restlessness, by embracing a data stream that defied resolution.

But nightclubs end. The music stops. And the spellbound, eventually, return to their realities. As big Ben chimed 3am across London, the music in Nick's nightclub evaporated into harsh white light and Nick, along with hundreds of others, awoke from their peaceful state of free love. Their consciousness and individuality returned. The club transitioned out of a single organism moving as one, into a collection of competing parts – most of them pushing for the toilet, the exit, or the coat room.

Where hundreds of people had miraculously swirled and swayed gracefully and confidently within a confined space for hours on end without conflict, awkward bulbous growths sprouted throughout the club in minutes. Cliques formed and personalities asserted their dominance: they occupied, seized, and defended territory.

"Where's Fred?" Nick said to Heeta, as they squashed into a queue for the exit.

"He'll find us outside." She said pressing her chest outward to give her small body the presence it needed to warn others of pushing her inadvisably hard.

Nick had burnt a lot of the alcohol away in the club. He didn't feel drunk. He felt parched. Sweat dripped down his neck as if he had been in a gym for 3 hours. Bea and Tom were close by. Sweat too dripped down their faces, but it didn't stop them from dipping their dehydrated tongues into one another's mouths. The masses pushed them to the exit like a wave carrying driftwood.

Outside, they claimed a bit of pavement as a group and waited for Fred to find them. Bea lit up two cigarettes, passed one to Tom, and inhaled the other. They stood and waited. It was technically the end of the night, but the masses of people did not seem to thin. A third layer of the evening seemed to unfold, the long post-club, pre-kebab goodbye.

Fred rocked-up with a tall older man attached to his waist. His voice was husky: too many cigarettes, dehydration and shouting at the top of his voice for the man beside him to hear whilst inside the club – not that they had spoken all that much.

"Who's your friend?" Nick said. He did not want to know. In fact, he was irrationally annoyed at Fred turning up with a man.

"Come on, let's get some food." Tom said. They drifted toward the crowds sitting on kerbs while either holding chip-wrappers or balancing kebab boxes on their thighs as their legs stretched into the road. The temperature was cool, but everybody wore beer jackets. Deep fat fried potato and cheap bits of meat slid down throats that appreciated the weird mix of grease and fresh air. As everybody ate, Nick stood and began to hunt a taxi – he rightly predicted that it would take a while.

He stood on the edge of the road ready to wave his arms. Fred and his new man cuddled on the kerb. Nick scowled when the guy looked in his direction, preventing any conversation. *He looks an absolute knob*, Nick thought as he stared into the road avoiding anybody's gaze. He didn't know why he was so annoyed. The night had been great. He'd had a great time. He wasn't interested in Fred, and he definitely wasn't the sort of person to begrudge the happiness of others. Nick was painfully thoughtful. He was off. *Fucking Sasha.* He thought as he stood by the edge of the road. Memories of her kissing him; of her sitting on the swing telling him that he didn't love anybody; of her telling him it was ok... all flooded his consciousness. He argued with himself; told himself that it was sorted, but the more he told himself, the angrier and more emotional he became. Sasha had punctured him like an invisible hole on a bike wheel. He hadn't noticed at first, but with time, his energy, his composure had unquestionably flattened. *The fucking bitch.* He thought. He hated himself for thinking it. *I'm not that person. Am I?*

An empty people carrier truckled along the road. Nick pounced so that it had to stop. The driver lent out of the window and Nick began to negotiate the 100-mile journey across the country. They had to pay a lofty amount up front and hand over two mobile phones as a deposit, but they reached an agreement.

Still feeling out of character, Nick picked a fight and offended Fred's new man as they climbed into the taxi. This caused Fred and the guy to wander-off for a private chat. The others were too exhausted to intervene or chastise Nick – though Heeta did make clear that he was being a complete dick. It wasn't meant to be this way around. Fred was the dick, not Nick.

Fred returned to the taxi alone. His face threatened that he and Nick would end-up in a police cell if he said anything to him. Sheer necessity forced them into the car together; both would have given anything to be as far away from the other as possible.

The taxi door slammed shut and the engine spluttered to life. Bea and Tom snogged in the boot-seats while Heeta leant her head into the passenger headrest. Without Fred's man, it remained empty. Nick sat in the middle seat and Fred, with his arms crossed, sat behind the driver. Their arms bristled and functioned like two walls, pointlessly, built adjacent to one another.

Before the taxi exited London, everybody, save the Bengali driver, was asleep. Nick's head rested on Fred's shoulder. In sleep, their cement-like arms crumbled into flopped limbs. They folded into one another. Their drama and feuding yielded to exhaustion.

Chapter 5 – Let's do it, let's go

Nick awoke on the sofa next to Fred. They had done it again, but unlike last time, they couldn't run away from what they had done. They were to do the walk of shame together. Nick lived much closer than Fred, who lived at least an hour walk away. Nick felt obligated to offer him a lift once they got to his. He hoped Fred would decline and walk home a different way. He didn't.

"How long will it take to get to yours?" Fred asked.

"Twenty-minutes."

"You sure you're ok to drive? … I can walk the rest of the way."

"Don't worry. I'll drive from mine."

The walk was awkward. Part hungover, part sobor, part sleep deprived. Neither had much energy to make conversation and neither had much motivation to sweep the reality of their encounter away with empty talk. Silence bobbed along between them, interrupted only by occasional words, which lacked meaning. Nick's apartment thickened in their horizon and when they finally arrived, Fred sat down on the kerb outside. Nick twisted to stare. He assumed he was sitting down to wait while he fetched the car keys.

"Come sit for a minute." Fred said.

Nick didn't understand. He wanted to go inside, to get away from Fred; to leave him sitting on that kerb while he climbed into his clean bedsheets. "What are you talking about? We're here."

"I just thought I'd sit for a couple of minutes." Nick rolled his eyes as he stood behind Fred who began to waffle on about his life in Nuneaton. *Why has he chosen to go on about all this now?* Nick released an internal sigh as he strolled back along the path. He joined Fred on the kerb.

"Do you see your life here?" Fred asked.

Nick tended to dislike these overly reflective conversations, considering them too fluffy and indulgent. He didn't have an issue with the topics in itself, but tended to lack respect for the type of people that got into them. From his experience, they were the Freds of the world: talkers, who bemoaned their actual life; talkers, who gave away their emotions, their power, to ideas, imagination and make-belief, rather than influence and deal with the actual world around them. It felt dangerous, a rat-hole. He couldn't afford that and so generally stayed away, but Fred pulled him in.

"Nuneaton makes just as much sense as anywhere." He said.

"Come on, you really think there is a future for us here?"

That 'us' pissed Nick off. He played dumb, as if he didn't understand the shared identity to which Fred referred – their sexuality. He'd come out years ago, but he had a dislike of being forced into groups that placed him exclusively with Fred. It made him feel powerless, like he wasn't in control of his own destiny; his own life.

"So, this is what you want your life to be – a flat with Sasha?"

"Of course not." Nick snapped.

The discussion prickled onwards for a few minutes. Nick picked at Fred's language; instead of trying to see the point Fred was attempting to make, he approached the discussion with literal interpretations like some archaic teacher that nobody liked, who fussed with the letter rather than the spirit of things said. Fred didn't notice though. To him, Nick was sitting on the step and engaging in a profound discussion. It didn't matter that Nick was uncomfortable and counting down the seconds until he could get of the step and go back to his own world. Fred didn't notice that.

"What does everybody want?" Fred said in response to one of Nick's rebuttals.

"A partner. Love." Nick said rather to his own surprise. Fred had hooked him – against his nature – into the conversation. He softened, physically and emotionally. His back eased as he pressed his hands into the pavement behind to take some of the pressure off his core. After a long pause, he tilted his neck back and the sky became his vision. He spoke into it. "Ok. I get it." Fred's mood perked. He turned his head and smiled at Nick who twisted his flopped head ever so slightly toward him to make brief eye contact. They never looked directly at each other in that way, not when they were sober. He elaborated to Fred's delight. "If I'm honest I can't see my proper life here either."

Fred's teeth twinkled as a large smile extended on his face. Like a puppy, he became over excited and began to list of foreign capital cities: New York, Paris, Barcelona. He pleaded that they could go emigrate together; and pleaded even harder that he was serious. And then like a child post-high, he flickered into a sombre, dramatic come-down – the rush wearing off.

"I'll die if I stay here." Fred said, tears building behind his dramatic eyes. The tears didn't shock Nick. He expected them, but his own feelings did surprise him. He sat looking at Fred, and felt a terrible truth buried within. An awful, sinister truth about an unhappy destiny if his life didn't change. If he didn't take courage and stray from his current path, the life he had worked hard to build for himself. To his amazement, he turned to Fred, looked into his teary eyes and said. "Let's do it. Let's go." He could hardly believe what he said.

They would go as friends, of course. Nothing romantic. But in his heart, Nick knew he had to go. Sasha moved the curtains aside in their apartment behind. She was watching him and Fred sitting on the kerb. She watched as Nick clutched Fred's hand in response to their decision to leave Nuneaton. And somehow Nick knew she was watching him. He knew that he had to move out; he realised, at that point, sitting on the kerb, that he had built himself a mock-life. Pretence. He did not want that. He wanted a proper life, a life he felt connected to. Things had to change. He knew his current life was over. He was moving on, shaking things up. Starting again. Away from Sasha – away from Sashas.

Chapter 6 – No longer his

"Shut the door on your way out." The headmaster said to Nick.

His office was painted a diseased yellow, a mock-sun colour trapped in the walls. It was how staff felt when they went in there: strapped into a forced, insincere smile. Happiness stapled to their faces as waves of panic and an urge of self-preservation pulsed within – *get out alive. Don't agree to anything.* The headmaster of Eliot High was a modern-day mafia don disguised as a hippy. He used the language of peace and love, but he was a tyrant beneath it all. Hierarchy existed for its own sake, for his sake. Staff weren't expected to have strong voices, to champion excellence and intellectual rigour. They were expected to kowtow. To model obedience and deference to his greater good. Conformity not cooperation. Discipline was the end, not the means. It's why the school didn't perform particularly well.

Nick went in prepared. His decision was firm. He wasn't taking the promotion. He was quitting. The headmaster's intimidation couldn't sway his thoughts; threats of a poor reference wouldn't derail his plans to leave. This was happening. This had happened. No matter what. Nick turned away from the Headmaster whose eyes bored into the back of his head – *how dare anybody desire to leave his orbit.* Nick passed over the imaginary line separating the carpet of his office and the corridor outside. A feeling of safety – relief – returned. A single step transported him out of a danger zone, but he was not home and dry.

"Nick?" The Headmaster called as Nick gripped the door handle. "This decision cannot be undone. You understand that, don't you?"

"Yes, Sir." Nick said, almost automatically, like a young Victorian school boy who hadn't actually listened to what had been said; like a drilled machine, who responded affirmatively irrespective of what the request actually was.

The Headmaster broke eye contact. His voice changed from a severe, suffocating intensity to an icy, cruel indifference with unnatural speed, and a calculation that made his former affection completely disingenuous. "Close the door." A cold command. A sneer. One last exchange that let Nick know he no longer belonged to his regime; that he was no longer under his protection – that he meant nothing and was fair game. That if he could be replaced immediately, he would be.

The door clicked shut and Nick stood on the spot. A warm smile spread across his face. He had done it. Nick didn't do this sort of thing. He didn't give up security. He pursued it. It felt liberating. The Headmaster's attempt to sow doubt had not worked. With the barrier between them – the closed door – he was certain that he had done the right thing. There would never be a good time to leave. In fact, he appreciated that it would only become more difficult. He looked at the empty corridor and thought about the space he had created in his future. For the first time in quite a while, he felt unbound, a thrill at the prospect of not knowing where he was going. He stood and smiled, a proper heartfelt smile.

The Headmaster's PA called his name from an office along the corridor. His pause broke. He walked over.

"Hi Lisa."

Her lips curled to imitate a sad faced emoji. "Don't leave us, Nick." She allowed the affection in her words to take effect before ploughing on. "This place needs more people like you." She was sincere – she liked him. "But I'm happy for you, I guess." She winked at him.

"Thanks Lisa. Has Fred been in to see him yet?"

"God no. You think he would have been that calm if you were the second or third person to resign in one day?"

"Third? Who else is leaving?"

"Sasha." Lisa pointed at the door, implying that Nick ought to close it. The large square of glass left them visible, but they could talk without being overheard. "You didn't know?" She said.

Nick sat on one of the tatty chairs with fabric in need of a good wash. He leaned forward to speak. "I knew she's been having a bit of a hard time since I told her I was leaving… but the truth is that we haven't really spoken much. I mean, we're polite; say hello; chat a little bit about work; what we're having for dinner; you know, simple stuff… but it's not as it was. We mostly stay in our rooms – give each other space."

Lisa nodded. She loved gossip, but only as much as she loved people. She wouldn't use anything she knew to harm or hurt anyone. She just loved knowing things about people and assumed everybody else was the same. "She's booked a meeting to hand in her resignation. She's been struggling with her classes. They haven't been performing very well, and I think, you know, with what's happened between the two of you… it's tipped her over the edge."

Nick's cheeks flushed a little as a surge of embarrassment worked its way up his bloodstream. He knew Lisa wasn't suggesting it was his fault, but it didn't stop him feeling responsible. "I knew her results hadn't been the best, but her classes always seemed…" Nick thought of the neat piles of exercise books. The perfectly underlined dates and titles, objectives; the splashes of red ink splattered everywhere, reminding any onlookers of her presence; her involvement; her teaching. He had assumed that Sasha was ok professionally. She certainly gave the impression that she had everything under control. Her books looked beautiful.

Lisa read his thoughts. "I know. She gives the impression that everything is rosy, but there are some pretty major problems."

Nick showed surprised. Lisa continued. "There've been more parental complaints than usual. No issues with behaviour or anything like that. But loads of complaints about the kids not having a clue what they're doing. Lots of pretty handwriting, but if you speak to her little buggers, they haven't got a scooby do what any of their work actually means."

Nick nodded. When it was said aloud, it made sense. Sasha loved a sticker; she could repeat and enforce a rule; dictate a process. But when it came down to it, she struggled to think on her feet and get into depth. She wore too much armour. Doubt was dirty, unprofessional. She was afraid of showing her thought process to the children in case there were kinks.

"She doesn't really get it." Lisa said. "She's taken him too literally." Lisa's eyes rolled toward the wall: The Headmaster sat on the other side. "She thinks it's enough to just exert authority. It isn't. Not really. You can get away with that when you've got his job." Her eyes rolled toward the Head's office again. "But everybody else knows that they actually have a job to do… and it isn't dishing out a shit load of stickers and red ink. I've told her that she's got to share herself with the kids; show them how she's thinking; how she's got to a perspective or point of view. To loosen up a little – be a bit humble – but she just doesn't get it. She looks at me like I'm talking shit."

Nick nodded. He could picture Sasha doing this. He was developing an appreciation that beneath her façade, Sasha had deep insecurities and this actually made her come across pretty judgmental. "She would be mortified if she could see herself." Nick said trying to muster a defence on her behalf.

"Oh, I know she means well and that it's all just insecurity." Lisa added in her casual voice that downplayed perceptive observation as common knowledge. "But there's only so long you can ignore it in this job. You know that Nick."

Nick wasn't sure if he knew that. He hadn't thought about it. But it did make immediate sense. Teaching was about the kinks, the misunderstandings, the not knowing. In his experience, kids warmed when they sensed humility in an authority. It made them respect it more. "I guess." Nick said.

"Come on, Nick. It's more than 'guess'. This job isn't for the faint hearted. You've got to know who you are. The kids don't need prissy closeted Adolfs modelling how to be a bossy, intolerant diva – they need people… people they can relate to; people they can trust and think things through with…"

"Yeah, I know, but it's not exactly like I'm *out* with them…" Nick said beginning to voice his own insecurity.

"Being honest doesn't mean climbing into bed and telling them about your first gay shag."

Nick laughed. "We probably shouldn't talk about climbing into bed with children."

Lisa cut him off. "See that's what I mean! You just have this way of handling things. It doesn't matter how provocative, taboo or plain wrong the topic is, you've got that ability to put people at ease. To calm the energy; to steer a conversation into a measured productive place without burning or chastising people in the process. That's what I'm talking about." Lisa stopped for a moment to reflect on what she'd said. It was an unusual action: her thoughts and words usually came as one. She thought aloud. She wasn't one to mull things over to herself; like many children, she spoke first, thought later. "You're sensitive… that's what it is."

Nick laughed. He wasn't expecting that, but he enjoyed Lisa piecing him together as if he were a jigsaw puzzle. She continued. "I don't mean in a soppy wet way. I mean it in the sense that you listen to people, like properly. You sort of assume the person's good, and so anything they have to say doesn't faze you. It's like you separate the words from the person, in a good way… if they say something stupid or insulting, you don't overreact… you…" she went silent again as she searched for the next piece of his puzzle… "You, you… you…" she searched harder for the piece… "You sort of see or hear the kink in the comment, in the thing said, and show it back to them; expect them to go deeper… and I suppose this is what makes them feel comfortable. What I meant about being open… You're not afraid of responding to them; encouraging them to think harder. Sasha wouldn't do that – she'd be far too afraid to see who they really are."

"And petrified of where they might go."

Lisa slapped her desk with the flat of her palm. "Exactly – She can't connect with the reality of who kids are; what their thoughts and opinions about the world might be. She hasn't figured out her own... she's no real sense of place or purpose; no vision, and so she has no real appetite for change... no proper expectations for herself, let alone the kids. She doesn't know where to lead them and so it's easier to keep the conversation simple."

Nick nodded to Lisa's slotting of the pieces together. Though, the truth didn't make him feel better. "I know she's your friend." Lisa said, picking up on the throb of Nick's sombre heart. "We're not slagging her off, or pointing out her faults."

"Aren't we?"

"No. We're understanding the problem so that we can help her." Lisa meant what she said and this helped. He straightened his back and some of his guilt escaped in a deep exhale that gushed into the office.

"I know." He said. "It just feels shit that I've lived with her for so long and none of this has ever come up... why haven't I ever tried to speak to her about it?"

Lisa smiled, a tender compassionate smile. "Nick, you can't blame yourself. My guess is that you have in your own way. But that she just wasn't ready to hear it. I think this is her beginning."

Nick's neck cricked a little. "What do you mean?"

"Unlike you, I think it's a good thing that she's resigning. She needs space to open up; to find out what she likes; what she wants. This isn't a job where you can easily do that."

The truth is absolute and Nick heard it like a blacksmith's hammer pounding hot iron. Loud. Distinct. Unmistakable. A slight squirming sensation wriggled within. "Perhaps there's a bit of me that needs that space too." He felt embarrassed for saying it.

Lisa laughed, not unkindly. "Nick the fact that you can say that so easily, is exactly why you don't need it – not in the same way. You know who you are. You just need to put yourself out there more. Have more confidence with it. Sasha is a very different situation. She has no idea. We're not talking about shaking things up – new school, new friends. She's got some serious soul searching to do, and it's going to be brutal and dramatic and beautiful – eventually."

For the first time, Nick didn't fully get Lisa's point. He assumed there was probably one there, but it eluded him. His nose twitched and his eyes scrunched slightly. "Don't worry." She said. "You'll understand one day."

Fred's face appeared at the glass window of the office door. He had clearly run out of hair product and was overdue a trip to the barbers: wisps of dry hair sprang neurotically. "Speaking of brutal and dramatic." Lisa said. Both she and Nick laughed aloud, a deep guttural laugh, a deep pleasurable laugh that is only possible when it is at the expense of somebody else, but a somebody that is loved, deep down.

The door of Nick and Sasha's apartment closed without making a noise. The music to the BBC's 6 o'clock news sounded from the lounge as Nick placed his shoes onto the rack. His black socks pressed against the strips of laminate wood; the bottom of his work trousers remained a couple of centimetres above, never touching the floor. The door separating the corridor and the lounge was ajar. Nick, with a flat palm against the white panelling, pushed it open gently. He walked through.

Sasha sat on the sofa holding a mug of tea in both hands. Her gaze was directed at the T.V but she wasn't watching it. Nick knew that he had to speak to her, properly speak to her. His socks pressed into the white carpet rather than the laminate of the corridor. Before he sat down on the sofa beside her, he took the remote from the coffee table and silenced the news presenter pumping unhelpful anxiety and emotion into the room. He sat and leant into the cushions, his red and blue striped tie rested along his perfectly ironed shirt, which looked as fresh as it did first thing that morning. "Sash." He began.

The white mug of tea raised to her lips and she sipped. It was too hot to drink. The mug settled back into her lap. "Sash." Nick repeated.

"Nick." Her voice was empty and hollow. The sound of it lingered like a miserable ghost meandering around the flat; too pathetic to scare anyone, but haunting nonetheless. Nick watched the streams of alarmist fragmentary sentences sliding across the yellow ribbon sucking-up words like a conveyor belt at the bottom of the screen. Item after item of alarm disappeared as fresher, bigger catastrophes cycled in.

"Sasha?" He said again. "Why didn't you say anything?" He allowed a space for her to respond, but elaborated into the silence… "About work?" The silence continued and so he specified further… "About resigning?"

The white mug rose again and the same hot tea brushed her lips. She didn't allow any of the liquid to pass through. It was still too hot. But she had to do something. The tea settled back into the mug and levelled itself, but Sasha kept the mug close to her lips. She spoke into it. "I need to do this, Nick… alone… I need to do it without you." The mug tilted as she went to sip the tea again.

"You can still speak to me."

"Don't." She spoke over him. "Please don't. I need to separate myself from you…" The mug returned to a perpendicular angle away from her lips. "You've been enabling me… enabling me to believe that I had a future here…" Her voice thickened. The emptiness filled with something far more dangerous. "You've known the entire time that this isn't your life; that it was only a matter of time before you left to begin for real…"

"That's not…"

Sasha cut him off. The mug held steady in her hands, but a hostile energy charged through her fingers. "It is… You have led me along. I invested in you. But now I need to stop." She sipped more tea. Although Nick was nicely settled into the sofa, he had never felt more uncomfortable. He was stuck in that relaxed position, unsure of what to say.

"I think you should go." Sasha said into her mug.

Nick rolled his tongue and then hooked his lower lip with his teeth. He breathed out of his nostrils without making any noise. Even though Sasha had told him to go, he wasn't sure whether it was the right thing to do. He continued to feel glued to the sofa, more out of indecisiveness as he also knew it wasn't the right thing to stay. *What do I do?*

The image of a rotating planet earth spun on the red background in the television screen. A news presenter replaced the globe and began silently talking to them.

"Nick, I think you should go." Sasha repeated.

Nick swallowed, leant forward and rubbed his right hand over his fisted left one. "Ok. I'll go. I get it." His thighs levered his body upward and midway to his ascent, Sasha continued. "Now, Nick. You should go now."

The fingers on his right hand rubbed the wedding-finger of his left hand. "I'll go." He said, walking away from the sofa.

Sasha stood with new found energy. She bent to place her mug onto the coffee table. It created enough noise for Nick, with his back to her, to know she had put it down. "Now, Nick!" Her voice was thunderous.

Nick's white socks landed on the kitchen lino, and he turned back. His own voice also much firmer. "I know. I'm going." His compassion had been replaced with frustration and a sense of his own injustice. He understood she was upset, but equally, he felt it wasn't fair for her to speak to him so aggressively.

Sasha raised her arm and pointed in the direction of the front door. "I mean you need to leave the flat."

Nick was tall. He stood like the BFG in the kitchen, dumbstruck, feeling extremely intimidated despite his size. He returned her direct stare. Their eyes met. Where Sasha had previously lost herself in Nick's hazel irises, she now stood solidly opposite them like a combatant ready for war; a different kind of annihilation. Her blue was the blue-grey of a sleety Siberian sky, defensive and offensive. And as if in some sinister Russian-western, long stares poured across the room; each knew that the next move could cause devastation.

"You can't live here." She said, her voice controlled, composed even.

"I can't just move out on the spot." Nick responded like a card player placing his cards without delay, the focus shifted as quickly as it settled.

"Go and stay with somebody from your real life." Sasha had never been nasty, and while she spoke with an eerie calmness, the bitterness charging her words was unmistakable. Nick's cheeks flushed, not quite the red of BBC news but enough to demonstrate that Sasha had embarrassed him. His head dipped and his eyes broke from her stare. The barrier dividing the carpet and grey lino filled his vision. "It's not appropriate, Nick. You need to leave. You hurt me; encouraged me to develop feelings for you. It would be wrong to stay; exploitative."

Exploitative? Nick's heart tensed. He hated how she was making him sound. He stopped looking at the floor and made the mistake of appealing the judgment she had cast on him. "Come-on Sash, exploitative?"

She exploded. "Get out! Get out! Get out!"

Nick's face winced backward as if her shouts were physical objects flying toward him. Then, her mug did fly toward him. He ducked and avoided its torpedoing spiral across the flat. His large torso twisted downward. His head bowed toward the floor, which his knee lightly brushed. Hot tea stained the carpet and lino and pieces of the mug fell onto the kitchen surface beneath the wall upon which it had just smashed. Nick lifted his head and saw Sasha looking down on him from the same spot she had threw the tea. "Get out." She said, her voice drained, and once again, hollow. "Please Nick, just get out." Her power dissolved into desperation.

Nick's hand pressed onto the lino so that he could leverage himself up. Droplets of tea had splattered onto his white shirt. He raised his hands into a semi-surrender position, unsure as to how she would next react. He thought about just leaving. He wanted to. But he emphasised a twist of his neck that drawn attention to his looking in the direction of his bedroom. He wanted to suggest his thoughts to Sasha before expressing them. He maintained his stare at the wall for a few seconds and then spoke, his words travelling toward the bricks even though they were for Sasha. It was as if directing the words elsewhere would disguise the fact that they were Nick's. "I'm going to get a few things, and then I'll go."

Sasha sat back down on the sofa and stared away from the kitchen. She looked out of the front window. Nick glanced to check that she had definitely stopped looking at him. He took this as her acceptance: an agreement for him to collect a few things from his room before leaving. He left the open planned living area with a sense that he needed to hurry-up. He knew she wasn't looking at him – that nobody was looking at him – but he felt as if he were on a stage with thousands of people in the audience critiquing the minutest movement of his muscles. He had never felt more self-conscious, more exposed.

He tossed the largest bag he could find – his old gym bag – onto the bed and began stuffing it with clothes. He prioritised work shirts, underwear and socks, and then crammed as much else into the bag as he could fit. He stretched to grab the frosted 'Happy 18th Birthday' glass from the top shelf of his storage unit, and removed the wad of cash notes stored within. The strap of his gym bag wrapped over his shoulder, and a coat and jumper hung over his arm. He was leaving. He assumed he would come back for the rest of his stuff when Sasha calmed down, but unsure as to when that would be, he inwardly said goodbye. But it wasn't just to the room. He said goodbye to the life it represented. 'Perhaps Sasha was right', he thought… *perhaps I have been exploitative – hiding, using this place… well, not anymore…* He felt nothing. He had spent the last four years of his life sleeping in that room. His late twenties. Nothing. He had nothing to show for it. Nothing to feel for it. He didn't feel sad, nostalgic, apprehensive about potentially missing the place. He was glad that Sasha had pushed him. He thought about that mug flying over his head toward the wall – the violence, the passion, the energy of it – and realised that it was the most alive, the most present, he had felt in that flat than at any other time within the last four years.

He took one last look of his room and to his surprise did feel something: excitement, elevation, emancipation. The dull décor, the familiarity, the inevitability slid away from his shoulders. The room detached from his possession. It was no longer his. He cared nothing for it. Sasha could have it. He walked back through the living area and neither he or Sasha acknowledged one another. They didn't know it then, but they would not see each other again.

PART 2

ESCAPING THE MONSTER

Chapter 7 – Two years later, building a life

People sat cross-legged on the fake grass of the gentrified South Bank. They drank pimms & lemonade from plastic cups and chatted about pop-up restaurants and funky new club openings. The Thames took on a less brown-grey colour under the beautiful blue-sky that blessed London's eccentric mismatched skyline, its architectural pick-a-mix make-up. Nick's legs stretched-out in front of his bottom. His flat palms rested on the grass and supported his torso so that he could lean back.

The man he was with had popped to the toilet. Nick thought about how far he had come since leaving Nuneaton and Sasha. They were behind him. He'd cleansed himself of the drama. He still saw Fred occasionally, and every now and again, he even indulged in thoughts of a future where they stayed together. The thought of it lit a fire in his heart. He had grown to love Fred in the flat they shared; in their trips back to visit Fred's family; in their London life. But the relationship was not romantic. It was intimate, in one the most special ways: Fred had become Nick's first true friend and for that he would remain grateful. Fred was the chaotic, melodramatic yin to his otherwise ordered, serious yang. They were not destined for one another though. The courage that brought them together – the determination to disrupt the provincial life that neither of them wanted – was also the thing that drove them apart. After finding their feet in the big city; after helping one another adjust and settle, they needed to let each other go. To properly integrate themselves into lives of their own.

The sunshine warmed the top of Nick's hands. The beams flowed down the inside of his stretched-out fingers, and he sat on the fake grass, feeling warm inside and out. His lips curled at the side, and a slight chuckle surfaced as he thought about Fred.

"What's amused you?" The guy said as he sat himself back down beside Nick.

"Nothing – just thinking about Fred."

"How's he doing?" The guy asked.

"Good." Nick said on autopilot, the way people do when people ask about a friend that they don't really know or care about. "To be honest, I haven't seen him for ages. The last time was at that guy's funeral."

"What funeral?" The guy lifted his plastic cup out of the little mound formed with his jumper. He sipped the Pimms and lemonade and then held it with both hands. His feet and bottom were flat, and his knees arched into the air.

"I never told you about Michael?" Nick continued as the guy shook his head. "It was this rich guy that Fred went on a date with before we moved to London. He ended up randomly bumping into him again, like a year later, just before we moved out of our flat. Anyway, the guy had cancer – no family or proper friends left – so Fred moved in to live with him for the last few weeks of his life."

"Why?"

Nick knew the answer but it felt a bit too intimate to say. "You know."

"Not really." The guy said taking another sip. "Did he expect something out of the will?" The guy's teeth shined as his face transitioned into an open-lipped smile. Cynicism was cool in London.

"Fred's a dick, but he isn't a gold-digger…" Nick said taking a sip of his own drink – he hadn't become a full Londoner yet. "Besides, he hasn't got the discipline to be a gold-digger – he'd never be able to do anything he doesn't like for two days let alone three weeks." Nick lowered the cup away from his face and smiled as he thought about Fred's impulsive nature. A short, comfortable silence breathed between them. Nick rounded-up the topic of Fred: "He was being kind – didn't want the guy to die alone."

They both drank and then Nick wedged his cup back into the mound he'd made to stop it falling. "So, what're you up to this afternoon?" Nick asked.

"Start work at 7 – sticking around for a drink?"

"Might do – although I said I'd meet Heeta in Soho so I will have to dart off soon. We've hardly seen each other for the last few weeks and we agreed that we'd make a bit of time for each other." Nick looked at his watch, the sleeves of his work shirt were rolled up slightly tanned arms. "In-fact, it's quarter to six already, so I should probably head of after these."

"I'll walk over with you – I need to pop into Foyles and then grab something to eat before I start work. Ready now if you are?"

"Sure." Their little plastic cups clinked, and the remnants of brown liquor disappeared down each of their throats. "God, I don't know why we buy this crap – Pimms never tastes as good as you think it's going to."

They stood together. It was still too warm for jumpers, so they carried them. The grey concrete staircase allowed them to exit the sky-garden of fake grass and re-join the embankment proper. The black railing separating the walkway from the Thames, shimmered in the sun pouring onto it. Nick and his friend strolled beside. Although they had plenty of time to cross the river and head into the West End, they sustained a respectable London pace that prevented them getting dirty stares and huffs from fellow pedestrians.

"Oh shit." Nick said as their feet landed onto the top step of the outdoor staircase that elevated them onto Charing Cross bridge. "I've left my sodding work bag." Nick turned and took-in the bird's eye view of the embankment, the walk they had just done. "I'll have to run back for it." Nick lent in and hugged his friend, their arms wrapped across one another's shoulder and their hands softly patted each other's back.

"Cool – pop in for a drink after you've finished with Heeta." Their hugs loosened and Nick began stepping back down the stairs, squeezing between rows of people climbing up.

"I will." He called back, waving his hand into the air behind him. He jogged back along the embankment to the sky-garden. Nick was in excellent shape and so despite the heat, the exercise didn't come anywhere close to causing him to break a sweat. His bag was where he had left it. He walked, calmer now that he knew his bag wasn't lost, and also because running through the sky-garden would have disturbed the energy of the place. He mumbled to the group that had claimed the space, that he was just getting his bag. They nodded at him while sipping their mostly full cups of Pimms. They looked pleased that the ownerless bag had been retrieved by somebody. The single strap pressed itself against Nick's work shirt and bobbed against his side, as he set back off. He traversed the same stretch of the embankment for the third time.

Once he had crossed the river, he checked his watch again. He had plenty of time. Crowds layered on top of crowds around Charing Cross Station. People left bars and restaurants, but even more people entered in their place. The West End was electric in the evening regardless of the day of the week. Nick slowed his pace as he approached the crossing – it was safer to stroll on this side of the river. Tourists outnumbered Londoners, and the Londoners that were around were increasingly drunk. The business strides of the day were transitioning into the stumbles of the night. Doubled decker buses stopped on either side of the crossing, and hordes of people exchanged their side of the road. The grandiose columns of the National Gallery glittered ahead. Baby blue sky filled the spaces between each column and the effect made the Romanesque grandeur of the building live-up to the high expectations conveyed by the symmetrical fountains, protective lions, and large open spaces of Trafalgar square. Nick begun many of his dates at Trafalgar Square. He never tired of it. He loved the romance of the place.

He checked his watch once again. There was time for a quick drink before he needed to meet Heeta. Nick crossed the road to make a little detour. Trafalgar Square right-angled into his side view, and a dingy old-looking tavern took centre stage. Nick ducked to enter the pub without banging his head on the wooden frame. He avoided the shabby drab bar on the ground floor, and instead took the staircase down toward the basement.

With each step, the melody to Cher's *If Only I Could Turn Back Time,* became louder. However, a voice less brilliantly scratchy and soulful, sang the lyrics. Nick twisted around the dark corner, ducked his head to avoid another wooden beam, and then entered a terrifically camp Karaoke bar. There could not have been more than twenty men in the bar, yet the place felt completely full. A man wearing a blue vest strutted over to Nick. From afar, his skin looked smooth and gave the impression of youth. However, as he came close enough to lean in and kiss Nick on either side of his cheeks, the illusion of youth melted instantly. The man was easily in his fifties, and his five face lifts did not alter that fact.

"Nick darling! It's been too long. Too long. What are you drinking?"

"I was here literally last night." Nick said.

"Oh, hush darling. Gin and tonic, Xavier!" The man shouted across to the bar to his husband. "Gin and tonic for our Nicholas." The man hooped his arm around Nick and began chaperoning him through the clumps of men singing along to the lyrics floating across the two cubed television screens hanging from the low ceiling. Nick's head didn't touch the ceiling, but he instinctively lurched because of the feeling that it couldn't be that far away. The man serving behind the little bar, Xavier, was also in his fifties. He didn't seem to have had the face lifts of his husband, who was still attached to Nick. He filled a glass half full with gin.

"Hello Nicholas." Xavier had a Spanish accent that emphasised the 'hola' in Nic-hola-s. He held a spray gun in his hand. "Tonic or lemonade, darling?" His 'darling' sounded more like harling.

"Tonic please." Nick said.

"Sweetie, I am so happy I see you again tonight. You es beautiful, eh?" He said as he sprayed the tonic into the glass of Gin. Nick removed his wallet and went to remove his debit card. The man put the spray gun down, pushed the glass forward to slide it across the bar. He slapped Nick's hand, quite hard. "Don't be estupid. No pay. You sing me a beautiful song." The man pursed his lips into a scrunched air kiss and winked afterward.

Simon, his one arm still linked through Nick's, shoved his other hand in Nick's face. His index finger straightened onto Nick's lips, gesturing he should be silent. "Don't argue with us love. Now tell us what you'll be singing."

Nick liked singing, and he had a good voice, but the thought of singing Karaoke after only a few drinks filled him with dread. Yet he felt obligated and to Nick, obligation trumped personal comfort. As a good Geordie, Nick hated the idea of not reciprocating generosity. They had welcomed him into their bar as if he were an old friend, when the reality was that he had been in the pub a dozen times at most – and they had just given him another free drink. He had to sing. It was the least he could do. He expected them to pressurise him, but they usually waited at least half hour. Their speed caught him off-guard – the plan had been one drink. Now he would have to down his gin for Dutch courage, order another one to not look cheap; drink that for more Dutch courage, and then one more, just for the road.

"Fine." He said to them both, taking a large gulp of the gin and tonic, which was easily at least two parts gin, to one-part tonic.

"Fantastic." The man behind the bar said – *fantastique.*

"Oh Nicholas, you sweetie, what are you going to sing?" Before Nick responded, the man unhooked himself and dashed off behind the bar. "Sorry darling, one second." He returned from the stock cupboard with two bags of pork scratchings. "Here darling, you are too skinny." The man opened one of the packets and shoved them into Nick's hands. He placed the other packet on the bar for afters. "Too skinny." He repeated. The man was thin as a rake and the irony was completely lost on him. Nick lifted a large pork scratching and began crunching on it. He was hungry. The fat melted in his mouth and the salt tingled his tongue.

"Now, what song do you want?" The man returned to his question. "We've had ABBA and Madonna already, so perhaps something else sweetheart..." He was about to suggest another singer, but Nick interrupted. He knew what he wanted to sing.

"Fast Car – Tracey Chapman."

"Ooo, lovely. Haven't heard that one in ages." Simon locked his eyes onto Nick and his smile intensified. It wasn't creepy. It was tender. Nick's song choice had surprised him. It was an intimate song; of course, people sang intimate songs at his Karaoke bar but usually toward the end of the night when everybody was pissed. The early hours – anything before nine – typically involved something safely camp.

Nick thought about it afterward and regretted it immediately. He downed the gin and tonic, and Xavier began making him another without Nick asking. Nick reached for his wallet. He would definitely pay for this one. Xavier sprayed even less tonic and poured even more gin than the first drink. The 3:1 ratio widened with each round until the spray of tonic was more for appearance. He slapped Nick's hand again. Xavier too appreciated Nick's song choice; it earnt him another free drink.

Nick finished while another patron sang Kylie Minogue. Xavier had another gin and tonic waiting for him on the bar. Nick did actually pay for that one.

The patron was coming to the end of the song and although his beard kept blocking the microphone, it did not stop his voice screeching throughout the room. He was terrible, but everybody cheered anyway. That was the etiquette of gay Karaoke in Halfway to Heaven.

Simon took the microphone from the bushy beard Kylie Minogue singer during another eruption of cheering. "Ok. Ok. Calm down ladies." He said to the men. "While I know it is virtually impossible to top that performance – love you really Bernie." The pub roared at Simon's soft aside... "We do have someone that was blessed with an actual voice... up next – put your hands together, gentlemen – Mr. Nicholas Du Bois."

Oh fuck, thought Nick, *I'm up already... and why on earth is he building expectation.*

"Come and share that gorgeous Geordie voice." Simon began clapping and the rest of the pub copied. However, as the soft rifts of Tracey Chapmans' guitar began flowing into the room, a hair-raising charge of silent energy overcame everybody. Nick looked at the floor as he squeezed through the clusters of men wedged together like flamingos at a watering hole.

The microphone rested on a stand. Nick's arms dangled to his sides, unsure of what they ought to be doing. The melody repeated a couple of times and Nick internally tuned into its emotion, its desperate longing for escape coupled with the tiniest flicker of hope and possibility. He sang the first line, the simple monosyllabic words came together and set the tone of the performance: soulful, heartfelt, unpretentious. Like Aretha Franklin, it didn't need big words: *"I want a ticket to anywhere."* The men of the bar filled that *ticket* and *anywhere* with their own memories, their own moments of escape and arrival.

His voice gained momentum and rolled two sentences into one; the audience submitted and rode its stronger waves. And like a wave breaking against sand, they enjoyed its lulls too... it's emotional back and forth. *"Any place is better."* Nick's voice, bittersweet, in its simultaneous ability to express bleakness and romance; reality and fantasy; here and there.

"I got nothing to prove." His voice crescendoed as passion begot passion; as reckless confidence struggled through his overly controlled self. His rationality joined his emotion and soul. His brown hazel eyes locked onto to the men in the audience, who gazed in silence, enraptured in his rendition. His vulnerability and insecurities flowered. He shared his romance, his intimacy with every man in the room. Grandeur unselfconsciously contrasted with poverty in an age-old allure of a story elevating its protagonist from rags to riches. *"Finally see what it means to be living."*

Nick laid himself bare. It was more than performance. It was truth. Personal and somehow the audience knew – felt it. This *was* Nick's story: *"My old man's got a problem… Mama wanted more from life than he could give."* Nick's mum hadn't left. He'd wanted her to. But she never did. The audience didn't detect that though – the performance had become autobiographical in spirit if not detail. He continued. The literal inaccuracy didn't weaken Nick's energy and ownership. The song consumed him; he gave it everything; embodied it. He became the lyrics in spite of the lack of compassion he felt for his own father. Of course, he wasn't conscious of it – he was barely conscious of the room at all. He felt as if he were back in his bedroom, lying on his bed, door shut, headphones-on, listening to the song on repeat; singing along in complete privacy. *"We gotta make a decision… Leave tonight or live and die this way."* He sang the words to himself. Those words helped him to acknowledge his own existence; to love and to allow himself to care about his own desires; to make him feel as if he mattered.

"Speed so fast it felt like I was drunk." The heartiest smile spread across Nick's face. The audience assumed he was reliving memories of some romantic elopement, but Nick had never eloped or developed a thrill for dangerous driving. The words were enough. The thought and fantasy alone was enough; the sheer possibility of being with somebody and sharing such exhilaration was enough.

Suffering dripped lavishly – proudly – from his voice. The simple image of an arm wrapped around a shoulder referred to more than physical affection: it was liberation, an allowing of himself the possibility that a man one day might love him; that he might receive the kind of love he wanted. *"I could be someone, be someone, be someone."* His voice decreased in energy and enthusiasm upon each repetition. Saying the same words over burst the illusion. It reminded him of where he was. He returned to the room. He left his memory and imagination and brought the doubt of his wider adolescence into the bar. The more expansive sadness of his childhood replaced the rarer optimism and hope of his bedroom. Yet, his voice never fell into futility. His sombreness wavered like a violin string, which always contained the potential for monumental uplift, no matter how heart-crushingly devastating it could sound in any one moment. With a slight flick of the wrist, the instrument could change everything. The audience hung onto Nick's instrument. They awaited its next move, its next flicker.

They were not disappointed. The emotional journey continued throughout the song. Nick's voice raised and lowered expectations of love and the happy ever after he secretly wanted for himself, despite it being a wild fantasy throughout most of his youth. He rounded off the song by projecting the question away from himself and onto the audience. He made them feel as if it was no longer his story, his fantasy – or Tracey Chapman's – it was theirs. It took that group of twenty gay men back to their own adolescent dreams of coming out: *"Leave tonight or live and die this way."*

A thousand hands began clapping, or it sounded that way to Nick. The men applauded him so much that he had no space to be embarrassed. Of course, it was his natural instinct, but the sound beat down the red blush surfacing under his cheeks. Simon walked to stand beside Nick. "Sorry Bearnie, you're barred." He said into the microphone. The pub roared adding to the noise of the thunderous clapping. Bernie, the bearded Kylie Minogue singer, raised both hands into the air, gesturing defeat.

"I'll give you this one." He shouted over to Nick, over the laughing and applause that was beginning to calm.

"Ok. Ok. That's enough, that's enough." Simon said into the Microphone. He turned toward the laptop resting on the side. He fingered a couple of buttons. "What do we have up next…?" He said more to himself than the room. "Lovely!" His back unsprang to its erect position. He called the name of the next poor sod to go up, followed by the name of the song and its original singer: "Cyndie Lauper - Girls, they just wanna have fun". Like goldfish, the men forgot the last four minutes of intensity. The electro-pop beat brought out in them a carefree, happy-go-lucky, loose-hipped enthusiasm. They were ready to dance and bob along to the next song, the new playful rhythm.

Simon strutted back through the bar, his hand locked onto Nick's as he pulled him along. He imagined how rock stars must feel after they come off stage. This performance felt different from others he had given. London was helping him connect to people; to be more open. The lack of reservation made his voice stronger. It wasn't so much that he could hear it. Quite the opposite. He stopped hearing himself. When he used to perform, his consciousness was separate from his words. A part of him held back so that he could monitor and check everything that came out. In public, he had never been able to master the art of giving himself totally to the song; to get lost in its story and emotion. He had always given technically good performances. But a critic lingered in them. Nick had lacked that capacity to suspend his supervisory role; to let go, give it everything, and allow others to judge, exclusively. As he strode across the floor, his hand in Simon's, he recognised that that had changed: he had just put himself out there, and he felt proud. In moments of that song, he accepted that he was good enough, and sang without any thought of how he would be received.

Lucian, another bearded regular, found it all too easy to let go. He butchered Cyndie Lauper through the mic. He screeched the chorus as if he needed to release twenty years of passion all in one go, through a medium to which he lacked talent entirely. Singing wasn't for Lucian, but he didn't care and neither did the patrons. They screeched back and sang along with him. Nick smiled another hearty smile. He could sing – he might be the only person in that bar that could sing – and yet he seemed to be the only person that had been worried about being judged.

"Bravo, Nicholas." Xavier said placing a fresh gin and tonic onto the counter: 4:1 gin to tonic ratio. "Es beautiful, eh?" He added, waving his hand to refuse payment for the drink. "Nicholas, es true!" His voice boomed in response to Nick's modesty – his chin lowered itself, and his eyes swept the floor. Xavier stretched his hairy arm across the counter and cupped Nick's chin. Skin pincered between his thumb and finger. "Boy, es true." He repeated, this time to Nick's face, which Xavier had lifted upward. "Hon-es-tly, Nicholas, was beautiful." Xavier dismissed the rest of the patrons with a scrunch of his face and sprawl of his hand, the sort of facial gesture provoked by a sour lemon or something that tastes bad. "You no like these guys. You is proper singer. Why no sing for job?"

Nick almost laughed. The idea of singing for a living was preposterous. *How could I depend on that for a living?* He thought to himself. "Es risk." Xavier said intercepting Nick's thought. "Of course, risk, yes." A pleasurable smile lingered on his face, as if something sweet and tasty rested on his tongue. "But life!" He pronounced 'life' as if the word itself was, and not only conveyed, abundance. "Life!" He repeated, in a wicked medusa gaze. "Life es risk. No have risk. No have life." Nick understood his argument, and appreciated his friendly, father-like pep-talk, but he was not convinced. He smiled in return, acknowledging Xavier's warmth, and suggesting that he would think about what he had said. Xavier burst into an animated laugh and his hands sandwiched Nick's cheeks, taking Nick slightly by surprise. "You no listen! But one day, you will know I speak truth. You come here when." His hands released and Nick felt as if he had been lowered back to the ground even though he never physically left.

He gulped the gin and splash of tonic, emptying half of the glass, and then lifted the glass immediately afterward to finish the rest of the drink. Xavier continued laughing. A gin bottle already tilted in his hand, its crystal-clear liquid falling like a miniature waterfall into the glass. The tonic was now for appearance: 5:1 ratio. Nick took his debit card and Xavier allowed him to pay. He stood at the bar and drank this one a little slower. He enjoyed watching the others sing: Madonna's Material Girl replaced Cyndie Lauper, and Whitney Houston's *I wanna dance with somebody* replaced her. Xavier continued making drinks for the other patrons. His expressive enthusiasm never faded.

Nick snuck-out of the pub – Halfway to Heaven – as Belinda Carlisle returned for the second time that evening. He didn't say goodbye as he knew they would insist on giving him another drink, which would entrap him into buying another in return. He had to leave if he was going to meet Heeta on time, not to mention, get up for work, alive, the following morning.

The sunlight struck him as if it were a sheet of lightening that stayed permanently switched-on. He'd only been in the bar a forty-five minutes, but he'd knocked back four of Xavier's gins, which translated in real terms as ten to fifteen singles… or as Nick had begun to measure his alcohol consumption: half a bottle of gin; and that was on top of a few shots of Pimms at the Southbank, which he didn't really count toward his total intake of alcohol due to the stingy measures they poured.

The heat of the day remained in the atmosphere. It had blended with the bus and taxi fumes lingering across London's hodgepodge road-network, the smog that would keep its night owls warm. It wasn't yet the height of summer, but it would remain light for at least another hour. Nick had become used to the slightly metallic taste in the air – it bothered him when he first moved to London, but now he expected it, had even grown fond of it, kind of like an environmental Stockholm Syndrome. The National Gallery glittered ahead. Nick strolled toward it. The warm fuzz of alcohol spread through his bloodstream. It brewed an emotion that distorted his perception of everything going on around him. It softened the hard edges and spikes atop of the railings along St. Martin's church. It dulled the horns and de-escalated the aggression of pissed-off taxi-drivers; slowed the criss-crossing, chaotic commuters, and tourists. The world calmed but continued its business. The alcohol made London easier to process.

A simple side street merged Trafalgar and Leister square, which despite depictions of tube stations were practically next to one another. Crowds blossomed over the pavements around the inner gardens, and clusters of small groups ate and drank overpriced beers, super-sugared cocktails, and banquets of crap food, albeit al fresco, on the numerous bar and restaurant patios bordering each side of the square. Nick enjoyed watching the haze of chatter as he strolled past them.

Chinese lanterns flickered overhead as Leicester Square ricocheted into China Town. Peking Ducks dangled and rotated in windows. Behind them, large circular tables covered in white table cloths hosted groups of noisy people chatting to each other while smearing plum sauce for their self-constructed spring rolls. In other restaurants, hordes of hungrier customers bobbed along all-you-can-eat countertops, squeezing small mountains of food onto barely visible plates. Nick's tongue rubbed at the space where his teeth met his gums – he was thinking of the pork scratchings, checking for any tiny remnants that lingered. He was peckish, and as he crossed Shaftsbury Avenue, the main road dividing China Town and Soho, he decided that he would order a little something when he met Heeta.

Nick walked past the rather stark church, which was fenced in by a low brick wall and a serious wire-mesh barrier. It was like an inverted prison, a space that considered the rest of the area barbaric and dangerous, and itself a safe haven, a barriered fortress that could keep the world out. Nick thought that it looked out of place, which is a pretty big statement for a building in a city that manages to harmonise Gherkins, Giant Clocks, Palaces, Tenements and Abbeys. He wondered about its History and made a note to himself to find out. The music from the bear-bar across the road soon caused the thoughts to dissipate. Rather rotund men with thick beards and thinning hair stood in small groups drinking pints of beer. Next door attracted a fruiter cliental – Nick quite liked the place. Its neon coloured sign set a friendly, camp tone, *The*

Village. However, the almost naked guys dancing around a pole attached to the bar inside, balanced the effect. The bar had funky, bright branding on the outside that made itself welcoming to anyone wanting to venture in, but it unashamedly made clear that the inside was bold and uncompromising in what it was about. It proudly peacocked its sexuality to the street: the dancing men were positioned close to the entrance and front windows, just enough for passers-by to sneak a peek at their muscular smooth flesh.

Nick peered into the open door and stared as he walked past, but the dancer never returned even a whiff of a gaze. He was trained to remain elevated, god-like in his outlook and perspective; his attention reserved for a higher reality than that of the mere mortals worshiping at their feet (and thighs) beneath. They were pagan, not Christian Gods – characterised by power, personal strength, and ambition. A kind ear and benevolent eye, they were not.

Nick's stomach rumbled as he turned the corner into Old Compton Street. Heeta stood with her back pressed to the window of Balans. Her thumbs tapped into the mobile phone she held. As Nick approached, the phone slid into her pocket and she looked-up, a warm smile stretched across her face. Despite her shortness, Heeta had presence. Her projected grandeur had only increased since moving to London. Her high heels announced to the world, *don't fuck with me,* and in general, it didn't. She leant forward and hugged Nick. He lowered himself so that her arms could wrap around his shoulders without her having to lift onto her tip-toes. Even though they didn't do much together, their relationship had grown strong since the move to London – since her replacement of Fred as Nick's flatmate.

"You're twated already."

"Nah – just had a couple after work." Nick said, his words slightly slurred and husky. He was surprised at himself, at hearing his own voice. The last time he had used it was in the bar where everything was loud; where sound was in a constant state of competition. He experienced a slight wave of disorientation, as if it ought to be 3.00am in the morning, post-nightclub.

"Fuck off." Heeta laughed at him whilst linking her arm into his. "Come-on, let's get a table and you can tell me where you've been." Nick did as he was told. The glass door opened inward and arm-in-arm, they entered the gay-restaurant. A chic lady with half of her head shaved, and the other half dangling in curls across one side of her face, welcomed Nick and Heeta.

"Hey – do you have a reservation?"

"Seven, fifteen – we're a bit early. Hope that's ok." Heeta said, smiling at the woman in more than a platonic manner. The woman reciprocated the flirtation with a flick of her hair and a sultry blink of the eyes.

"No problem. We've got a table by the window. It's ready for you now. Follow me." The woman took two menus from her little counter and strutted toward the table without looking back. She expected them to follow, and they did, Heeta ahead of Nick. The woman placed the menus onto the table and slightly pulled one chair ajar. Heeta slid her delicate frame into it, her head high and breasts held firm as she sat. The woman kept one of her hands on the back of the chair and Heeta's back brushed the top of her fingernails. "Can I take your drink order?"

Heeta met her gaze. "Gin and tonic."

"Hendricks, Bombay Sapphire, or Gordons?"

"My ex used to call me Bombay Sapphire, so I'll have Hendricks. Time for something fresh." The woman was impressed. She scribbled something onto her pad and grinned. She looked at Nick, expecting his order without having to ask.

"He'll have the same." Heeta said. The woman scratched onto her pad again.

"Ok. Somebody will be right over with your drinks and to take your order." The woman brushed Heeta's back with the subtlest increase of pressure in her finger nails, enough to let her know it was intentional, but not so much to make it obvious or invasive.

"I didn't realise you'd booked a restaurant." Nick said once they were alone.

"I assumed you wouldn't have eaten dinner – you haven't have you?"

"No. I'm starving. It's perfect – just hadn't expected it."

"Oh good – thought you were going to make me eat alone for a second." Heeta picked up the menu.

The items absorbed their attention: quail eggs sounded too insubstantial and pretentious; lasagne, too heavy and simple. "Think I'm going to settle for the burger." Nick said. The truth was that he had not been to many restaurants in his life. As a child, takeaways were a real luxury, and they pretty much consisted of Fish & Chip shops. His mum had brought a Chinese meal home once from the supermarket, but it had caused such a terrible argument that most of the meal ended in the bin, uneaten. He didn't know food. It wasn't that he was particularly unhealthy; more inexperienced and unconfident. The London restaurant scene was an aspect of the city he was yet to discover. The prices scared him too. The £15 printed in a fancy italic font beside the burger made him think of a £3 Big Mac Meal. Nick wasn't cheap: he was prepared to spend money on things he wanted and valued. The problem with food was that he had so few reference points. The prices just seemed wild to his statistically savvy mind, a bad deal. *Would this burger be five times better than a big mac?* He thought. *Probably not.*

"I'm going for the Halloumi moussaka." Heeta said, her eyes scanned up and down the page as if her choice could shift. It wouldn't. Heeta was a decision maker. Nick wondered how a Halloumi moussaka would look and taste.

"So, Nikki-boy, let's get down to business." Heeta said.

A poker-game silence bounced between them. Nick considered the intrigue of her words. "I knew you'd be up to something... Making out like you wanted to spend a bit of quality time together." His teeth sparkled within a warm smile, and hers imitated.

"Oh, shut your face. We've got our own lives and we love that about each other." The woman returned with the gin and tonics. She plonked Nick's glass onto the table and placed Heeta's. The difference was noted. Heeta's tongue ran over her lower lip as she gave a small, deferential nod of appreciation. The woman brushed her nails against the side of Heeta's arm as she walked away.

"When did you become such a power lesbian?"

"Oh, fuck off. I've got years of catching-up to do." She took a sip of her drink, inspiring Nick to do the same. Unlike the glass in Halfway to Heaven, it contained fancy ice cubes, intricate frosting, and wedges of lime carved into fancy spiral patterns. However, also unlike Halfway to Heaven, the gin was diluted in a small ocean of sugary tonic. Nick felt himself sobering up as he sipped. Their glasses returned to the table and Heeta continued. "I've been looking at places."

Shit. The crevices of Nick's lips tilted downward and his cheeks sank at the thought of having to flat share with a stranger. He liked living with Heeta. She was clean and reliable without being anal, overly domestic or fussy. The best bits of Sasha without the crazy or neediness. Heeta put him out of his misery.

"For us, you moron."

"Ah!" Air gushed out and his body leant forward. Both hands pressed flat onto the table. "I've had too much to drink to have to think about living with some crazy wierdo." The poker-game silence returned as they examined one another briefly – they knew how the other felt, but they needed to be sure... "So, you're pretty happy then, with how things are?" Nick asked.

She nodded. "Yeah. You?"

In his inebriated state, affection flowed easily. He stretched his arms across the table and took her hands into his. "Heeta Patel… will you continue living with me?"

"Nikki boy… Abso-fucking-lutely."

They stopped testing each other and relaxed. Heeta continued. "But I am ready to move. The flat is nice and all, but we're both commuting, and socialising in the city and West End…"

Nick interrupted. "I get it… I think it's a good idea."

"I was hoping you'd say that…" Their relationship was mature and honest. They respected the reality of their both needing to be happy with the arrangement, and gave each other space to flag concerns and voice reservation. That involved conversations about money. "Can you afford it?"

The £15 italicised price of the burger glittered and caught Nick's eye. "How much are you thinking?" He said.

"I'd prefer to spend a bit more than we currently do – work is going well and I've acclimatised to London; figured out how to financially navigate it better than I could a year ago… but it's got to be right for both of us…"

Numbers flickered through Nick's head in the form of excel rows and columns. He kept a spreadsheet to monitor his finances: rent, travel, food, utilities, phone, holidays, gym, toiletries, nights-out, savings. Most of the expenses remained fairly static, but the sum in the *nights-out* box had been increasing month on month. "I'd have to cut back a bit on going out, and I'm not fussed on a holiday this year… but generally, things aren't bad, so I'm sure I could spend a bit more on rent."

"But do you want to? It's got to be something you prioritise…" The ellipsis at the end of her statement left a larger than expected whole for Nick to fill. He wasn't sure how to answer.

"Yeah…" He said thinking on the spot… "No, definitely." His enthusiasm picked-up and momentum gathered in his voice. He visualised a more adult home and began to think more specifically about where he was going over time, rather than that evening. "I'm thirty-three this year… I should be thinking about finding a nicer place to live."

Heeta agreed. But his response did not give her the confidence she desired. "I think that's great, Nick. But you skirted the question: is it something you actually want, or just something that you feel you ought to be doing? Because in my experience, if it's the latter, it won't work."

"It's something that I want." Nick responded assertively. He gulped a large portion of his sugary gin and tonic, and as the glass settled back onto the table more empty than full, he recognised that he would need to slow down, again not just the drink in front of him, but the amount he was drinking generally. *It would probably cost a tenner*, he thought. "I need to cut down on the drink anyway."

Heeta smiled a little more earnestly than before. She wasn't fully convinced, but Nick was considering the situation properly. That was enough for now. "Probably not a bad thing." She said.

"Who would have thought Heeta would be discouraging drinking?"

"Oh, come on – there's a difference between getting shit faced for a night out and habitually slinging back half a bottle of gin on a work night." A seriousness settled across her face. "I say it with love, Nikki boy, but it's becoming a lot. I'm not judging… just…"

A slither of anger ran through Nick. He wasn't used to it. Anger wasn't really his thing. There were situations in his life where psychiatrists would have told him feeling angry was normal, but the truth was that he rarely felt proper anger. The unusualness of it – the impulsive urge to argue or dismiss, to argue and dismiss Heeta – shocked him. Fortunately, the feeling of shock trumped the feeling of anger, enough that it did not take hold and translate into action. Nick looked puzzled rather than bitter. "Nick?" Heeta said. She sensed his drift.

"I know." He said, his tone confessional. "I'm going to get on top of it."

"Look – I don't think you need to check yourself into the Betty Ford Clinic or join AA; you just need to perhaps, you know, acknowledge how much you are drinking. Decide whether you are happy with that amount. And if you aren't, then decide on a quantity that you would be happy with."

Nick felt mortified that this conversation was happening. Everything she said was so basic. Why had he allowed the situation to get to a point where somebody was spelling it out? His buzz was definitely wearing off. The soft edging of the world that the alcohol brought about, faded away, and a horizon of hard, sharp edges filled his vision.

"Nick, I'm not judging or encouraging you to go teetotal. I just want to know if you're serious about the move."

A different waiter arrived at the table to take their orders. His pen scratched onto a little notebook as Heeta ordered the Halloumi moussaka. A little tally joined the scratch as Nick ordered the same. Heeta's intervention pushed him out of his comfort zone. He would step into the unknown via a Halloumi moussaka.

"I'm serious about the move. I want it." He said, returning the conversation to their move. "How much extra are you thinking?"

"Well the mortgage adviser thinks that we can borrow up to £400k between us…" Heeta sipped her gin and tonic to conceal her facial expression. The information registered immediately. Nick might have been drunk, but he wasn't stupid.

"You think we should buy together?"

Her glass returned to the table. "This is why I need to know if you're serious. I'm not Mother fucking Teresa. If you want to drink your salary – which I estimated for the mortgage advisor by the way – that's your business. C'est la vie and all that French shit, but if you're interested and serious, then I'm up for this. It's the logical thing to do." She stopped speaking. She had put herself out there and needed to see where Nick was at.

He hesitated. His mouth opened and closed as he went to censor himself. "Just say whatever you're thinking… if we're going to do this, we need to be honest with one another and that won't happen if we hold back." Nick nodded, and even though he found it uncomfortable to share his thoughts, he did.

"I suppose I thought that I'd buy a house when I fell in love; with the person I fell in love with."

Heeta sat calm as if she were a therapist. The comment hardly surprised her. She left a comfortable silence, and then broke the patient-therapist convention by speaking into it. "I never did. I never allowed myself to get caught up in that romantic vision. Not because I was opposed to the idea of loving and sharing my life with someone, but because I never – I mean never – envisaged loving and sharing my life with a man. I knew I never wanted to do that. Fuck. There was no way I was ever going to replicate that part of my mother's life. Not ever. And I suppose the possibility of doing it with a woman never entered my thoughts – never something that I could even consider or think remotely possible… So, I guess, I've had a lot more space to think about how else I might do this."

Nick went to pick up his drink. His hand reached the glass, but he tamed his autopilot. Instead of wrapping his palm around it, he glided his index finger around the smooth rim in soft, unrushed loops. He thought about what Heeta was proposing.

"You don't need to decide immediately. It's a big decision."

"I want to do it." Nick said, his finger was still on the glass but it no longer circled. "It makes sense. I'm in a position to buy… sort of… if I calm down the partying a bit. Owning a house has been something I have always associated with a serious relationship. Not something you do with friends. But hearing myself say it aloud I can hear the insanity and offence in that."

Heeta smiled. She saw the same liberating channel of thought that she had swam. It was opening within Nick. Her instinct to have this conversation felt validated. He continued unspinning the new thinking webbing-out before him.

"I mean I am convinced, was convinced, am unconvincing myself… I don't know… that I shouldn't be reserving my trust and commitment for some fantasy; some idealised person that I may never meet. It's more than that actually… it isn't just reserving, it's withholding: I'm withholding myself from making commitments with real friends – actual relationships – people that I know and like… trust." He connected with her. She was so happy that he was coming to the same conclusion.

"One Halloumi Moussaka." The waiter sprung upon them sooner than either expected. He held one plate toward Nick's part of the table, and the other in the air, reserved for Heeta. "And another Halloumi Moussaka." The second plate descended onto the table. "You guys need anything else?" They shook their heads and lifted cutlery from neatly folded napkins.

"This looks great." Nick's risk had paid off. An obese man on the table opposite, lifted the burger that Nick was going to order. He had no food envy. Warm oozy cheese bubbled across diced aubergine, and as their knives split the dish open. Gushes of steam pushed wonderful smells of Moroccan spice into the air.

"But what if we meet someone?" Nick voiced his one concern.

"Then we meet someone." A slice of Halloumi disappeared from Heeta's fork. She mustered a cheeky smile and a shoulder shrug. She chewed her Halloumi and then swallowed it.

"Look, of course it's a possibility, but so is divorce. There's risk in everything." Nick was reminded of Xavier: *Life es Risk, eh?*

"This is so good by the way."

"I know, right." They shovelled mouthfuls, only slowing to allow the steam to escape. Heeta sensed that Nick needed more reassurance. A slight rupture in the conversation had surfaced. She could tell that he was trying to will his anxiety away. And that never works. "Look, you probably will meet someone way before I do." He was grateful that she had returned to the conversation. "But even if you meet them next year..." Nick squirmed his face. He didn't want his forever relationship to start that soon. He had only just begun to enjoy his London life. "Exactly!" Heeta said, reading his thoughts. "But let's say it happens anyway. You meet someone within twelve months; you date for a year or two; start going on holidays together; stay at each other's place more and more; break-up for a bit; get back together; and, then, then!, you might decide it's for real and that you want to merge your assets and buy a place together... at that distant point... three, four, even, five years down the line, we sell our place. I cry. You cry. But we both walk away having paid down a mortgage, and with a piece of house that will be worth a hell of a lot more than when we bought it." She shovelled another forkful of cheese into her mouth. "I know it's not the most romantic of propositions, but I can't see the downside." The aubergine ground into even smaller pieces.

Nick was sold. "I think it's much more likely to be ten years down the line anyway – minimum." How long do mortgages even last? We could own a place outright before Prince and Princess Charming come along... oh god, we could be Prince and Princess Charming..."

"Twenty or twenty-five years are most common." Heeta got straight to business. The taste and flavour of the Moussaka egged her on. She was determined to make this happen. She was hungry for it. "We would need to go for the longer term though to make it affordable."

"And what sort of places would that allow us to get?"

"Well a good sized three bed flat off Clapham high-street; a small two-bed in Brick Lane; or a manor house in Hull. It depends on the area and what we want. Where do you fancy?"

Round two began. They crossed the first hurdle of agreeing to commit to one another, now the fiercer negotiation of location, location, location, began. It wouldn't be resolved over dinner though. They enjoyed the food while speculating about their future home. No longer would they live in some dingy rental: they would have a proper home, a place that would be theirs. When the boiler blew, they wouldn't have to wait for a non-engaged landlord to dally around for weeks on end while they endured cold-shower after cold-shower; they could sort it, and properly. Not a quick, cheap fix that tied the place over until the next poor tenant came along and suffered through the same thing.

Heeta called for the bill, and the woman with the half-shaved head, half dangly curls reappeared. The waiters weren't stupid. They knew how to maximise their tips. Nick handed Heeta some cash, and she plonked her debit card onto the small receipt in the white dish, paid and then left.

London's daylight had moved East. London was joining the night already upon its Western sisters. "We've got to have one more to celebrate." Heeta said. Her high-heels clacked against the stone pavement of Old Compton Street.

"Well I should probably say no."

"But…" Heeta linked her arm though his.

"But I don't have the mortgage quite yet, so I guess I can make a few more unwise decisions."

"That's my boy." They strolled along Old Compton Street. "Fancy one in O-Bar?"

"Nah." Nick said unenthusiastic. "It feels a bit too coffee shop upstairs, and hardcore downstairs… we're soon to be proprietors, Ms. Patel… We need something suitably sophisticated, a place of ambience and elegance where hardworking professionals can kick back for a late evening aperitif."

"Aperitif happens before meals." She laughed. "What you really mean is that you want to go to The Village? … *Hardworking professionals?!* More like dirty old perverts that want to stare at go-go boys."

"Well there's that too." Nick also laughed.

"Oh, come-on then." They joined the short queue edging along the pavement outside. Two bouncers wore black duffle coats. They scanned the customers, judging whether they were suitable cliental: gay, gay friendly; basically, not too underage, and not going to cause trouble. They raised their eyebrows approvingly at Nick and Heeta.

The music was surprisingly loud after being in the restaurant. The nearly naked men danced on the bar while patrons ordered drinks beneath. "Find us a seat. I'll get the drinks… Put the money towards your first mortgage payment." Heeta said.

The thin bar throbbed with people, and Nick had to press against so many bodies in order to pass through to the back of the room where there was usually a spare table or two. Most people preferred to stand and be a part of the action. He exited the blob of people like a hopeful man escaping a dark wood. He quickened his pace toward the one empty table, a plastic cube with two very low stools beside it. Nick placed his brown satchel bag onto one of them and sat on the other. It was uncomfortable given his size, but he didn't care. After eating, he'd take a seat no matter how impractical.

Heeta returned with two gin and tonics. They were stronger than the ones in the restaurant despite being presented in crude plastic beakers. Heeta popped herself onto the stool, which suited her delicate frame much more than Nick's dangly torso.

"How's work?" Nick asked, as he re-settled his satchel bag between his legs now Heeta had taken the stool.

"Good. I thought it would take longer to sort the department, but things have settled quicker than expected. I'm thinking of applying for an Assistant Headteacher position if this year's results are good again."

"Wow. You'd be great." Nick believed it. She would be great. Heeta was a brilliant teacher – she loved her subject; she loved stories – and so her students' results followed naturally: her classes absorbed her thoughtfulness and regard for the literature they studied. She didn't obsess with Power-Points, spreadsheets and gimmicky gluing and sticking. She stood and conveyed expectation that the books were worth their consideration and time. Her students sensed that Heeta was quietly happy, not unnervingly happy in that forced fake way that suggests a chaotic, unstable, despotic core, beneath a surface of manic bubbliness. They read in her an easy-going contentedness. She seemed good at life. They combined this awareness of her with their understanding of the way she invested in books, to conclude that it was a good investment for them to make too. They got on board, expected the stuff they read to contain meaning, and low and behold, they found it. Self-discipline flowed from engagement and so her classes were simultaneously relaxed and productive. She didn't need to impose order with an iron fist because her students respected and valued her. They weren't being bent against their desire, corrupted away from possession of their own agency.

"I've been reading a bit, and it seems that three years of good results is what they're really looking for." She reduced her knowledge, expertise, and experience into educational currency: exam performance.

"Who are?"

"Senior leadership. It looks especially good when you've led a core department too." Heeta took a sip of her gin and tonic.

"I know I'm still young, but I will have the track record, so I'm thinking, fuck it – what have I got to lose?"

"Absolutely." Nick entered the bar with the determination to drink slower, but he lifted his beaker, and drank almost half of it in one go.

"I didn't expect to get the Head of English position when I applied – thought I was too young, but fuck me, doing the job has made me realise how incompetent half the entitled middle-aged wankers doing the job, are – I'm sure senior leadership will be no different."

Nick raised his beaker and pushed it through the air toward Heeta. "*Vive la revolution!*" He said in a French accent. Their beakers clinked and more gin disappeared. "Seriously though. I think you are dead right. The Head of Maths at my place is alright – she gets it. The kids like her, and they do well. But the leadership team: Jesus, apart from the Head, they're awful. They fanny around the corridors *patrolling* as if they're bobbies on the beat. I think they've forgotten what it's like to teach; what children are about."

"I agree. I call it the big man syndrome." Heeta said. "It's when a school has lost its way. When it relies on big personalities to enforce order because deep down its succumbed to xenophobic fear."

Nick smiled. He wasn't used to listening to her be so serious and intellectual. "Xenophobic fear?" He repeated her phrase.

"It's true. When the leadership team aren't comfortable with difference, it trickles down into policy and practice. They need to control everything – make everything the same. The trust and individual judgment that schools ought to be encouraging disappear, and process enthrones itself at the expense of diversity. It doesn't take a rocket Scientist to appreciate you don't teach *Great Expectations* in the same fucking way as Photosynthesis or fractions. The lessons will obviously feel very different, have totally different flows. That. Is. Ok." She emphasised each word, rebuking the dumb perspective of uniformity. "Every experienced teacher knows this, yet the moronic PE Deputy Headteacher – in charge of *Teaching & Learning* – don't even get me started on this pseudo-scientific occupation! – will insist on conformity under some vague notion of consistency. When did their degree in rounders make them spiritual gurus of the dark mysteries of the human psyche?"

"I love it when you rant."

"Fuck off. I don't do it often, but it really goads my shit when I get going." She gulped her gin while winking at Nick to let him know that she was still calm beneath her costumed rage. Her beaker returned to the table and the liquid now matched Nick's in terms of its quantity. "I am serious though. There is so much waste. So much. And I don't even blame the dumbasses for taking the jobs. They mean well, but fucking Christ, shoot me, if we have to sit through another training session on starter tasks or plenaries." She stuck her fingers together to imitate a gun and pressed her thumb to suggest it firing into her brain. "It is beyond stupid. Most of my department don't need indoctrinating into believing the benefits of the five-part-lesson, they need to re-charge and practice the thing they love. They need to fucking read – to have some space in their lives to enjoy a good fucking book." The beaker sprang back to her lips. "You would not believe the number of English teachers who do not read outside of work while bemoaning in the staffroom that kids don't read anymore. Seriously, they say this without irony or humiliation. None. How do they not recognise that they are talking about themselves? The kids certainly do."

Nick's teeth shone like pearl moons in the darkly lit bar. He was enjoying Heeta letting out the steam from her inner pit of fiery passion. She continued, encouraged by his smile.

"I'm not even blaming them. I get it. The day is loaded with classes, the evening with marking; feeding, washing – if there's energy and time left, playing with the kids. I get it. Life is busy. Tough. But come on! Don't fucking teach English, if you don't love books." Her voice flickered to a plea and then strengthened into a calm factual voice of authority "… And don't bitch about the kids not reading when you aren't yourself. Kids feed of our energy. They are hungry for experience and want to try all sorts of loves and passions until they find that thing that floats their boat."

"Heeta for Headteacher… although perhaps less sexualised, and less mixing of metaphors." Nick hid his smirk in the remainder of his beaker, but she mirrored it anyway.

"Enough of the fucking pseudo-science and vanity projects! Let teachers fall in love with their subjects; draw out the inner geek. Excellence will follow that. Proper excellence, not a pony-show of praise for jumping fences elegantly, or filling and ticking boxes with the neatest handwriting. Give staff the space to shine. Stop. Making. Them. Be. *Consistent.* Fuck! I hate what that word secretly harbours."

"Sounds like a good title for lesbian fiction – *secret harbours.*" Heeta burst into a roaring laugh.

"It really does!" She slapped her own leg… "definitely something I would read." The laugh transitioned into a series of snorts. "Ok. Ok. I'm done. No more ranting." She went to drink from the beaker to realise that it was empty. "Seriously, no more. Otherwise, people will think I've turned into Fred. How is he by the way?"

"Infuriating." Nick said lifting his own beaker and drinking the remainder of gin. "I will get us one more…"

"One more, but we should go then."

Nick ventured back into the dark forest of men. Several hands fingered his bum cheeks, while others patted his waist. He was served quickly though, which meant he returned speedily.

"When did you last see Fred?" Heeta asked.

"He popped over last week – Ryan had a work thing." Heeta laughed as Nick's eyes rolled unintentionally. "God, he's so evangelical at the minute. Honestly, every other sentence was reconnection this, reconnection that. I bloody wish he would go and lose himself again. He was at least bearable when he was a selfish cunt."

"It'll ease. He's in love."

"I know. That bit, I'm fine with. In fact, I wish he would talk more about him and Ryan. Well, you know what I mean – not that I want him to speak more, just that it might result in him speaking less about the other stuff." Nick sipped from the beaker. "The most irritating thing is when he goes on about making peace with your family as if it's that simple for everyone, just because things worked out for him." Heeta lifted her beaker and left it pressed to her lips. She knew that it really wasn't that simple for everyone. She nodded and Nick acknowledged the pain and maturity in her. He moved on, assuming that she probably didn't want to discuss it. "The worst thing is that he makes out as if his family have been through some enormous revelation; as if his parents were barbarous advocates of conversion therapy prior to his coming out. He forgets I've met them – several times. They are lovely. Like really tolerant and fun – they got wasted at his gran's funeral, danced together for half the night in some shack on the edge of town; then, they invited everyone back to their home for a house party where people were welcomed to crash, and they did. His dad played the fucking guitar, had a Johnny Cash poem framed on the living-room wall, and put Bob Dylan on repeat for half the night. The only thing missing was a spliff being handed around. Of course, there was probably a bit of homophobia when he was young – fuck where wasn't there when we grew-up? But in the grand scheme of things, he was born into a pretty good family."

"It still hurts though when you know you're different; maybe even more so when everything else seems so great." Heeta cushioned some of Nick's criticism.

"I know I shouldn't be so judgemental. I guess, you don't know anybody else's full story."

Heeta smiled. She sensed that Nick had caught hold of his own downward spiral into an oceanic moralistic tirade, and so felt comfortable in joining him for a bit of further, soft mockery. "He can be infuriatingly evangelical though." Her smile extended.

"I knew you thought it too, Mrs Non-Judgmental."

"Of course, I do. It's true. Fred's an idealist and so minor kinks of reality that don't conform to his vision of the way things ought to be incite his fury. Thank God, he's got a good heart, and fairly good ideals. Imagine him without those."

They both laughed. Accepting reality for better or worse, always made them feel better. Unlike Fred, Heeta and Nick were earth walkers. They dealt with what was in front of them. They edged and shaped the aspects of their lives where and when it was possible. "I think he burnt witches in a previous life." Nick said.

"Nah, not his style. I'd go with something a little more Stalin-esque… grandiose without the ceremonious trimmings of religion."

Chapter 8 – Taking sides

Two weeks later.

Nick grabbed a coffee on his way to work. A queue stretched along the glass counter in front of him, but the baristas bobbed along the other side taking and preparing orders before people reached the tills. Nick felt the gin from the night before, but relatively speaking, he was fresher than most mornings. The house that he and Heeta visited yesterday evening wouldn't leave his thoughts: dirty floral wallpaper failed to hide damp walls and shoddy electrical repairs; the kitchen looked like it needed a good fire to cleanse it of cockroaches; and the neighbouring properties seemed to be grooming drug mules. It was a disaster. The figure of his salary multiplied by four thickened on his visualisation of the house. *How can half of that place come anywhere near to that amount?* The barista removed a slice of carrot cake beside a £4.95 placard.

"Anything to eat, Sir?" She asked. Nick returned to the here and now.

"No thanks." He said on instinct before considering his hunger. "Actually, I'll take a chocolate chip cookie."

"I'll pop it on the counter by the till for you." She moved-on to ask the same thing to the customer waiting behind.

He ate his cookie on the way to the station taking small sips of coffee while it was still in his mouth. He arrived with time to spare. It was one of those easy mornings where things happen effortlessly. No rushing. No drama. No splitting hungover headache. The train shot him into central London with a thousand other passengers without delay or fuss. Nick stepped onto the 186 bus and unintuitively headed back in the direction he'd come. The dirty windows on the upper deck filtered the bright sunlight. Its dazzle muffled. Nick closed his eyelids nonetheless. He felt the engine and the rays of sunshine warming his face. His satchel bag rested on the next seat, one of the few empty ones left.

The bus veered out of the station, and the sunlight changed direction. It rested onto the back of his head rather than his face. Nick opened his eyes and as the bus rumbled along. The side streets caught Nick's attention. He wondered about the hundreds of properties snaking of Borough Market. Perhaps his home was there.

Children in Asda-trousers and cheap blazers where the badge had been ironed on, joined the bus in increasing numbers. More people stood than sat. Hands gripped the poles and handles dangling from the roof. Backs leant against the plastic barrier between the downstairs aisle and the doll-house staircase to the upper deck. Space on the 186 through Elephant & Castle was more premium than New York real estate. A passenger took the seat beside Nick on the upper deck.

A vibration pulsed against his thigh, a text message from Heeta. *What you think about this?* An incomprehensible sequence of conjoined blue letters formed an unintelligible sentence: it was a hyperlink. Nick knew that he needed to click on it, but he wasn't used to seeing them on his mobile. He thought about waiting until he got to work – it would be better to load the webpage on a computer where the internet connection would be more reliable. But his desire to see the property outweighed the frustration of not knowing for sure whether the page would load correctly, how long it would take or how much it would cost. His thumb pressed the blue squiggle of underlined text, and the mobile automatically switched itself to a web page that attempted to load. The phone vibrated again as he held it in both hands, another message from Heeta. *Bit small, but good location – close to work?* Nick read the message as it appeared, but he didn't want to touch it in case it removed him from the webpage and the loading would have to restart.

A block of emerald-green filled the bottom of the screen, followed by a crimson red italic font that spelled out the name of the estate agent. Then a flash of lightening rolled across, and the rest of the page loaded instantly. A four-story terraced building dominated the space. Above the picture, a simple font read: *Upper-*

ground floor two-bedroom flat. Close to Borough High Street. Nick pulled the phone closer to his face. He held it with both hands and like a grandma struggling to read, he squinted and moved his face forward too. He examined each of the windows on the building, and began to work out which ones belonged to the flat. He concluded that it must be just the one beside the front door, which hovered above four or five steps stretching from the pavement.

Must be tiny. He imagined standing inside. *I wonder how far back it stretches?* He glanced at the *More Photos* tab but decided it would be too painful to proceed. He closed the webpage and responded to Heeta's text message. *Will have a proper look when I get to work – looks interesting though.*

Cool – I think I do fancy London Bridge… You're not at work yet??

Nick clicked the button to send his phone into oblivion and slid the device back into his pocket. He would message her back later. The thought of living in the area took his attention. He stared out of the window at the bars and cafes. He liked it. If it came down to a conflict between location or space, he decided firmly that location ought to win. He wanted to be a part of the action. He was fed-up of spending thirty minutes on a train before he could jump on a twenty-minute bus that would take him to where he wanted to go. That was it. He mentally discarded all property beyond zone 1. Although he had been living in London for several years, he felt like he was now moving to London proper. This was no longer his first rodeo – he was doing it for real.

Lambeth High was a 1960s rectangular slab of a building. The 186 sighed relief as it reached the school gates and farted out its passengers. Nick lowered his head, squeezed down the staircase and followed the masses. He looked sharp in his suit. Several kids, mostly girls, expressed a larger than life "Hello Sir" as he strolled along the narrow path, which forced people into thinner cliques.

The leadership team welcomed the students and staff passing through a large foyer. It was mostly pleasant: the Head was one of those genuinely warm people. He had eyes that saw everything, but in a way that didn't make people feel judged – acknowledgment eyes. Whereas the Deputy had eyes that let people know she could see their flaws. Her glance at Nick told him that she noted he was arriving at school later and later. It didn't acknowledge that he was still early, or that his lessons were well planned and executed. It focused on his weakening deference to her authority, his audacity to not care enough about conforming to her parochial expectations. She reminded Nick of the Headteacher at Eliot High. Usually, he kept his focus on the blue carpet as he walked past them. He would give a small hand wave, upward glance and polite conscious smile that gestured an apology for his timekeeping, but overall, he would avoid real connection. He wasn't interested in workplace politics. The objective for Nick, was to pass through as unnoticed as possible; to get into the building and teach children Maths. But the combination of the dirty property he had visited yesterday evening, the sugar from the cookie, and the thought of buying a fancy, albeit tiny, property off Borough High Street, emboldened him. *Fuck you.* He thought to those judgemental eyes. He was a grown man – as long as he wasn't late – he would arrive at work when he wanted and not feel ashamed. He lifted his gaze from the carpet and met their eyes, not for a millisecond glance, but for a fuller multi-second moment of intimacy. The Head seemed delighted. He noticed the difference, the increased confidence. The Deputy noticed too. She released a Jaws like smile. She knew she had to officially endorse the act of confidence. It's what schools are officially about nowadays. But in her heart, Nick's upward (slightly lingering) gaze challenged her egoistic authority – what she was about. They both felt the act of creation in that moment. They both recognised it as the moment they became rivals.

Lesson one was when Nick would have had Year 11, but exams had finished and so they were gone; tossed out into the adult world to fend for themselves. Realistically, most of them would be back for Sixth Form, not out of passion for advanced study, but boredom and because it was the next step on their conveyor-belt life.

Nick hovered a no-frills white mug beneath the hot water tap attached to a mini-boiler that seemed to clutch miraculously to the wall. A waterfall of near-boiling water fell and allowed the teabag to stain and thicken the liquid. A splash of green milk plopped in. Nick stirred it with a tatty teaspoon and placed the plastic carton back in the staffroom fridge. He sat on one of the tables in the centre of the room, slurped his tea and began marking a set of books.

The need-to-be-marked pile decreased every couple of minutes. The room was empty and so he charged through uninterrupted. He wanted to get them done so that he didn't have any work to take home for the weekend. As he slid the last book toward him, the door hinge squealed. The Headteacher walked in. Nick had his back to the door: he wasn't overly social at work so didn't bother to turn around to see who had come in. His red pen scribbled corrections beside a complex algebra equation that had been worked through diligently, but still incorrectly. The Headteacher peered over his shoulder and watched Nick undo the mistake. He re-built the equation step by step with his red pen. As he approached the final step, the Headteacher patted Nick on the shoulder. Nick assumed the man or woman was making a cup of tea, not watching him do Maths.

"You're very good. That's tricky stuff." The Headteacher moved forward so that he and Nick could see each other comfortably. He pulled out one of the blue plastic chairs and sat at the table. "I like you, Nick."

Being told he was liked so directly reminded him of the experience with Sasha and that made Nick uncomfortable. But despite the inherent creepy potential of the statement, the Head's comment did not come across creepy. Nick smiled. "Thanks, I think…"

"You get on with the job." He nodded toward the book that lay open with the corrections visible. "You get that you are here for them and not your own power." His words were solid and heavy. He meant what he said, and said what he meant. But he didn't get to his position without being shrewd. There was also meaning in what he did not say. He did not reference his Deputy, but the fact he had chosen to approach Nick after she and Nick had informally declared a cold war was not coincidental. "You will have been with us for nearly three years, and in all that time I don't think you have made a single political move."

Nick was excellent at Math. He could undo and redo complex calculations seeing how an action now would impact an outcome five stages later: if he had joined a Chess club, he would have been the best. But when it came to politics and power, there were too many variables and unknowns – he avoided situations that seemed unduly reliant on luck, where there was less security to be achieved. Where there was a less linear relationship between effort and outcome. It was statistics that influenced Nick's conservatism, his apolitical disposition.

"… until this morning." The Head added.

Nick felt exposed. His instinct was to deny it; to plead ignorance. But then the Head laughed. "My God, she even pulled-out those teeth on you… I haven't seen them for a while." The Head shook his head as laughter petered out. "Like I said Nick, I like you. But there's a paradox now. So, listen-up Maths boy. Your likeability has correlated with your lack of drama. Your professionalism. Your ability to leave your ego at the door and get on with doing a damn good job. And you have. The results of your children are some of the best I've seen in years." Nick knew his classes performed well but he lacked the comparative perspective of just how well.

"But to go further in this industry, you are going to need an ego." Nick hadn't expected him to say that. "Education is not value-free. Leadership demands the strength and courage to make enemies; to insist on implementing what you stand for even when that means going head-to-head with people that have differing visions. And sometimes those people will be your superiors – you will need to learn how to manoeuvre and outplay them. Your challenge to Agnes this morning was the first sign of your suitability for my kind of leadership." Nick's impulse was again to deny the truth, but he had already made the move. Avoiding conflict was not the same as backing down once it was there. Nick was not a coward.

The Headteacher did not require a response. He had more to say. "I like you because you aren't a diva with an attitude: you compromise and make-do; defer to idiots, stroke their egos, and then get on and make things work once they are out of the way. But as my Assistant Headteacher, I need you to sometimes fight and challenge those idiots. That's going to require you to have your own ego, sometimes." The Head placed one of his hands over the other. It layered gently. He laid back into the plastic chair and had one leg crossed over the other. He looked at Nick, awaiting his response.

The door hinge sounded again as a young student-teacher tried to enter the staffroom. The Head raised his hand and strengthened his index finger to gesture that she should give them a moment of privacy. She turned away and let the door close. Nick turned to see who it was and noticed her telling another member of staff not to go in.

"This is part of it. You will need to feel comfortable with people having an opinion about everything you do, their ascribing meaning to often meaningless interactions."

"Is this a job offer?" Nick felt gunge in his throat.

The Head, although fairly relaxed, seemed to relax that little bit more. "You are going to be excellent." He stood up and patted Nick on the shoulder. As he began to walk away, he made a comment about the equation Nick worked through when he first arrived. "Teach him the Greek method too."

Nick peered at the red scribbles in the book and pondered on what the Greek Method could be – he'd never heard of it. The door hinge squealed, and the Head left. The two members of staff came in. They scanned Nick's face for information: They assumed he had been told off.

Nick took his mug back to the sink, swilled it out with tap water and loaded it into the dishwasher. He collected the pile of books and left the room as the bell struck and shook the building. By lunchtime an e-mail pinged into every staff inbox. It advertised an Assistant Headteacher post.

Chapter 9 – Quick trip, big news

"Tell me again exactly what he said to you." Heeta sat onto the sofa and cupped her hands around a fresh cup of coffee. She placed one for Nick on the coffee table. Rain pelted the windows of their flat like small bullets flying into protective glass. It made a lot of noise but there was no chance of the window breaking.

Nick leant forward and took the coffee. "Cheers." He sipped before answering. "That I would need to learn to manoeuvre and outplay superiors if I wanted the job."

"He offered it to you there and then?"

"No – I asked him but that's when he said I would be excellent. It was cryptic, but also not cryptic at all."

"He was telling you that he wants you, but that things need to go through official channels."

"I think so."

"You know so." Heeta sipped her coffee. "It's brilliant. A) You will be amazing and B) He sounds like a total James-Bond dream. How many bosses would approach you in that cool espionage way; confide in you despite the power differential."

"I suppose."

"There's no supposing. He came to you and revealed that he thinks his Deputy is a cunt. That is enormous. He gave you his trust – that's the sort of person most people dream of working for."

"I guess."

"What is wrong with you?" Heeta was ecstatic on his behalf and couldn't understand why he looked like somebody had taken a shit on his face.

"I dunno – it's not a done deal."

"Fuck off. If the Head approaches you in that way, then nobody else is getting that job. Do you want it?"

"Of course." The speed of his own response surprised him. He did want the job. "I mean, I hadn't really thought about it before today. I haven't even been a Head of Department – how will it look?"

"Fuck how it'll look. Is that why you're being so moody and depressed about it?"

"I'm not being depressed about it."

"You're not exactly jumping for joy." She placed her coffee onto the table and reached out for Nick's. "Give it." Nick scrunched his face at her, confused as to why she wanted his cup. He kept it wrapped in his hands, testing whether time would encourage her to change her plans; whatever they were. "Give it here." She repeated. Nick obeyed. "Now jump for mother fucking joy."

Nick smiled, a defence mechanism to hide his anxiety. *I am not jumping on the spot.* He thought and Heeta assumed as much.

"Yes, you are. Stand-up and jump for joy."

"Oh my god – you are so bossy." Nick was stalling for time. He did not want to do it.

"This will be over a whole lot faster if you just do what I say." A mischievousness leaked from her dimples. Nick knew she was right.

"Fine." He shuffled forward to perch on the edge of the sofa, psychologically preparing himself to stand and jump for joy like some evangelical devotee to the lord. He shook his dangly arms and legs on the spot, swayed his head, and rolled his shoulders. It changed him: he left church and walked into the boxing ring. His self-consciousness melted into energy that charged his emerging, rocky-esque passion and determination. The soundtrack to *Eye of The Tiger* played in his mind, and he not only jumped on the spot, he began mock boxing the air in front of him. Heeta slapped her thigh, and shouted "Yes, white boy! You get that nasty Agnes!" They both burst out laughing. Nick crashed back onto the sofa and they lent into one another still laughing uncontrollably.

"Thank you." Nick said.

"You are welcome, white boy."

"I do want the job. I'll be good at it. I don't exactly know what it is that I'll be good at…"

"You'll figure it out. And once you know, you can tell me. We can then take over a crappy school and run it together."

"Do you want to be a Headteacher?" Nick asked.

"Yeah… I think so."

"You think so?"

"I do. One day, I want to be a Headteacher. My name is Heeta Patel, and one day I want to be a Headteacher." They laughed again.

"I would send my children to your school, even if it was in the roughest area."

"You want children?"

Nick paused to think. He had not had this conversation for a while and he intuitively recognised that his feelings had changed. "No." He said firmly. "I did… I think I always did… but I don't anymore." His speech was slower and more deliberate than usual as if he were declaring important information that had to be correct, like a passport application.

"Me too." Heeta said. "I don't think I ever wanted them as strongly as you did, but I thought it would probably happen at some point. It never made much sense, because there was never a man… but there was always a baby, somewhere. It's gone though… and… I don't feel unhappy about that."

They offered one another a small comforting smile. Heeta handed-back the coffee to Nick, then clinked her own cup against his. They made a caffeine cheers and sipped together. "To fulfilling careers."

"To fulfilling careers."

The rain continued firing at the windows. It was a miserable Friday evening. "How about you? Do you want to be a Headteacher?" Heeta asked as her legs folded onto the sofa.

"Not really. Teaching was never my dream job."

"What was?" She asked.

"I'm not sure if I had one. I knew that I wanted to be paid well."

"So, you picked teaching?"

"The pays not as bad as people think… but I get your point. I think I chose it because it was safe: I knew that I would be able to get a job after graduating and it's not as if the teaching industry is suddenly going to go under…"

"You're really good at it." Heeta chipped in. "Are you glad though? Glad you became a teacher?"

"Yes." Nick said without hesitation. He was glad. The job had helped him ease into adult life and he had put a lot of effort into mastering it – he was proud of what he had accomplished, especially given nobody in his family had finished school let alone taught in one. "But I don't see it being my forever job." He said as if he were at confession. "Like it's fine, more than fine: pay is good, holidays are good, and now that I know what I'm doing, lesson planning isn't overly burdensome; I can mark much faster than I used to."

Nick listed the benefits emphasising those impacting his personal life. "It's not as overly stressful or challenging as it was early on, especially once you've developed relationships with the kids… so I don't have that much to think about of an evening, meaning that I can enjoy…" He imitated Heeta's smirk. "Yes, I can enjoy a drink and get through the morning a little hungover."

"Don't say that in your interview."

Nick sighed. He leant back into the cushions on the sofa. "I'd be stupid to not go for this right?"

"Yes." Heeta replied instantly. "I mean as your friend, I am supposed to tell you to follow your dreams and never compromise. But as an even better friend, I am telling you to find some passion and get that job before you do anything else. If you really want to change careers, great; go for it, but don't do it on whim, and definitely don't give up an opportunity in the here and now unless you know exactly what you want to do instead." Nick nodded. He agreed with her. "Because at the minute, it sounds as if you have no idea what else you would want to do." Again, he agreed with her. She had read him completely. He threw a cushion at her face, playfully.

"Mrs know-it all."

She screeched in surprise and then threw the cushion back at him. "Whatever, Fred." She deliberately said before imitating something he would say. "Oh, I am so lost! I have read Foo-Caught." She mispronounced the French intellectual. "… and now I am 'aving an *existential* crisis…" She used a French accent. "I am *so confused* about what I should be doing *wiv* life!" *Confused* and *Wiv* sounded particularly French.

Nick leant over and pushed the cushion toward her again. "Existentialism was Jean-Paul Sartre, not Foucault."

"Sorry Fred!" She called from behind the cushion. Her voice increased in pitch as Nick's hands wormed their way to tickle her covered sides. "Ok. Ok." Nick retreated. She moved the cushion forward so that it rested as a low barrier between them. "When's the deadline for the application?"

"Next Friday."

"Speaking of which, I've booked a few viewings around London Bridge for next week. I sent the links to your work e-mail. The one I like the look of couldn't do anything until the Friday…"

"The one you text?"

Heeta nodded. "What did you think?"

"I had a quick look on my phone and properly at work. It's small, but I liked it. I like the area a lot."

"Me too." She paused like a chess player considering her move. "I'm pretty sure I would rather go for somewhere smaller in order to get a better location." She held a breath hoping that he would want the same thing. They had discussed locations non-stop since agreeing to buy a place together, but Heeta had been considerably more militaristic in the search. While Nick looked only at the properties that she sent to him – pleasant distractions on the bus to work – Heeta had been putting in serious effort. She had searched hundreds of properties online. Each one she sent to Nick had been whittled down from hours of screen scrolling, google map searches, transportation vs. mortgage calculations, commute time estimations and the rest of the minutia that mounts to a small mountain of effort when it comes to house hunting in London. She had thought hard about it; her little reveal of wanting somewhere small but a better location, was the iceberg tip of a much deeper, considered desire. It would cause conflict if Nick didn't share her position and she didn't want that.

"I agree." He reached his arm across the cushion and gestured an intent to tickle her again. She slapped his arm as if she were playing a whack-a-mole game. "Seriously – are you genuinely happy with London Bridge? It has to be right for both of us."

"Yes – absolutely. I know you've been doing loads of research, and I can tell you've already decided, but I want it too. I pass through the area every day on the way to work, and I like it. A lot. It's close to the city, close to the West-End, but there's plenty going in the immediate area. I'm up for it. Honest."

She smiled. "You have no idea how happy that makes me. I've been getting pretty into the search and…"

"And you've settled your heart on the area. You aren't the only Mrs Know-it-all." Nick poked his tongue at her.

Heeta imitated the French accent she had used to reference Fred's existential crises earlier. "Oh, *I am so 'appy! I am found.*"

They laughed and even though Heeta's comment didn't make complete sense, it didn't matter. The thought of Fred always brought joy to them, and senselessness was apt in relation to him. "So, what have we got booked in?" Nick asked.

Heeta detailed a list of properties and they spent the next hour sitting on the sofa discussing them. They clicked to enlarge pictures on their phones and passed their devices back and forth to draw attention to appealing features: an open planned kitchen, a nice landing, a quirky layout. Between floor plans, they ordered a Chinese takeaway for dinner, and as soon as the chow-main had depleted, Nick fetched himself a glass and poured a gin and tonic. "Do you want one?"

"Nah. I have a yoga class in the morning, so I want to wake up fresh."

Nick poured the glug he would have given Heeta into his own glass. He added a splash of tonic, and given his mood of sophistication, he found a lemon from the back of the fridge and added a slice to his drink. He plonked himself onto the sofa, and gulped at least a third of the glass before lifting to rest his feet on the coffee table. They decided to watch a chick-flick, but Heeta yawned too many times before half of the film had played out. She slapped Nick on his thigh and removed herself from the lounge. "See you in the morning. Don't open another bottle."

"Night Heets." He moved his legs from the coffee table so that she could squeeze past. His white socks landed back onto the wooden table as soon as she passed. Her bedroom door closed. He went to take another sip of his drink and realised his third gin was empty. His legs came off the table again. He took himself to the kitchen counter and poured the rest of the gin. There wasn't enough left in the sky-blue bottle to match the portions of his first three, so he opened the cupboard to reach for a fresh bottle. "Shit." He said becoming aware that the cupboard was empty. He closed the door and topped-up the glass with tonic. He abandoned the lemon slice after the second drink. The chow-main, chic-flick movie, and knowledge that the rest of his evening would be spent alone dulled his earlier sophistication. He just wanted to feel the effects of the gin. *Fuck the lemon.*

As he cushioned himself back into the sofa, he became irritable in that way a smoker does when they know they only have one cigarette left in the packet. He sipped his gin, but by comparison to his other glasses, he could now only taste tonic. He looked at his watch: it was only quarter past ten. He couldn't go to bed before midnight, and that would be early. He removed his feet from the coffee table once more and lifted himself up with an energised determination. He fetched his waterproof jacket and committed to a short journey to the corner shop. It was the lesser evil. Short term pain: he would soldier through the horrendous wind and rain for a bottle of gin. He left the movie playing so that Heeta would not notice that he had popped out. He placed his key into the outside of their flat door to minimise the sound of the latch clipping shut. He gently unturned his key and removed it. The door closed without sound.

Before leaving the main entrance of the apartment building, he covered his head with the hood of his jacket. He blended into the estate. He shuffled along the pavement in his tracksuit bottoms, hooded-head and white trainers. Nobody was about, so he walked alone through the darkness. As he joined the main road, headlights from the oncoming cars brightened the otherwise austere light begrudgingly leaking from houses with closed curtains and crap streetlamps that conveyed the council's cheapness.

He reached the strip of commercial buildings and the light improved. The kebab shop's red and yellow neon sign added colour to the street while the off-license's green tinted windows contributed to a Christmas effect. Nick pushed open the door and entered. The man sitting behind the counter of confectionery wore a turban. He waved at Nick, who returned a wave as he approached. "Bottle of gin?" Mr. Ameer asked turning to reach for a green bottle on the shelf behind him.

"Yes please." Nick took a mint Areo and placed it onto the counter.

"Miserable weather isn't it?" Mr. Ameer placed the bottle onto the counter beside the Aero. He fingered the number pad of the till and then wafted a black plastic bag so that he could pop the bottle and Areo inside.

"Horrid." Nick said handing over a twenty-pound note from his wallet, which the man exchanged for a few coins from his old, and rather angry looking, till.

"Well you go and warm yourself up with this." Mr. Ameer passed the bag across the counter whilst giving an affectionate wink to which Nick felt only slightly creeped out. He had popped down to buy a late-night bottle too often and so Mr Ameer's cheeky wink had become familiar.

"Cheers. Have a good evening." Nick said. He leant forward to open the door and left. By the time he was back in the flat, his socks were soaking and his jogging bottoms were damp. He would need to change. The black plastic bag rustled a little as he carried it through to the kitchen. He landed the bag onto the counter like a pilot – quietly, lacking fuss. He was so relieved to be back with a fresh bottle that would see him through the evening.

Despite the third of a bottle he had already drunk, his movements were controlled and confident. He removed the gin and Areo without causing the bag to rustle, then placed it into the bin. He compressed the existing trash so the bag could drop deep into it. He didn't want Heeta to know that he had popped out; that he had needed to get a fresh bottle at 10.30 in the evening.

The jogging bottoms flung into his washing pile, which mounted in the grey basket beneath the window of his bedroom. His damp socks joined and formed a summit on the pile, a trip to the laundrette was imminent. In his loose black boxer shorts and t-shirt, Nick wandered to the chest of drawers and pulled himself a fresh pair of jeans from the bottom drawer. The flat was warm so he decided to leave the socks – he only had a few more pairs and wanted to save them just in case he couldn't be bothered to go to the laundrette over the weekend.

Although his hood had covered most of his head during the trip to the shop, the rain had managed to somehow wet his hair. Droplets rolled off the smeared spikes of fringe stuck to his forehead. He walked back to the gin as his fingertips brushed the droplets of rain-water aside.

A larger measure flowed into the same glass, followed by a peppering of tonic – no lemon. He collapsed into the sofa and watched the ending of the chick-flick movie. 11.00 o'clock flickered by. His mobile phone caused the wood of the coffee table to shake beneath its vibration. Nick's mum was calling. He lifted the phone and pressed the side button to stop the vibration without formally declining the call: the screen continued to show three little curved lines pulsing away from an image that was meant to represent a mobile phone. He watched the screen until the *Mum calling* turned into a *Missed call. Mum.*

Nick tipped the remaining liquid from the glass into his mouth. He took his phone to the kitchen counter. He knew that she would call again and didn't want the phone to vibrate onto the coffee table while he was making himself another drink. The counter started to buzz as his mum rang again. He silenced the vibration but again refrained from declining the call. Rejecting the call required firmness. The action in itself carried a message – *I don't want to talk.* Whereas, a *Missed call. Mum*, which for the second time displayed on his phone, left space for an excuse: *Sorry I didn't see your call… I was in bed… I was with a friend… I wasn't ignoring you because I didn't know you were calling.* Not answering hid his desire to not speak to her in ambiguity and it gave him distance.

Three more miscalls piled onto his screen. The movie had finished, and it was only the awfulness of late-night TV that motivated Nick to get off the sofa and put something fresh on. A text message from his mum flickered onto his mobile, but he tossed the phone onto the cushion. The text message was a sign that the calling would stop. He strolled to the DVD shelf and his finger drifted across the titles, from left to right. As he read each, he pondered whether its mood was sufficiently easy. He stopped to think about the main events in one or two contenders, but he knew it was a no by the fact that the title was making him think. He wanted something that could play in the background and demand nothing of him. He didn't want to think. He wanted to drink his gin and zone-out on the sofa for an hour or two. *The Devil Wears Prada* won. The case unclipped and the disk popped out. His index finger slid into its inner hole where it remained hooked while he ejected the finished film from the DVD player. The new disk flopped off his finger into the device. He pushed the play button on the device itself so that he didn't have to faff with the remote. He plunged back into the sofa, but forgot to reach for his phone first. It slid into the crevice between two cushions. He would recover it later. He swigged his Gin, and for the first time he recognised the effects of the alcohol. His wrist movements were delayed and messier, and his glass made a slightly louder thump as it landed onto the coffee table with force that was less aligned with his intention. The relationship between cause and effect was loosening. Nick noticed that drunk sensation in which the world was slightly oceanic; surfaces like waves, never quite settled or fixed into place. They more truthfully represented the ever-changing nature of reality.

Onscreen, Meryl Streep swept her assistants with looks of disdain, her lips pursed to convey her thoughts: high levels of moron in everybody around her. Nick took another drink and the glass settled with another unpredictable rumble on the coffee table. The cushion vibrated beneath. His mum was calling again. It was not unusual to receive five or six miscalls in a row, then a splurge of incoherent messages. A miscall after the messages though, that was more unusual. Nick tilted his solid and tall torso and raised his buttock so that he could dip his hands into the crevice and reclaim his phone. He silenced the vibration and let the phone ring out as before. He wanted to check the messages she had sent.

Don't ignore me. Honestly, it's important this time.

Please pick-up xx. Nick read the messages backward, most-recent to oldest.

Fucking cunt. I'm your mum. Just ignore me then xx.

Mr bigshot now – no time to speak to me x.

somets happened, serious pick-up xxx.

Nick's face remained stoic throughout. The messages were what he expected and although it was untrue to say that they did not hurt him, their repetition certainly lessoned the impact. The idea that love is absolute, that either a person loves somebody completely or not at all, proved problematic for Nick. He knew he loved his mum – he wouldn't consider her call if he didn't. He would block the number and be done with it. But equally, her power over him was no longer limitless. She could only make him feel so much. Her insults and needs had clipped impact because he had also clipped what she meant to him. He did not love her fully because to do so would make him too vulnerable to her unpredictability, too hurt by her despair and lashings. Boundaries layered over the years and those boundaries diluted the love between them. It was there, but awkwardly so, sagging and stretched over a boundary, a metaphorical brick wall that blunted authentic sentimental exchanges and shared experiences.

His glass hovered on his lip as he considered whether he had the energy and inclination to speak to her. The glass tilted into the air and gravity pulled the liquid into his throat like a changed tide, a river pulled into a new direction by the strength of the stars above. *Fuck it*. He thought. The glass banged the coffee table much more loudly than he intended. His thumb pressed into the menu button on his phone. He would call her back.

He made himself another drink as Meryl Streep gave her employees another bollocking onscreen. A good portion of the new bottle had already disappeared. Nick pushed his thumb onto her name and then lifted the phone to his ear. He trod across the carpet. His jeans loosely hung around his bare feet. The ring filled his earlobe. Time seemed to slow exaggeratedly, such that he felt the wave of each ring loop along the canal before passing through the drum. Another ring. Another. Another. *Is she playing tit for tat?* He thought.

"Hello." His mum answered. Her voice was coarse and husky; unsure of what to say.

"Hello." Nick repeated. He spoke quietly so not to wake or be overheard by Heeta. A powerful silence settled between their greeting, a dark silence; thick and textured like a physical beast, who was making itself comfortable despite knowing it was unwelcome.

"What you up to?" She asked just to fill the silence.

"Nothing – just watching T.V." Nick answered immediately so the focus rebounded to her. She was the one that needed to speak.

"Which channel?" Again, she asked something to stop the silence.

"It's a film." He did not want to discuss *The Devil Wears Prada* with his alcoholic mum.

"What film? I'll have a look." She tried to make a connection.

"It's a DVD. Just a chick-flick." He down-played the film and genre. He didn't want to describe what it was about. He judged that describing a woman living in New York seeking to establish a high-powered career in the fashion industry whilst juggling a relationship with an unambitious, unsupportive boyfriend, would only provoke self-pity, condescension and further alienation. *How could she relate?* He thought.

"Oh." Her enthusiasm dropped: the energy and tone of her voice changed like a ball thrown-into the air that had reached its zenith. It turned sharply and fell with force downward. "You don't have to tell me about it if you don't want." She was not being reassuring. The little energy she had disappeared.

Nick acknowledged the passive-aggressiveness in her response, and he shared a re-framed version of the story's essence that he thought better fit her self-identification. "Mum it's about a make-believe woman moaning about a make-believe boss." Nick did not do it consciously, but he viewed his mum as a victim in need of protection from everyday life. It set the parameters for how he related to her: he censured topics or approached them with high cynicism, which did not reflect his true thoughts and feelings.

"Where's the woman?" She said changing the topic away from the film, and not meaning to sound quite as sharp as she did.

"She's in bed, and her names Heeta."

"I know her name. I just don't understand why you're living with her." She was referring to his leaving Sasha, implying he was repeating the same mistakes.

A fresh silence injected itself into the conversation. This time it originated from restraint. Nick had become fairly immunised to her attacks on him, but he had not learnt how to avoid the darts she threw at people he cared for. He has misinterpreted his mother's jibe as a personal attack on Heeta when it was not meant that way. "Well?" She said pressing him for a reaction. "She's not your girlfriend obviously, so why live with her?"

Nick's tongue rubbed against the front of his teeth. He regretted calling. "Mum, it's pretty late." He said ignoring her question. "What is so important?"

"Oh, perhaps I should call you in the morning." The slur in her pronunciation was more prominent. Nick knew how this went: there was still something that mattered, and this was a game of drawing-out his desire. She wanted him to beg for the information.

"It must have been something important." Nick began the back and forth.

"I shouldn't have called. It can wait."

"Clearly it can't, or you wouldn't have…"

"I don't have to have a reason to call you." She cut him off.

Nick censored his impulse to whip a response in which he told her that she should when it involved calling in the early hours of the morning. But he caught himself and allowed a silence to shape his language into a polished form that didn't expose his conservatism: "Yeah but you probably have something important to say if you're calling this late."

She now thought about the next move. There was logic and truth in his statement, which meant it was less easy for her to react impulsively. She was a drunk but a drunk that could hear truth no matter how many bottles of Vodka swirled through her liver.

Nick and his mother were both headstrong and rational despite the intensity of emotion. When his mother was a nasty cow, she meant it. And when she was tender and generous, she meant that too. Things did not happen by accident. They both had inherent bull-shit detectors. Unlike Nick, his mother embraced her self-awareness and turned it into a weapon: when she heard lies or manipulative language, she interpreted that as an invitation and green-light to enter her own manipulative and provocative state; to mirror the bull-shit and fire her own missiles of crap. Whereas Nick shrivelled and became tortoise like. Bull-shit made him want to withdraw from further conversation. He did not like it. He would rather the relationship end, then for it to continue with hostilities.

"You're right of course. You're always right." She said. Nick wanted her to just tell him what she had to say. He wanted to be over and done with it.

"As are you." He expressed honest feeling for the first time: bitter passive-aggressiveness. They were finally in the same place. They had finally acknowledged one another's frustration toward the other, and let it be. They did not try to control or manipulate the truth of their relationship, and consequently, the gristle-like connection between them eased. They became more comfortable. They eased with one another.

"I'm not though." She said with more tenderness. The bitterness and self-pity in her voice evaporated. Her words conceded another truth: her *I'm not though – not always right* was an acknowledgment that she didn't handle conflict and relationships particularly well. It was a sincere apology for not being more like Nick; his choice to withdraw from hostility rather than contribute to it. But it was equally not a plea for forgiveness or a promise to change, which would have been bullshit. His mum had no real desire to change. She had become used to this way of life; knew how to survive when she matched fire with fire, shit with shit.

This enabled Nick a comfortable silence. He could leave that truth unanswered without it causing offence or implying his condescension or judgment of her. He was not accusing or calling out her behaviour. She was confessing it, and like an honest priest, he had no interest in judging her. "So, what was the news?" He asked and for the first time, had expectations of receiving a response.

She lingered. Her response was delayed; no longer because she was drawing-out his desire, but because of the brutality of what she had to say. The reality stuck in her throat, and she had to choke it out. "Your father had a heart-attack." Nick waited for her to elaborate, but the prolonged silence communicated more than words ever could. Nick knew before she eventually said it. "He's dead."

The rain stopped hitting the window and the final droplets smeared down, not to be replaced.

PART 3

CONFRONTING THE MONSTER

Chapter 10 – Someone that gets it

The crematorium overflowed with people. Eric had not been a particularly good husband or father, but he belonged to many places. Men from his life in Newcastle travelled to Nuneaton to pay their respects. Scallywags from the local pubs padded-out the back rows, acquaintances the middle, and his small family took the front.

Nick stood beside his mum and younger sister. The crematorium had a colonial aesthetic. It could have been mistaken for an African or Mid-West church were it religious – wood was everywhere: it framed the floor-to-ceiling window at the front of the room; the roof pitching into a central spike; and, the doors from which everybody entered, to the door that everybody will leave.

Green fields and blue-sky glimmered on the other side of the window. The pseudo-wilderness put everybody in their place. It announced that the world span long before them and would continue spinning long after. It was a metaphor of humility, a declaration that ultimately, nobody matters in and of themselves. That meaning is ephemeral and temporary: here today, gone tomorrow. Make of it what you will.

"Welcome." The non-vicar said. "Eric Du Bois was a loved man as his friends who have travelled far to be here today attest." The non-vicar smiled as if he were about to perform a wedding ceremony. "Eric was a popular man. While his blood family is small – only his wife Evelyn, his late daughter Eve, his son Nick, and his daughter Brook – he considered everybody here today part of his extended family."

Nick cringed. His father did not think of the people in the room as his family, and neither, did the people in the room think of his father as their family. Family did not need referring to, not in this context. Family was not his father's thing. Everybody that knew him, knew that. *Why is this non-vicar so shit?*

"Eric was a fun-loving man." *Wrong.* "Eric was a tender and generous man." *Wrong.* "Eric was…" Nick stopped listening, but he chuckled at his mum's adaption, which she said under her breath for only Nick and his sister to hear.

"Eric Du Bois was a piss artist." It put a smile on his sister's face too, and made the non-vicar's droning easier for them to tolerate. He continued waffling impersonal platitudes for ten minutes, re-writing who Eric Du Bois was. He edited-out his grubby, messy life and made his existence fit neatly into a timeless account of an unrealistic man that did not reflect his experiences. The non-congregation kept their heads bowed like uncritical, obedient children. They were not listening either, but ensured they looked respectful and as if they were, for the duration of the service. It was the expectation. They knew how to behave and appear respectful. They said nothing, thought nothing, felt nothing. They kept still and tried to breathe as quietly as possible. The crematorium was an extension of the state and this was how to behave before the state. Deference, or at least a commitment to appearing deferential. Nick's mum had never been much of an actor. Her eyes rolled and her face conveyed that the service was a burden. However, the non-vicar read her dissatisfaction with him as her upset and emotional distress for her lost husband. He offered a patronising long stare the few times he noticed her sighs as if the sight of his pursing lips and puppy dog eyes had a magical power of healing. The worse part was that he took her subsequent lack of sighing as positive feedback: his fat face had connected with her delicate soul, easing the distress, and egging on his fervour. The reality was that it had simply become the lesser evil to contain the way she really felt. Toward the end, she even feigned a smile to appease his longing need for a reaction from her. The service had become a platform for the stroking of his ego, not acknowledging and remembering the good, the bad and the large ugliness of Eric Du Bois.

The service eventually ended, and the non-congregation stumbled out of the room like brow-beaten children leaving an austere assembly hall. Nick held his mum's hand, and his sister held her other hand. They did it out of protection more than sentiment. If they were their own group, it left less space for others. Like a closed-circuit atom, they could drift around the mass without it transforming them. They could be left alone.

People stood between the flower beds and mowed lawns. They contributed to bland, uninteresting conversations lacking substance. The service had drained everybody's agency. People tried too hard to not be themselves, sensing that it was somehow inappropriate. "I fucking hate funerals." Nick's mum said loud enough for people to hear. "People become moronic and false, more so than usual."

The three of them walked together like a Victorian trio doing the rounds on the Titanic's upper deck. His mum held her head high and controlled the direction, while Nick and his sister battled incoming targets: they smiled and nodded at onlookers as if ticking them off a list of people they needed to make an appearance for, like brides at weddings. Occasionally, they exchanged a few words to acknowledge the person's attendance, but mostly the nod and smile sufficed.

"Oh come-on, let's get a drink. I can't walk around any longer with these people staring at us." Evelyn said more to herself than to Nick or Brook. As they turned the corner of the terrace for the carpark, Nick's face lit-up. Heeta and Fred stood chatting, more normally than anybody else. They looked stunning. Fred had trimmed-up and the clean suit made him look sharp. Heeta wore an elegant lilac dress made of silk with black high-heels. They had their backs to Nick, Evelyn and Brook. Fred tossed his cigarette onto the pavement and squished it with his polished shoes. As he pivoted his foot on the butt, he noticed Nick. Heeta followed his turn. Their conversation stopped immediately.

The hostile frown of Evelyn contrasted with Nick's enthusiastic smile. She was not happy to see them and made no falsity to pretend otherwise. "We're so sorry for your loss." Heeta said to them, but looking more at Evelyn.

"Why? You didn't know him or anything about our relationship." Nick's mum spat the words as if they were barbed wire uncoiling from her mouth.

"Mum." Nick said. He clipped her barb with metaphorical cutters. "Don't be a cow." He surprised himself with his calm directness. It surprised Evelyn too. She smiled earnestly; her hostility dissipated in reaction to the firmness.

"Well... you're doing something right with him." Evelyn said self-directing the change in her stance and energy. She let go of Nick's hand and walked on with Brook. "I'll see you at the pub." She did not turn back. Nick waited for them to be out of earshot.

"Sorry about that."

"Please." Heeta replied, shaking her hand in a stop gesture, to emphasise that he did not need to apologise. "She's lost a husband that she clearly didn't like all that much, and I'm the bitch that lives with the son she clearly misses."

Nick squinted at the thought of his mum missing him. He knew it made sense, but the frequency of her nasty messages and frosty interactions made it feel equally absurd. He didn't argue with Heeta. He wanted a bit of space from thinking about his mother and so seized the opportunity to change the topic. "I'm so glad you're both here." He hugged them, one at a time.

"Man, we have to be here for one another. Family is so important." Fred rubbed the sleeve of Nick's jacket and, without meaning to, imitated the earnestness of the non-vicar.

"Oh Fred, don't make it weird." Heeta said punching him in the arm. "We talked about this on the way here." Nick burst out laughing and several of the non-congregation clusters perked-up at the injection of energy. Nobody judged.

"Come-on." Nick said to them. "Let's get a drink." In an unusually proactive display of affection, he linked each of their arms. "I've missed you Fred."

"Give it five minutes." Heeta said, rolling her eyes in her elegant outfit.

"I love you too Nick." Fred said without hesitation, and as unapologetically as an evangelical. Heeta lent across and punched him in his other arm.

"Stop being creepy." She said.

Nick laughed again. "Thank you though; both of you, for coming. It does mean a lot." They walked together in a horizontal line to the carpark. Heeta rubbed Nick's arm affectionately and Fred rubbed his own sulkily. Heeta took her keys from her handbag and they climbed into the car.

Fred stretched the waist-only seatbelt over him as he perched in the centre of the backseats. "Where's the wake?" He asked.

"The liberal club on the Green, but I thought we could get a pint somewhere else first, if you want to."

"Where are you thinking?" Heeta asked.

"Well we could park at the Arms, have one there and then walk to the liberal club... pick up the car tomorrow?"

"Good plan." The engine revved as Heeta accidently applied too much force to the acceleration pedal while attempting to find the biting point. The non-congregation, which had followed them to the crematorium carpark, stared at the noisy car. Again, they did not judge.

The rev settled into a sweet spot that enabled the car to get on its way. The little red micra swept around the crematorium's wide arching roads and catapulted itself onto the main road. They sped past the industrial units and the new housing estates, slowing only for the series of mini roundabouts, which were mostly empty at this time of the day. Nobody spoke. Each of them absorbed the sites of their prior home: the steel bridges spanning the iron railways, the terraced houses of Attleborough, the old peoples' homes; the nice flats, and the not so nice flats. The car passed the side street that fed into the rec where Nick and Sasha had their moment. Her words echoed in his mind. *You don't love anybody.* Although she had not intended them harshly, Nick heard the words with the hostility and bile she dished out in their flat when she broke down. He remembered her throwing the coffee cup at the wall, the tea staining his shirt. His mind fused together the two memories. Her *You don't love anybody* chased the coffee cup. It ricocheted off the wall following the splintered pieces of broken porcelain. Hard. Dangerous. He pulled himself out of his own head as the posher part of Attleborough flickered by.

Past the snooker club, semi-detached properties replaced the terraced houses, and a buffer of beautiful oak trees emerged to line either side of the widened road. The car slowed and Heeta popped on its indicator. Several cars overtook them as they waited for the oncoming traffic to disappear and turn into the carpark of the Attleborough Arms.

There were plenty of spaces. "So seriously man. How are you? Like were you close with your dad?" Fred asked as he unclipped his seatbelt and began to shuffle out of the car.

"Why do you keep saying, 'man'? You never used to say that." Heeta said closing her car door.

"Didn't I? Well, I've grown a lot over the last few years, and my language…"

"Oh God. Forget it. Pretend I never said anything…" Heeta pressed the lock button on her car keys and placed them into her handbag. Nick thought about the question. He knew it was coming, and although he had asked himself the question repeatedly since his mum told him the news of his father's death, he still had no answer.

"I don't know."

"And you don't need to." Heeta said rubbing her hand on his back.

"Yeah, but it will probably help if you talk about it." Fred tried to not add 'man' to the end of his sentence, but it didn't stop Heeta frowning.

"Fred, not everyone wants to talk about themselves all the time. He'll speak if he wants to, and only if he wants to, when he's ready."

"I wasn't saying that he had to, but just that it will help him if he does."

"He doesn't have to talk if he doesn't want to."

"I didn't say that he had to."

"But you did suggest that he wouldn't be ok unless…"

"Well, he won't."

Heeta lost her temper. "Stop pressuring him to speak."

"Guys – I am here." They had all stopped moving toward the pub. Heeta and Fred avoided each other's gaze, but side glanced to check in with Nick. "I appreciate you both looking out for me, but please stop being weird with each other. Fred, I do want to talk, but Heeta is right, I can't just do it on demand. Let's go in, get a pint, and you know, just let the conversation flow."

Fred nodded at Nick. "Of course, man. I just think you really should…"

"Fucking hell, Fred!" Heeta blew. "He just told you to back off and you're going at it again. Just because things worked out for you, doesn't mean it automatically will for everybody else. Give it a fucking rest."

"This hasn't got anything to do with me."

"Exactly!"

Fred swallowed and the space gave Nick a window to calm things down. "Guys – please. Enough. I really need a drink. Can we go inside and not have the pub stare at us like bickering children?"

Fred and Heeta glowed a slightly purple colour but conceded. Nick pulled the brass handle attached to one of the external doors and walked through. Heeta clutched the edge of the opened door and held it for Fred to enter.

Red floral carpets spanned the large room and a large amount of people sat at tables drinking even though it was midday and mid-week. The busyness surprised them, and it shook-off a bit of the tension.

"What can I get you?"

"Pint of Newkie Brown, a large gin and tonic, a shot of whisky." Nick said to the barman. "What do you guys want?" Nick made the request in a serious tone. He was not making a dad-joke.

"Make it three shots of whisky, three gin and tonics, and three pints of Newkie Brown… And Fred, you can get this round being as you've grown so much."

The barman reached under the counter for pint glasses and began preparing the order without challenge. Fred frowned, but he and his boyfriend, Ryan, had opened a joint account, so paying for the round didn't worry him as much as it would have in the past.

Three shot glasses lined the counter after the barman rested the pints of Newkie Brown on it. A bottle of Jack Daniels tilted downward, and honey coloured liquid poured out. Fred, Nick and Heeta took a glass each, clinked them together, and shot the whisky. The aftertaste burnt their throats, and all three gushed, making a sound like the ocean hitting the shore.

The barman had already begun making the gin and tonics, but Heeta told him that they would have three more shots of the Jack Daniels first. Fred looked alarmed. "Oh, calm down. I'll go halves with you really." Heeta said, allaying his unease at the bill.

"My dad has died. I haven't become bankrupt – I can still pay."

The barman glanced at Nick, as if to determine whether what he had said was true. The sombreness of Fred and Heeta's response let him to know it was.

"Have one on the house." He said refilling the shot glasses. They clinked the glasses and tossed the liquid back. Heeta waved her fingers at the shot glasses again.

"That's very kind of you." She said implying that the free round of shots would be the third, not the already consumed second. The barman released a small grin and offered the palm of his hands in a gesture of submission. He pulled-out an extra shot glass from beneath the counter.

"I'll join you if you don't mind. I lost my dad too a few months ago."

Nick and the barman looked at each other for a few seconds longer than would have ordinarily been comfortable were the context not flirtatious. He was handsome, very handsome.

"Of course." Nick said.

"To Dads, whether you love them or hate them." The barman toasted. They clinked and tossed-back the shots. Fred and Heeta pulled out a £20 note each. The barman took them and began entering digits into the till.

Fred, Heeta and Nick took the pints of Newkie Brown from the counter. The barman said that he would bring the gin and tonics and their change to their table. They thanked him and went to search for somewhere pleasant.

"Forty quid isn't bad for three pints, three double g&ts, and ten shots." Fred said, calculating the price of each item.

"Six shots – pretty boy was paying for four of them." Heeta said. "…But I agree – it would have cost a fortune in London."

"Finally, some common ground… so you two are playing nice now?"

"Oh, shut it, Mr. I've just pulled at my Dad's funeral." Heeta said. She wasn't sure if it would be too raw, but the whisky had warmed her up, and it came out before she could censor. "Sorry." She added immediately.

The comment did not offend Nick. He smiled. He was glad that they were not tiptoeing around him. "It's fine. I'm glad you're being normal." They settled on one of the large tables with seats built into the window. It could easily fit ten people around it. "He was flirting though, right?" Nick sought reassurance from them.

"Absolutely. You have been out of the game nearly as long as Fred if you need confirmation on that one. Who was the last guy anyway?" She sipped her Newkie Brown. "Oh, fuck. Please tell me it wasn't…" She looked at Fred and then Nick to indicate that she was talking about the two of them.

"No!" Nick said, with earnest disgust.

"Alright. It has happened before if you don't remember." Fred sulked into his pint.

"I remember." Nick sipped more of his Newkie Brown.

"What is this shit anyway?" Heeta asked referring to the drink.

"You have never had Newkie Brown?"

"Obviously not. Otherwise, I would have ordered something else. It's awful."

"It grows on you. My dad used to drink it."

The barman arrived with the gin and tonics just as a sombreness swept the air. The tray settled onto the edge of the table, and the barman lifted the drinks to each of them. His Adam's apple rolled down his throat as he plucked the courage to speak to

Nick in front of the others. "Look I wouldn't normally be so forward, and tell me if I'm out of line, but I'm going for a cigarette out back in a moment, if you want to chat to somebody…" He gave Fred and Heeta a look that let them know he didn't mean any offence. "Somebody that's been through it… then join me."

The man's black T-shirt wrapped tightly around noticeable biceps. They were big, but not obsessively big. He clearly took care of himself without becoming one of those gym buffs on restricted chicken and spinach diets: his torso was flat with modest layers of fat. Nick was attracted to him – unusually so. Nick rarely experienced that instinctive raw attraction, especially for a man that seemed to be interested in him. Nick caught a glimmer of the tattoo beneath his T-shirt.

"I will actually." He said, causing the barman's white teeth to shine. "Fred, could you slide out so that I can get past?"

Fred shuffled off the seat and Nick slid past the cushions. "Give me a minute to take over some drinks, and then I will meet you outside." Nick nodded and the barman left.

Heeta and Fred smirked, but said nothing. Nick strutted out of the pub through the same side doors they entered. The sun flooded the carpark, and the atmosphere was increasingly humid. Nick rubbed his fingers beneath his armpit to check for sweat. His shirt was a little damp, but there weren't any marks. The cars drifted along the main road at a leisurely pace, and one or two turned into the pub and passed Nick who leant his forearms on the black handrail separating the small terrace and driveway.

The barman squeezed Nick's shoulder as he approached. "Sorry, didn't mean to startle you." He said, opening his cigarette packet and holding it toward Nick. Nick shook his head instinctively – he didn't smoke – but as the barman lit a cigarette for himself, he reconsidered.

"Actually…"

The barman's teeth shone as the cigarette moved into his mouth. "I thought you don't smoke?" He said re-opening the packet indicating to Nick that it was his choice.

"Never have… But I don't know, it feels appropriate somehow." Nick took one of the elongated white cylinders, and placed it into his lips, unlit. The barman took the cigarette and exchanged it for the already lit one in his own mouth.

"Here, have this one." The man's lighter sparked and a gentle flame allowed him to light the other cigarette. The butt had been ever so slightly wetted by Nick's lips.

Nick attempted to breathe in his first cigarette. "Easy…" the man laughed as Nick spluttered and coughed over the handrail. "Perhaps you shouldn't inhale." He pushed-out and patted his throat to reinforce what he meant. "Don't swallow the smoke." Nick sucked on the cigarette again, but blew the smoke out before swallowing. He didn't cough, but the fumes made his eyes water as they drifted back into his face.

"I think smoking isn't for me."

"I think you're right. I wouldn't ordinarily push them onto a guy either… terrible habit…"

"… but my dad died." Nick said explaining his exception.

"Well, yeah. When that happens, the usual rules stop applying for the day."

"The usual rules…"

"Yeah…" He considered his words for a moment… "Like coming onto hot, straight men in broad daylight." The barman reached, and it worked: Nick flushed before accepting his advance.

"Well guess you're playing by the rules because I'm not straight."

"I didn't think you were, but guess we know for certain now that I am flirting with you."

They smiled at each other. The barman inhaled a long drag of his cigarette and on the exhale added. "I don't normally do this."

"What?"

"You know, approach guys so casually." His smoke fired out of his mouth in a neat plume. "I meant what I said about just having a chat, you know, about your dad. No strings... I knew when I lost mine, that people just didn't get it. Of course, there were people that tried to relate via their own loss, but it didn't help. I was both close, and at the same time, not close." He inhaled and exhaled again. "Being gay changed the dynamics between us, I think."

Nick synchronised with the feelings of this hot man, who spoke with ease and simplicity. Nick returned his generous openness by revealing his own thoughts. "I get it. In some ways, it would be easier if he were an ogre. People would understand the lack of feeling... but he wasn't, I liked my dad... or you know, I didn't not like him."

"You mean you didn't love him." It was a statement, not a question.

"I don't know... I guess not properly... not in the way that people are meant to; that people expect."

"You end up feeling stuck; trapped between displaying enough sentiment to put people off being concerned about you 'opening up', but equally, not so much that it exposes you as insincere or callous."

"Exactly." Nick tossed the cigarette on the floor and squished it with his foot – he was done trying to smoke. He interlocked his fingers as his hands merged into a single cluster. He rested it on the rail. "It feels like I can't be honest. People don't want to hear that I don't have particularly strong emotions... they want me to be distraught... they don't understand that, yeah, it's sad, and of course, I didn't want him to die... but will I miss him? Not overly. I barely saw him – and I don't mean that in a sentimental, woe-is-me, way. We were happy not seeing all that much of each other. He enjoyed doing his thing and I enjoyed doing mine. The relationship worked. We neither wanted, or objected to each other's company. It just sort of happened now and again… and that's not exactly something that you can overly miss, or feel distraught about." He paused and worried that he was waffling; that he was incoherent.

"I get it. And it's exhausting." The barman gripped Nick's forearm, just above the wrist. His thumb pressed into his skin enough to emphasise his presence and compassionate intent, but not so hard to come across aggressive or dominant. "And I mean it's exhausting, all the time – not just around other people. It's exhausting to keep questioning yourself, questioning whether you do really feel so little; doubting whether you are actually in touch with your emotions, or whether you're secretly repressed and unaware of who you really are. The self-doubt and existentialism; it's exhausting."

Nick felt lighter than he had in months. This beautiful barman from Nuneaton with large but not too large biceps, working in the Attleborough Arms on a Wednesday afternoon, was making more sense of his life than any cosmopolitan dandy or sophisticated metropolitan. "You are beautiful." Nick said, his armour down.

"You aren't too bad yourself. Rather forward, but that's not a bad thing."

Nick leant in and kissed the man.

The man returned the kiss. Just before their lips pulled apart, a green Peugeot rolled past the rail and honked its horn several times. Young men cheered "Oi, Oies!" from the window.

"So perhaps it might be a good idea to know each other's names." The barman said.

Nick blushed. "I don't normally do this either." He said referencing the barman's earlier comment about not normally chatting-up men let alone kissing them.

"I can tell." It wasn't an insult, more of an observation, a way of conveying that he could read Nick's character; that he could acknowledge the specialness of the kiss he had just planted.

"I'm Nick."

"Nice to meet you, Nick. I'm Jim."

"Jim?" Nick repeated his name as if it sounded suspicious.

"Something wrong with Jim?"

"You don't look like a Jim. I've always thought of it as an older man's name."

He laughed. "Well check you out. Two minutes ago, you were worrying about voicing your feelings, and now you're dishing out insults."

"Sorry – I didn't mean…"

"Relax. I'm not offended. Besides it's not actually my proper name – luckily for you." Nick cricked his neck and the man continued. "People started calling me it at school to differentiate me from the other Jack, but it sort of stuck – even to me."

"So, your name isn't Jim."

"Not officially, but everybody calls me it."

"Your real names Jack?"

"Well my birth name is…"

"Nice to meet you, Jack."

"Nice to meet you, Nick."

Chapter 11 – Joining the fight

"Good luck, you'll be great." Heeta said as she left the apartment with a piece of brown toast in her hand.

"Thanks – have a good day." The door closed behind her. Nick dipped his finger into the tin of wax and rubbed it through his hair. He sprayed a few additional squirts of aftershave and left the bathroom thinking through the list of questions he would likely be asked. The toaster's compressed spring released two more pieces. Confident answers rolled through his mind to a range of technical questions as he crunched into the slightly burnt toast: how would he do this? How would he do that? But there was one question that slapped and stopped his thoughts, repeatedly: *Why do you want this job?* Nick mustered responses. He could string together something logical and coherent, but his heart was missing. He was landing flat, and this question was about energy. The panel didn't care about the words, in and of themselves – his cleverness did not matter, not for this question; they were hunting for passion: technicality and experience deferred to raw intent and desire. *Why do you want this job?* Nick needed to assert his desire; to show them he wanted, really wanted the position more than his competitors; that it meant more to him than the others. But Nick struggled with desire.

He was good at his job. Very good. Students liked and worked hard for him. Staff liked and worked hard for him. *Why do I have to bloody show them that I want it, and perform like some dancing monkey, yoyoing on the spot to win the position of Lord Sugar's apprentice – fucking reality T.V* – Nick thought as he crunched on more of his toast. But he knew that bitching and moaning about Lord Sugar was not going to help him. He needed to pull himself together and find some inner desire.

It took him the usual 50 minutes to get to school – not a bad commute for London, but one that would be cut in half when they made the house move. After the train ride, he decided to stop thinking and internally practising answers to the range of interview questions. *It will be what it will be.* Instead, he returned to thinking more deeply and honestly about why he wanted the job. The panel disappeared. The purpose and context for the question disappeared. He was left with himself. He tried to think about the truth, not what would sound good. *Why do I want this job?*

He scratched money from the list. Money didn't fundamentally motivate him. Of course, he wanted more, and wasn't a martyr that would work for free, but it wasn't as if he had or was planning to have a large family of dependents. Money wasn't what made him get out of bed in the morning. It mattered but didn't dictate what he did with his life.

The idea of superiority and privilege dissipated too. Nick didn't care about appearing better or more elevated than his colleagues. In fact, he found that part of the job distasteful. He enjoyed helping people, and found that it worked best when people felt equal and unthreatened: hierarchy tended to foster awkward and clunky interactions. The person needing help tended to not ask the questions that needed asking, and the person doing the helping tended to conceal their ignorance on a subject out of fear and insecurity that they would be exposed for the mere mortals they actually are. Nick wasn't into superiority at all. He enjoyed the problem or the project that he was working on, in and of itself – *the thrill of resolution*, he thought to himself. And he tried the sentence again: *the thrill of resolution*. He interrogated it. *Sounds a bit douchey... as if it could have come out of a self-help book or MBA guide... but it's seems true.*

He remembered his advice: *you don't need a perfect answer, they just need to feel convinced that you have passion, an authentic eagerness and desire for the job. Truth.* And the truth was that he believed this about himself. Sitting on the upper deck of the 186 he believed that he wanted the job because he was motivated by the thrill of resolution... the feel-good satisfaction of seeing a school work properly; of students receiving the education they deserve; of teachers feeling the pride and satisfaction of being able to do their job. He liked the thought of being able to influence those things; make them better. It was that simple.

With hordes of children, he exited the bus. He entered the building and smiled at the leadership team patrolling the main foyer.

"Morning Mr. Du Bois, looking forward to seeing you interview." The Headmaster said.

"Yes, good morning. Although you will need to get into school earlier should you get the position." The Deputy said.

"Thanks. I'm looking forward to it too. I can bring a lot to the team." The confidence poured out of Nick as if he weren't himself. He didn't sound boastful or arrogant. His words presented as non-emotional and fact-like. Professional. They ignored the nit-picky irrelevant preciousness of the Deputy Head.

"I think so too. There's a lot more to the job than just being in the building early – I'm excited to see what you can bring." The Headmaster axed his Deputy's parochial put-down and she was not happy about it. Her back stiffened and her eyes forced forward ever so slightly in their sockets. She wasn't used to being rebutted publicly, especially by the Headmaster. It was a declaration of war. Nick knew it. She knew it, and the Headmaster knew it. The other assistant Headteachers didn't have a scooby-do. Like younger children, they merely sensed a bit of tension between mummy and daddy, and the new love interest of daddy's, of whom they were not yet fully aware.

The interview would last the entire day, and if he got through, most of the following day too. Nick had not appreciated how competitive the process would be. He sat in the fancy conference room and the Head Teacher's PA offered him a cup of tea or coffee. She knew that he would choose tea – she knew him – but she asked anyway; asked as if she had never met him before, so to reinforce the sense of impartiality for the sake of the other five candidates; to give the air that they had a fair chance. They didn't. The Headmaster wanted Nick. The other candidates were unknown. He knew, respected and desired Nick. He just needed him to not fuck anything up and do enough of a good job that he could argue his case against the Deputy. The chair of governors would vote with him as long as Nick didn't do or say anything too ridiculous, and as long as none of the other candidates were spectacular, which was a low probability.

Nick toured the school that he had worked in for several years. Two of the candidates tagged along, and two of the school's best pupils led the way. Although Nick had not taught them, he knew them: he let them play chess in his classroom during break and lunch. In return they played along with his charade, interacting as if they had never met him before. They enjoyed it. "What made you apply for the job at our school, Mr Du Bois?" The sassier girl asked, supressing a chuckle.

The thrill of resolution. Nick thought of his musings on the bus, and knew instinctively that he could not say that to a student in this context without coming across as a complete tosser. He was right: it was MBA bullshit. Besides she had asked why this school specifically.

"I like the ethos. There seems to be an effort for the students and staff to get along, which is special. I notice in a lot of schools that the staff can be a little uptight, treating the students as if they are inferior." Nick surprised himself again. Where was this confident, relaxed voice coming from?

The other candidates gave a discreet eye roll and felt a patronising smugness. One of them considered that Nick's response revealed his inexperience and that his liberal attitude would not play well to the students or existing leadership team. The man judged that Nick had not yet learnt the realistic demands of leadership; that it was necessary to stamp your mark through whatever means; that it was imperative to strengthen your position within a competitive hierarchy in order to be effective. He kept quiet and worked hard to create a sense of seriousness. The students did not like his reserve and interpreted his endeavour as aloofness – they didn't know that they didn't like him for that reason, but the reason for their disliking him didn't matter. They sub-consciously distanced themselves. They left a wider gap between him and them, than they did for Nick and the other lady. They also asked him fewer questions. He took this as a positive sign; that he was making a good impression. The children's austere behaviour was an indication that they were developing a respect for him as a viable authority figure.

The woman also considered that Nick had overplayed his hand; that he had been too earnest and naïve. She thought that Nick had the correct narrative – that it was important to say and to appear as if students and staff got along – but that in reality, the students needed and wanted to toe the line; that they secretly wanted an authority figure to boss them around… just that they should feel as if it's their choice… a democratic dictatorship. Her smugness originated in the false sense that the students shared her thoughts; that they too considered Nick a soft touch. They didn't. They respected the way he respected them, really respected their thoughts and feelings, and they could tell that this woman didn't, not deep down. She was shrewd and about appearances – they knew she would end up being one of those teachers that asked for opinions all the time, but was always pissed off when the class didn't climb into her head and imitate exactly what she thought and felt, word for word. Her lessons would be all about cutting and gluing established positions. They didn't want that. That wanted teachers who would give them space to think – to properly know stuff.

"What opportunities do you have for student leadership?" She asked, believing that they would be impressed by her formalised approach to celebrating the school's 'student-voice', as if a committee of wanna-be politicians were more impressive than the real voices of the other 1500 students used in the real contexts of everyday. She didn't get that. She was an old-school elitist with the mistaken view that a voice only mattered once it had been chiselled down and shaped into a bureaucratic form that professed to speak on behalf of others.

The tour guides were intelligent and polite: they played along and interacted with her pleasantly enough. But in the student panel they would never choose her as the best candidate for the job. It gave her false hope, and she became increasingly talkative as the tour progressed, boasting to everybody about the thousands of initiatives she had introduced in her own school.

Every now and again Nick and the students peeked at one another to share a private eye roll. It expressed, *please don't let them work in our school.*

After the tour, the Head's PA chaperoned the candidates back into the conference room. The tables had been rearranged so that the candidates could sit on a group table in the centre of the room, and be watched from all angles by observers who would sit on an outer circle behind them. The itinerary labelled the event, 'Fish Bowl Exercise'. Nick glanced at the outer ring of chairs and thought the set-up felt more like a dog-fight. *I'd get rid of this for a start.* He thought, pondering the things he would like to change.

The Deputy Head introduced the task once the other observers had entered and taken their seats. She spoke with an affected warmth and gentleness, the kind that lured little children into ginger bread houses. She ensured that she made brief eye contact with each of the candidates, including Nick. In her little speech, she declared – in violation of all the evidence that suggested otherwise – that they should feel relaxed and be themselves; that there was nothing to feel anxious about, and that they shouldn't overthink the situation. *Bullshit.* Nick knew that he would be an idiot if he was himself or didn't manage the situation in a highly thoughtful and strategic manner. Turning around and telling the panel that he thought this was an artificial exercise and an utter waste of school resources – that it helped in no way whatsoever and only reinforced flawed Lord-of-the-Flies psychology from the 1950s – was not what they wanted to hear. The clever ones thought it too, but like Nick they also knew that the panel didn't want to employ a tactless bulldozer.

Nick understood the real purpose for the Fish Bowl: it was an opportunity for the Deputy Head to gather evidence that she could use to argue against a candidate that she did not want to employ – evidence to argue against Nick getting the job. There were no winners – only survivors. Nick knew that. He didn't need to shine or stand-out; he needed to lose, just not as much as the others. His plan was to remain calm, offer sensible contributions, but on the whole, remain uncontroversial. He would shine later, in meaningful contexts. Real school life was not about short-term superficial interaction and competition. It is about long-term relationships and collaboration. Nick was firm. He told himself that he would win by not engaging faithfully in this farcical, forced exercise of social engineering; this attempt to inject a pseudo-scientific Darwinian competitiveness – survival of the fittest – into a context in which it is ideologically applied. The fact of slow adaptation of species over hundreds of millions of years is not justification for grown adults to act like dicks to one another, especially in front of even older grown adults, silently endorsing that dickishness for leadership.

"Your topic is vision. Together, you need to prepare a vision statement for your school. You need to outline your intent clearly – what is your school about? Then, outline your key strategies for implementation – how will you achieve your intent? And finally, describe your impact – why have you done it… what has changed as a consequence of the way you have run your school?" The Deputy said. She left a lingering silence in which she read each of the candidates' facial expressions to check they understood her instructions. Enthusiastic and overzealous head nods greeted her. Nick gave a more economic upturn of his lips, not quite a smile. "Ok, then. Of you go." She sat down and lifted one leg over the other. Her notepad rested on her skirt. She clutched her pen ready to scratch down Nick's faults.

"Powerful people." Mr. Dominant, the guy seeking to impress the tour guides with his austere ego, raced to get his vision onto the table first. The Deputy's pen scratched itself onto the pad instantly. A bulldog she could leash and take for a walk. Tick.

"Yes, but wisdom and compassion are arguably even more important. Power for its own sake, is dangerous. Our school needs to be driven by inclusivity and awareness." Mrs. Control, the power-driven woman from the tour rebutted him. It exemplified her. Nick saw it having spent an hour walking around the school with her blabbering waffle. She didn't give two shits about compassion or wisdom – they were tools for her to achieve the same objective as the man: power. Controlling the narrative was her thing.

The man didn't seem bruised or bothered by her challenge. In fact, it wasn't clear whether he had even listened. He was smug, congratulating himself that he had managed to frame – as he saw it – the agenda. Nick saw him glance at the Deputy scratching on her pad. He was counting his chickens before the eggs had hatched.

"Awareness of what?" A red-head woman asked. She had toured in a separate group and so Nick had less sense of her. Although, he already thought more of her than Mr. Dominant and Mrs. Control put together. It was a sensible question, and it indicated that she knew how to play this game. Like him, she wasn't playing to win, only to survive. They caught each other's eye and knew they liked each other. Nick offered a small smile of approval.

"It's a good question." Nick said allying with her. "I think schools have a duty to help children be sharp, to notice details and sieve rhetoric." Mrs. Control flushed a little, caught between embarrassment and offense.

"It's a little nit-picky. I think you could make the effort to understand my larger point. Awareness…" She repeated the word that had opened her to attack and left a short pause to emphasise that it still had relevance; "awareness…" She locked her war-lord eyes on Nick. "… of other people and contexts obviously… our children need to know how to use their power appropriately and awareness of the contexts in which they will need to exert their influence, will enable them to do this."

She was clearly a fighter. She redeemed herself from looking utterly floppy and perhaps impressed a few of the judges by demonstrating that she wouldn't roll over – that she could handle conflict and tolerate a bit of heat, even if it was mostly coming from herself.

"Perhaps." Said the red-head – the one Nick liked. "But it's a bit flaky, don't you think? This woman had self-confidence and less ego. She was comfortable with disagreement; she could play with Mrs. Control, who deep down was very uncomfortable at being challenged.

"Flaky?" She repeated. Nick had to stop himself from smirking at her irritation. "Please explain what aspect of my vision was *flaky*?" Mrs. Control played into the red-head's hands – she had invited advice passive-aggressively; in the process, establishing the likable red-head as an authority, a voice to be listened to, while reducing herself to a snappy, short-tempered diva.

"Well… you said that adults assert their interests and in order to do this well, they require knowledge on the possible scenarios they will face… It's too vague and open-ended."

"I think you're missing her point a bit." Mr. Dominant stepped back into the ring smelling an opportunity to present himself in the light of a saviour. "She meant our school should have a relevant curriculum."

Mrs. Control did not like having him speak on her behalf, but she was grateful for his moving the conversation forward. "Exactly." She said, forming an alliance with him. "It's about relevance – our vision is for a relevant curriculum that will enable our students to face realistic challenges."

"Sure. That's certainly clearer…" The red-head replied, removing the sense of dispute, which balanced her comfort of disagreement, with a character trait that was, otherwise, agreeable. She was running loops around the other two. Nick, to his surprise, found himself enjoying the task. The red-head finished with a silent 'but' – it was there, just not said – it left the space for Nick or one of the other candidates to continue the assault.

"But it's still too vague. 'Relevant' could mean anything, to anyone. If we are modelling the precision and sharpness we envision and want for the students, then really we should put more thought and effort into our own definition." Nick said, triggering one of candidates, who had not yet spoken, to join the discussion.

"I agree. Otherwise our brand comes across a bit sloppy. And given that a large portion of the students will end-up working – in at least some capacity – in marketing and advertising, we're not creating the best first impression." The guy taught business studies.

"Yes, but a school isn't a brand." Mr. Dominant said. "It's a community." He sought reassurance from his ally, Mrs. Control, who he considered to owe him a debt for his earlier rescue. She avoided his gaze, not subtly. Mrs. Control evocatively turned to the other side as he looked.

"It's both." The business studies geek clarified. "No one would dispute a school is a community, that's obvious. Whenever people are involved, a community exists in some form or the other. But a school has more than people. It has documents, policies, procedures, values, resources, buildings, uniforms. All sorts of things that obviously involve and serve people, but in themselves are something else. And all of that stuff needs steering. It needs a brand to pull it together."

Mr. Dominant knew Mr. Geek was right, so he changed track by attempting to create a false dichotomy, a rhetorical binary in which there are two types of people. "Well there are doers and knowers, aren't there? ... You clearly know a lot about the technical details and that's very important, but we're talking about the big picture here. Leadership. We don't need to get into the minutia of how a school is a brand. We need to make clear what we're about."

"Yes. We need to define the brand." Mr. Geek said, giving the man a disapproving look, as if what he had just said made no sense. "The two are indistinguishable. *Doers* as you call them are only able to be effective in what they do because they know a lot – they know what they are about."

Mr. Dominant backed down like a bully who had just been put in his place by a nerdy underrated colleague lashing back with a powerful combination of intelligence and hidden strength. Nick was impressed. It also seemed to have a humiliating effect on Mrs. Control. Her arrogance withered a little as she recognised that the competition wasn't so beneath her.

"You're right." The red-head said. "If our vision is for the students to be sharp and attentive to detail, to know a lot, and thus be able to do a lot, we need to be direct about that."

"It's that *a lot* that seems to need something." Nick said. The geek and the red-head nodded – they had formed a collegiate trio. Mrs. Control read the power shift and decided to join them. She dropped her competitive charge that was fuelling her one-upmanship. She stopped thinking about the panel sitting behind her and instead channelled her intelligence into honestly trying to solve the task.

"I think we need to be specific about the main branches of knowledge instead of saying 'a lot'." The red-head gave her a warm smile, instantly accepting her reformation and holding no grudges. She continued by reformulating what they had. "For example, 'Our vision is for students to be sharp and attentive to detail, to know, in breadth and depth, enduring world literature, mathematic and scientific principles, and a range of achievements in the arts, humanities, and design technologies'."

"I like it." Nick said. Mrs. Control blushed a little – she was not used to sincere praise. People sucked-up to her, but Nick genuinely endorsed her work. That felt different.

"Me too." Said the geek. "It's more on brand with the values of being straightforward and effective communicators."

"And then we can talk about confident, resilient, accomplished people as the impact. The effect of their school experience." Nick said.

The group continued discussing and rephrasing bits and pieces but the dynamics had settled among them – and ultimately, that was what the judges were interested in. The quantity of scratch marks decreased and one or two pads even closed.

Nick had survived. Mr. Dominant and the guy that said nothing were the clear losers. Mrs. Control had done enough provided the rest of her day had gone well. It hadn't. Mr. Geek, the red-head, and Nick were invited back for the second day of interview. The Head called them into his office at the end of the day and told them directly.

"Congratulations. We have been really impressed and would like to see the three of you again tomorrow." He shook each of their hands and mirrored their grateful, proud smiles. "Obviously, there is only one position, but whatever happens, I want each of you to know that I would employ you, and that I would be more than happy to write a recommendation to support you in any other application you have on the go, should you not get this position." He was easing their expectations. When all was done, two of them would not receive the job, no matter how successful or competent they were. "See you tomorrow – well done for today. One of the best interview days I've seen for a while.

They left the room and as they walked along the corridor, they saw the other three candidates standing with drooped faces in the Deputy Head's office. She was giving them the bad news. Nick sped up slightly. He did not want to be around when they came out.

"Congratulations." The red-head said to him and Mr. Geek. They repeated it to her too. "What school are you at?"

"I'm at an Academy in North London, but my wife and I are expecting our second and so are looking at buying somewhere a bit bigger. Places are cheaper south of the river, so trying to get a job down here to shorten the commute once it eventually happens." Mr. Geek said. Nick looked at him with fresh eyes. He had not expected the guy to be married with kids. He looked a similar age, and although two kids in your early thirties wasn't unusual, Nick felt struck to his core that it was impossible for anybody to be ready for children at his age.

"I'm just down the road. South-London girl, born and bred." The red-head said. Nick looked at her with fresh eyes too. She seemed more home counties than Lewisham. "I know right." She said anticipating their thoughts. "My mum was insistent that I attend elocution lessons. She was blind, and I think that encouraged her obsession with the way I spoke… I love her, but I'm glad the lessons have at least half faded."

"They have." Nick said. "You definitely don't sound South London innit? But you are not quite full Sussex either." He said with an affected posh accent.

"How about you?"

Nick didn't want to answer. It felt somehow fraudulent. He liked the two of them and wanted them to feel like they had a fair chance. The Headmaster's voice echoed in his head, *I want you, Nick – don't fuck it up.* "Actually, I work here."

"Oh, you're an internal candidate." She said, her enthusiasm did that weird thing where it increased externally – the pitch, the volume of her voice, the wilful optimism – but only because it was so obvious that her heart sank internally.

Nick didn't say anything – not by choice. He had nothing to say. Mr. Geek chipped in. "Well, it's been great to meet you both, and whatever happens tomorrow, it's quite a pleasure to meet two people that I would happily lose to." He meant it, and it softened the awkwardness. The red-head nodded.

"I agree. There are so many dickheads in school – it's nice to meet good people. Good luck tomorrow – and it's a small world, I'm sure we'll end up meeting again." She waved and strutted toward the exit. Mr. Geek waved too and followed her out. Nick popped back to his classroom – he had a bar of dark chocolate in his top drawer.

As he shut his classroom door and went to lock it, the Deputy strutted along the otherwise empty corridor. "You did well today." She said without stopping or looking at him. Nick was waiting for her next move. But she said nothing else. She passed him turning the key and checking the handle on the door. Her stilettoes clacked on the laminate. The volume diminished one step at a time. Her itchy perfume lingered behind though. Nick waded back through it and left the school.

Chapter 12 – More on than off

Heeta went to bed and Nick told himself that he would have one more celebratory drink before bed. "Do not open another bottle!" she shouted before closing her bedroom door.

They had been out-out to celebrate Nick's success at his second day at interview. He got the job. The cooker flashed 4.07 in its red angular digits. His voice was husky and his shirt damp with sweat from the club. While pouring a generous glug of gin, he gulped a full glass of tap water – he was desperately dehydrated. He couldn't be bothered to fetch the tray of ice and pop-out the cubes. Instead he emptied the dregs of tonic from the bottle in the fridge, spilling half of it on the counter. He dipped his finger into the glass and twirled it around the liquid. He sucked the droplets off his finger and collapsed into the sofa. He checked the messages on his mobile phone.

Jack: *'congratulations once again Nicky. Hope you've had a good night. Looking forward to seeing you next weekend x'*

Nick smiled goofily, and haphazardly placed his glass of gin onto the coffee table – it almost fell, but Nick barely noticed. The room was beginning to spin and so the little bounce of the glass was a drop in the ocean of his unstable perception. He tapped a response. *'I love you! x'*. He clicked send, his euphoric inebriation blocked his usual inhibitions. He flung the phone onto the other side of the sofa. His eye lids clamped his face. His torso lumbered flat. His arm flapped off the edge of the sofa. Nick was out. His body forced his consciousness into sleep.

Warm hands patted his cheeks. One eyelid unzipped itself like the bottom of a tent door. Light was already pressing through the material but the slight gap allowed a torrent of light to flood in. Nick grumbled.

"I cannot believe you slept on the sofa – you plonker." His body lifted slowly and the feeling returned to his numbed arm. It felt like a hundred thousand small needles jabbing him out of retribution. *Prick! Don't do that again.* His veins proclaimed as blood rushed back into them.

Heeta lifted the cup of tea she had made for Nick from the coffee table. "Here." She placed the cup into his hands. "Your phone has been buzzing too."

Nick slurped the surface of the hot tea. "Oh, fuck. It'll be Jack. I'm pretty sure I said I love you before conking out." Heeta laughed, a simultaneously wicked and compassionate laugh. "I know. I'm such an idiot."

"Well I told you not to do it." She walked back to the kitchen counter and pushed the toast back in – it wasn't done enough.

"I didn't exactly have a choice – the guy put it in the shot glass."

"You didn't have to drink it – I didn't... the guy was clearly dodgy as hell. Who wears a leather vest and ass-chaps outside of a fetish bar?"

"I didn't want to be rude."

"Oh, fuck off. You were shit faced and up for anything – good job there weren't any hookers offering heroin or coke. You would have been shooting-up and sniffing lines of their chests." She laughed as her back rested on the edge of the counter. The toast began to blacken behind. "I'm not judging. You were celebrating – it's not every day you become *Assistant Headteacher, Mr Du Bois.*" Nick slurped more of the tea wishing it wasn't so hot so that he could actually drink some of the blasted thing. "You just need to be a bit more careful. There's a lot of twisted perverts out there that will do anything to get into *Assistant Headteacher Du Bois'* underpants." She laughed at herself again.

"What do you think it was? I've never had a headache this bad before in my life."

"GHB." She said, turning around to manually pop the toast. It was nicely burnt around the edges.

"What the hell is GHB?"

"It's like liquid ecstasy."

"As in ecstasy? I took ecstasy!"

Heeta buttered her toast. "Well technically, you were spiked with GHB so you didn't *take ecstasy. Assistant Headteachers* do not *take ecstasy*, Mr Du Bois." She chuckled as she walked to the sofa with her buttered toast. Nick picked up his phone and noticed the low battery, the miscall from Jack, and a text message.

You are shitfaced! Wish I was there to take advantage ▢ *But seriously, I love you too… Give me a ring in the morning to let me know you are alive.*

Nick grinned in disbelief... "Bloody hell… he said that he loves me too." He tilted-up his head to look at Heeta.

"Well he must have been shitfaced as well. It was Friday night." She crunched her toast. "Gays – you are so fickle."

"Homophobia is no longer cool, you know. And besides, lesbians cannot accuse anybody of being fickle…"

"One: I was never cool. Two: you can't fight homophobia with homophobia."

"You were cool…"

Heeta dipped her finger in the pool of butter resting on her other slice. She wiped the grease along Nick's cheek.

"Urgh." He said swiping her hand.

"So, do you?" She asked.

"What?"

"Love him?"

Nick slurped more of his tea. He assumed it must have cooled given the number of slurps he had attempted. It hadn't – not enough. It burnt his tastebuds. "I can't – I've only known him a few months."

"Does that matter?" She said again, nonchalantly munching away.

"Well, yeah… I don't really know him yet: we've only been on a handful of dates."

"And droned on and on for hours on the phone nearly every night… I don't know…" Her tone emphasised that his reservation might not be justified. "I think we read people pretty quickly and that the rest of the time we're merely gathering evidence for what we knew right from the get go. I knew I liked you straight away."

"No, you didn't. When we first met, you were frosty, all the time. Sometimes I thought you were going to punch me right in the face, just for existing."

"Oh, don't be so dramatic. I didn't behave like that because I didn't like you."

"Why then?"

"Because I was envious."

"Really?" Nick was sincerely surprised. Heeta crunched her toast, chewed and swallowed it before answering. Nick couldn't think of a time that she had ever come across as envious.

"You were *out* and seemed at peace with your sexuality. Whereas Fred was struggling – there was such a contrast between the two of you and I suppose deep down, I identified with Fred more."

Nick smirked as if Heeta had bet on the wrong horse.

"Don't be a dick." Heeta mirrored his smirk involuntarily.

"Sorry." He said trying to contain his smugness.

"I think that's why I was so protective over him for so long. Beyond his melodrama, his thoughtlessness, and his tendency to be an utterly selfish prick, I saw myself in him."

Nick failed to fully contain the smirk. It leaked through his dimples. Heeta was none of those things and he found her identification with Fred amusing.

"Well obviously a little part of myself." She modified her proposition. It was not like her to be so vulnerable. Tenderness transformed Nick's smirk into a warm smile.

"It makes sense, actually… you know, thinking back. Although you were wrong about me."

"I wasn't wrong. I said you 'seemed' at peace… which is another way of saying, you weren't as fucked up as the rest of us." She patted the top of his hand which lay flat on the cushion, and the conversation rested.

Nick moaned as he stood. "Fucking hell – my head is throbbing. If this is what E does, I'm never touching it again." The tap released water into a pint glass, which tipped down Nick's throat in one flow. More tap water filled the glass and Nick returned to the sofa with it. "It's hard, accepting who you are." He sipped a more modest amount of the water. "I guess, I appeared further along with it back then because I didn't care."

Heeta frowned, unconvinced at his self-narrative.

"I don't mean that I didn't care, as in *I didn't care*." He affected his voice so that the second 'didn't care' sounded terse and charged with repressed anger, as if he were some teenager who actually cared very deeply and despite their will and determination to not do so. "I mean I just… didn't care." This time, he affected his voice to imitate a hollow housewife, dutiful and barren of desire, emptied of want; worn-down and emotionless after years of self-denial. "I think I was half switched off, and had become comfortable living that way… well, you know, not comfortable…"

"Used to it." Heeta helped him find better words to demonstrate that she understood and accepted this point. "I get it. It makes sense."

"Look at us. Growing." He smirked. "Fred would be so proud." They laughed together.

"Seriously though. I think I have definitely dialled things up."

"You're not a modem." Heeta said.

"Burr…. Derrrrrr….. ghurrrrr…. Huhhhhhrrrrr…. shhherrrrr…." Nick played out the sounds of his first computer as it connected to the internet. "Fuck my head." He said as his groggy pissed-off mind punished him for his poor decision to vibrate his dehydrated, hungover body for dramatic effect.

He rested his back into the cushions and sat still before elaborating. "I don't know… it seems a pretty good comparison if you ask me. I was going to say that I've definitely switched-on since moving to London, but I don't think it works that way… switching… On/Off. I was never 'off'… and equally, I'm not fully 'on', especially right now." He added as an ironic aside. "…but I'm more 'on' than 'off', whereas before I was definitely more 'off' than 'on'… if that makes sense?"

"It does." She sipped her tea. "… but if you ever tell Fred we had this conversation…" She drew a line across her throat, mocking a knife slicing it. "Besides, you haven't answered the question." She said returning to her initial point. "Do you love him?"

"I don't know exactly what love is meant to feel like; is it even a feeling? I'm crap at this stuff. How do you know?"

"You are asking the wrong person... my guess would be that it is something that you probably end up having even if you don't know what it quite is."

"I've never even thought about saying it before to anybody; surely that means something?"

"Yes. It means that you were shitfaced on GHB." They laughed. "Look I don't know. Do you like him?"

"Yes."

"Do you want to spend time with him?"

"Yes."

"Do you want to suck his cock?"

Nick blushed. He was a prude, not innately, but through upbringing. He and Heeta rarely discussed sex explicitly and he wasn't sure how to respond. He avoided laughing it off, motivated by an intent to honour his newly found regard for self-liberation: he wanted to be more open, to explore and understand all the parts of his life; that included sex. But just because he wanted to have this conversation, didn't mean that he could. Habits and attitudes are rarely uprooted with one endeavouring yank. Nonetheless, Nick decided to start pulling. He answered albeit in a safer zone of abstraction, avoiding specific details and particularities. "If you mean do I find him attractive; do I want to sleep with? Wake up next to him? Then, yes."

Heeta was grateful for his not completely shying away from her provocative question – she wanted to be less conservative too. She patted his thigh. "Well who the fuck cares whether you love each other or not. If you keep feeling those things, then, it sounds pretty good to me."

"I guess."

"Think of your little exchange as confirmation that you're both on the same wavelength. He wants to wake up next to you too."

"And suck my cock?" Nick tried it out, but it just didn't feel right, like a nun with a potty mouth. "Sorry." He said laughing. "… I'm just not sure I'm able to talk, you know, sexually - about that stuff. I want to, but…"

"Oh, me neither – don't worry. Let's just accept that we aren't completely perfect; that it isn't a taboo topic, just something we're both crap at talking about, with each other."

"Deal."

"So, what're your plans for the rest of the day?" She asked. Nick stared out of the window. The clear blue sky contrasted with the inner sleet of hangover.

"I'm going to bed for a few hours, try and shake this headache. Then, probably head to the gym to sweat out the next layer of alcohol. How about you?"

"I have a date." She dipped her smile into her tea cup to hide the insecurity it revealed. "You're not the only one around here with needs." She said, her words blowing into the tea and causing a little ripple to skim across the surface.

"Who is she?"

"The waitress from Balans."

"The restaurant? The woman with the funky haircut? You kept that quiet."

"Well, we've met a few times for drinks, and well, we've been getting along, so we're doing something a bit more formal."

"Good for you – time for some scissoring action?"

"Ok. We've tried and failed. Sex talk is now officially taboo, especially when you refer to lesbian sex as scissoring — where did you even get that from?"

"South Park." Nick confessed.

"Stop watching it. I'll give you a good book." Heeta lifted herself from the sofa and disappeared. Nick crashed onto his bed and let the GHB wriggle itself out of his body.

He woke-up five hours later, feeling parched and hungry. He weighed himself before drinking another couple of glasses of water. The scales generated the same skinny digits as they had for the last couple of weeks - bulking-up was not happening. Shorts, trunks, fresh socks, fresh pants, a clean T-shirt and a towel layered into his gym bag. The bus rumbled along the road as the doors of his apartment building clicked shut. He decided to walk rather than wait for the next one. His head needed the air, even smoggy London air.

The gym and pool were unusually quiet. Only a couple of the Victorian changing-booths at either side of the pool had towels tossed over the doors to indicate they were taken, and more importantly the lanes were mostly empty. *A quick swim to wake myself-up, then, I'll hit the weights properly.*

His jogging bottoms and boxer shorts fell to his bare feet. He pulled them off and neatly folded them, placing them onto the small wooden bench. He removed his T-shirt and did the same thing. He pinched the tiniest paunch on his stomach, beneath the light brush of blondish hair. He willed himself to lose it. Nick had a swimmer's build — he was lean and evenly muscular. He was definitely not fat. His trunks slid up his shins and thighs and settled into place.

His body sliced into the water, elegantly preventing much of a splash. His powerful arms cut into the surface repeatedly and drove the rest of his body up and down the lanes. Twenty lengths warmed him up. He re-showered and returned to his booth to change into his gym shorts and the T-shirt he wore to walk to the centre. He left his stuff in the pool booth rather than storing it in the changing rooms.

Like the pool, the machines were mostly empty. A tattooed man with jet black hair and a matching tank top looked over a few times. Nick noticed, but pretended not to. He wasn't sure if the guy was an intimidating meat-head just wanting some bro-banter or whether he was gay and checking him out. Either way, Nick wasn't interested.

The pile of weights built into the machine, elevated too easily as Nick pulled the bar down to his chest. Nick stopped, leant forward to pull-out the bolt from 32 and enter it into the hole beside 50. He knew which numbers the bolt generally needed to lock into for his strength. He re-pulled. The challenge was more appropriate. Grunts escaped his mouth with each pull and beads of sweat began to muster under his armpits. As the weights slammed back down to their starting pile, the black-haired beefcake squeezed Nick's shoulder blade, causing him to instinctively flinch.

"Hey there – I know you, sweetheart." His pecs seemed to flex beneath his tank top. Nick couldn't place the man, but now that he had approached him, a haze of familiarity gathered like puffy white cumulus clouds: they blocked the light, but only temporarily. Nick thought hard, tried to penetrate the cloud and tap into his memory. He was embarrassed by the reality of not being able to recognise the man when the man clearly recognised him. But just as a cloud's movement has no bearing on the intent, will or want of the person beneath it, the memory did not come.

"Sorry." Nick said, hoping that the man would relieve him from his discomfort. The man pouted and gripped himself around the waist making himself appear authoritative and commandeering. He was enjoying Nick's squeamishness.

"Bloody hell, Geordie – you must get around a bit if you don't remember."

Fuck. We can't have slept together. Nick thought. *I'd definitely remember. It's not as if I've been with that many men.* He didn't know why he was doubting himself. He knew he hadn't slept with him.

"We haven't slept together." He said, not meaning for it to sound so blunt and shrill. The man laughed.

"I'm exaggerating our relationship a little. I was enjoying watching you desperately try to place me. You are so sweet, Geordie. Most men would scowl and not give a toss unless they wanted to fuck there and then."

"So how do we know each other?"

"We had a little kiss years ago. Your friend pimped you out for a couple of shots."

"Oh god, you're that barman." Nick blushed. He had returned to the bar a couple of times once he had moved to London, hoping to bump back into him. His hair had changed.

"Well, I was a barman. I DJ now – well, I DJ'd then too, but there's enough work to support myself fully, so I gave the bar job up not long after our little kiss."

"I did go back once or twice on the off-chance that you were still there." Nick said with a slight flirtation. "Your hair is different."

"Did you now?" The guy laughed, ignoring the comment about his hair. He focused the conversation to the here and now: "What weight are you lifting?"

"50."

He laughed again. "You're lifting 50k – not bad." The man wrapped his open hand around Nick's upper arms to inspect his muscles. Nick did not flinch externally but within he tensed – he wasn't used to somebody touching his body in such a casual manner. He didn't have a conscious objection to it, but his body was unused and inexperienced when it came to random guys sizing up his muscles in public. He contained his discomfort, and acted as if he were used to guys touching him in that way. "Nice." The man said giving the bumps on his arms a little squeeze. He stroked the skin around his upper arms, as if he were some sort of dermatologist with the ability to determine the inherent composition of his skin with touch alone.

"I'm guessing you're pretty into it then?" Nick said.

"Five times a week. I work late into the night, so I'm free in the afternoons – you can guarantee I'm around about this time most days. How about you?"

"Well, I initially started coming just to manage my weight – I enjoy a drink and didn't want to pile on the pounds because of it. But I'm trying to proactively bulk-up a bit now."

"What are you taking?" The guy asked as if it were an utterly normal question, as if it were commonplace to be taking something. Nick felt ridiculous for having to give his spartan answer.

"Nothing?" He changed his voice to make his response sound more like a question, to imply that he was open to 'taking' something even though he wasn't.

"Geordie, you need to be taking stuff if you want to bulk-up." He leant down and hovered his flexed arm. His elbow appeared to rest on an invisible surface, and his muscles glimmered. He held it in that position, offering it for Nick to sample as if his arm were a fancy piece of meat on a deli counter. Nick felt uneasy at the idea of physically appreciating the sensuality of another guy in the middle of the gym. He waited for the offer to become explicit before extending his own hand to admire Mr. Muscles' biceps.

"Are you going to feel them or what?" The guy laughed, obviously finding it funny that Nick needed to be given permission. "Impressive hey?" Nick's fingertips brushed along the camel-humps of the man's upper arm. "You have to grab them. Lock your hand around and you will be able to appreciate the strength." The man talked about his muscles as if they were a separate item; a pet, rather than an integral part of his physical being. It was surreal to Nick, but the guy took that dazed, confused look as awe. "Steroids, Geordie. If you want to bulk-up, it's the only way."

Nick nodded, conveying to the man that he accepted his statement as unquestionable truth. But the idea of taking steroids made him deeply uncomfortable. Drugs made him uncomfortable, period. The irony wasn't lost on him. He imagined the GHB swimming around his arteries, its meandering in and out of his organs; his heart sucking it in and pumping it out in freshly oxygenated blood. The thought of it triggered a thick dose of hypocrisy. Nick felt as if it was chasing the E; as if his body had become a cat and mouse battleground, a paintballing arena filled with opposing agents trying to eliminate one another.

This inner drama reduced Nick to a state of passivity with Mr. Muscles. He nodded along to his waffling-on about the ins and outs of how the steroids worked, only half listening. His awkwardness over being physically touched-up, discretely crumpled away. The tension in his arms gave-way to the shame and anxiety of his gut. Mr. Muscles took Nick's now unresisting upper arm, and repeatedly prodded specific parts of his triceps, biceps, and whatever else existed beneath the skin. He vomited pseudo-scientific explanations of mono-fats vs. hydrofluoric-anti-proteins and a load of other home-grown, blog science. Nick nodded along, and willed himself to listen, not because he was interested, but because he thought it would stop him thinking about the drugs in his system and the consequential feeling of being contaminated. Mr. Muscles' hazel irises widened as they mistakenly perceived interest in Nick's. They glowed, and Mr. Muscles' evangelical enthusiasm for Godly steroids poured-out.

"Are you coming or what?" Mr. Muscles said. He had released Nick's arm and was standing a couple of feet further back. Nick had crawled so far into his own head that he had barely listened to him. His mind deleted the last few minutes from its time-space continuum as ruthlessly as the delete key removed a block of highlighted text on a computer screen.

"Sorry. I zoned-out. Where are we going?"

"Come-on, Geordie. It won't take a minute."

Nick climbed off the leather seat of the machine and followed Mr. Muscles out of the gym. *Shit, what have I agreed to?* He thought. *I'm not hooking-up with him if that's what he thinks.*

"My stuff – my phone – it's in the pool changing-booth." Nick said as he caught-up with Mr. Muscles in the gym's hospital-like corridor. He was assuming that they had gone to collect their mobile phones so that they could exchange numbers. "I'll go and get it." He said, giving himself an excuse to leave and sneak out of the place.

"No problem, which side are you on? I'll come over to you in a second."

Shit. He thought. *That's probably worse. Fucking hell! I wouldn't have agreed to hook-up with him, surely?* "Erm, ok. I'm on the right side as you enter." Nick lied. "See you in a minute." He almost sprinted away. He would actually run as soon as Mr. Muscles was out of visibility. He intended to grab his stuff and get out. Apart from an elderly man attempting to breast-stroke, the pool was empty. Nick ran along the right-hand side, on the tips of his feet to avoid slipping. As he passed the gap in the cubicles leading to the showers, he realised he had mistakenly crossed to the wrong side of the pool, forgetting his lie, and that his stuff was in the cubicle on the left, the only one with the towel hanging over the edge. The arithmetic calculated itself automatically in Nick's mind. He continued running knowing that it would be quicker to get to his booth by going the entire way around the pool. *Fucking idiot.* He thought to and about himself. The time he gained from running was completely negated. *Shit, I'm not going to have time to get my stuff and get out before he's back.*

The door banged the side of the cubicle, but the elderly man in the pool didn't notice over his own gasps for air. Nick grabbed his neat pile of clothes, but as they layered in his hands, he froze.

He stopped. He stopped rushing. He stopped running. He sat down on the bench with the pile of clothes resting on his lap and thought about his sister.

The adrenaline in his stomach fizzled out, and an overwhelming melancholy fogged his insides. Nick could not remember the last time he cried. He certainly hadn't cried as an adult, and although no tears dripped down his cheeks, he felt that salty, coarse suffering that tears are meant to cleanse from the body. The sadness glued him to that bench and weighed the soles of his feet to the floor. The suddenness of his immeasurable sadness felt like an internal Berlin Wall separating his will from his body. They disconnected from one another. A whole fragmented into unnatural parts. He felt helpless and no matter how much he did not want to feel it, it was there. *Why now?* He thought. *She died ten years ago.* The clean clothes fell to the floor; luckily, it was dry.

The memory of his sister sitting on the backdoor-step flashed onto the cubicle wall as his mind subordinated sensory reality for a dream-like projection of repressed experience. His younger self flickered onto the wall. He stared into his own childhood eyes and watched himself desperately long for his sister to stop feeling so wretched. The boy's eyes filled, like water rising within a tank. Logically, they would surely burst as more water entered. They didn't.

Nick watched the water drain from his younger self, presumably from the same source they were filled, because it was not outward. There were no tears. The image played-out like a movie rewind, but it wasn't a rewind. The boy's eyes were actively emptying. The desire for his sister to stop hurting dissipated second by second. The darker hazel of his irises faded to a soft wood, an eerie leftover fragment of the deep colour that was there moments before. The eyes haunted Nick. They meant no harm but they meant no good either. They meant nothing. They were vacuous. They faced the direction of his sister slumped against the outside wall of the back of their council house, but they no longer had the capacity to take-in the stuff they looked at. The subtle downward crescent of his sister's lip; the way one of her hands rested in the other like a wounded dog that could not articulate, but only show, its pain. The wave in her hair that tucked behind her pierced ear. The knock-off Nike trainers that were white once upon a time. The black tights that hid her fleshless, bony legs. The hand-me-down jumper that was too big for her even before she lost half of her body weight.

Nick saw his child-self block the image of his heroin-addicted sister. He watched his eyes develop the capacity to screen the world, out of self-preservation.

A knock on the cubicle door stabbed the balloon of Nick's dream-like projection. "Hey Geordie – I'm coming in – hope you're decent, sort-of." He entered and shut the cubicle door behind him. "Woh-man, you ok?"

Nick felt jet-lagged, as if he'd just woken from an unsatisfying nap on a cramp jumbo-jet. Mr. Muscle's concern irritated him like an air steward asking him if there was anything that he needed. "Yes, to get off the fucking plane." He mumbled to himself.

"Hey?" Mr. Muscle asked, uncertain as to what Nick had said.

"Nothing." Nick shook his head and flapped his arms to stir some energy into his body. "Sorry, sorry." He said, using the repetition to inject some energy into his voice. "I'm not feeling great… had a bit of a heavy night, and think I might have overdone it."

"We've all been there." Mr. Muscle patted Nick on the shoulder. "Move over, man." Nick scooted along so that they could both wedge onto the little bench. The outside of their thighs pressed together out of necessity.

"Look… I'm not sure if I gave…" Nick began – he intended to clear-up the situation by being direct. He was in a relationship, and wasn't looking for a hook-up – although the relationship hardly mattered: Hook-ups just weren't his thing.

"Don't worry, Geordie." Mr. Muscle interrupted. "It's cool. I'm not judging you. Relax. Seriously, I'm a DJ: I see people taking all sort of shit – that's their business. Personally, I'm not into drugs though. I…"

"You said you do steroids." Nick interrupted him.

"Yeah man, but steroids aren't drugs – not real ones. It's not like shooting-up on heroin or knocking back E on a Friday night. Nick swallowed, to preventatively stop the shame and anxiety from resurfacing. He'd had enough of thinking about whatever was in his system and the heroin in his sister's. Mr. Muscle tapped his exposed knee and gave a quiet laugh. "Look, man. I mean it. I'm not judging you. You're clearly into something, and that's your business."

"No – I'm not. I mean I had something last night, but I didn't mean to."

"Seriously, you don't need to explain." He squeezed Nick's thigh and pulled out a small packet of pills from his pocket. The see-through bag looked so sinister. Mr. Muscle took Nick's hand, opened it, positioned the packet into his palm, and then pressured Nick's fingers to tighten into a fisted close. "Look these ones are on me. But man, I seriously don't recommend you taking them with E, that stuff is majorly unpredictable – it'll probably be fine – but like, I cannot guarantee anything. Whereas, if you're clean, you can take one of these each morning, on a full stomach, and it will work: 100%. Trust." He patted his thigh again, and then leant in to kiss Nick. He stood immediately, clearly not expecting anything else. He stroked Nick's cheek with his fingers bent slightly inward so that the outside brushed the skin of his face. "You're sweet, Geordie. Too young for me. But you'll make somebody a very happy man. Use the steroids. Seriously, they work, and if you want anymore, you'll be able to find me here. Obviously, no more freebies. You're cute, but not that cute. Ah fuck it – one more for the road." Mr. Muscle leant down and smacked another kiss onto Nick's lips, his powerful body compressed into his slim frame. "Look after yourself Geordie."

Mr. Muscle left the cubicle. The elderly man clung to the edge of the pool. Nick sat on the edge of the bench. His fist untightened and he stared at the ominous plastic bag of pills in the palm of his hand.

PART 4

SLAYING THE MONSTER

Chapter 13 – Six months later, done with being earnest

Nick and Jack spent the summer together and after the school holidays ended, they knew they liked each other enough that they could begin having that discussion about how to move forward. Jack rented his flat in Nuneaton, but he had been left a bit of money when his dad died – not much – but enough to contribute to a deposit on a place. Nick and Heeta though, had proceeded with purchasing the apartment. They completed two months before the school year ended. Nick was a proprietor of a tiny apartment two doors down from a kebab shop in one of the best cities in the world.

His bed was empty for half of the week, and for the other half, it was occupied double. He and Jack were travelling back and forth between Nuneaton and London, to wrap around Jack's job. It was stupid.

"The travel is costing a fortune." Nick said as he lay beside Jack on the queen-sized mattress squeezed into a room that was too small for it and them. Jack rubbed his toe on Nick's shin.

"Are you asking me to move in, Mr Du Bois?"

"I might be… I know it's pretty premature…"

"Oh, so you aren't quite sure…"

"Oh, shut-up. You know what I mean." Nick took Jack's hand into his own. "But I like being with you, and it's been tough going back to seeing each other at weekends."

"I know. I've thought about it too… it would be pretty easy for me to find work here: it's not as if London is short of pubs…"

"But?"

"But this place is tiny, and it's yours and Heeta's."

"She won't mind you moving-in."

"Well, I'm not completely sure, but actually, I wasn't thinking about her…" Their hands remained together even though they had turned onto their sides to face one another.

"What are you proposing?"

"Nothing yet… but I would like to contribute…"

"Don't be coy. You clearly have something in mind – just say." Nick said. Their hands separated, as it was too uncomfortable in their position.

"I'd like us to get a place together… I have some savings – not a huge amount – and I know you've literally only just bought this place… So, I'm not proposing anything right now, just putting it out there; that if I did move in, I wouldn't envisage it being an indefinite thing… I'd eventually want us to be in a place that feels like mine too; ours…"

"I knew this would happen: not a relationship in sight for ten-fifteen years, and then as soon as I make a decision to get on with life… buy a house… settle down… a man comes along that I would have done it with…"

Jack laughed. "You haven't signed away your life. Houses can be sold, and I guarantee for more than you bought it: London is crazy at the moment – you wouldn't think there had been a major recession."

"There are still lawyers' fees, moving costs, and…"

"Those costs will be nothing in comparison to what you'll gain from the increase in the house price. I was reading an article the other day about an area that had seen prices double in five years – double. That means the owner had made more from his home than his job. Way more. His house was effectively paying him more money than his full-time job. It's insane."

"Yeah but that only works if you decide to eventually move out of London."

"Well who knows what we will want to be doing in ten years. And not necessarily – it depends on the areas."

"Fuck, you'll be in your forties, then." Nick said. "I'm not sure I can be with a forty-year-old."

"Look, Mr. hot-shot, I'd be more worried about yourself. You might be all bulky right now, but you wait until all that muscle starts drooping and sagging. Then, we'll decide who can be with who." Jack reached out to poke Nick's noticeably larger triceps."

He flexed them a little and smiled. Jack's admiration pleasured him. "So, when you say not a long-term thing… how un-long-term are you thinking?"

"I haven't thought about the details. I guess it doesn't have to happen immediately as long as I know we're on the same wavelength."

"We are."

"Good – so Christmas?" A jolt of fear stuck upward through Nick. "I'm taking the piss." Jack said. The fear sank back to its dormant state. "I imagine we could start having a look at places, perhaps next summer. It'll give us a year to find a flow; sort things out."

Nick rolled onto to his stomach but kept his head twisted to face Jack. The timeframe eased his feelings. "I can work with a year." Jack leant over and kissed him.

"So, I'm moving in."

"You're moving in."

"He's not moving in." Heeta said, uncharacteristically irate.

"Why not?"

"Nick, we've only had the place a couple of months."

"That's not a reason."

Heeta knew he was correct. "Look, ok. He can move in." She poured herself a glass of red wine, gulped half of it, and re-filled the glass before putting the bottle back onto the counter. "I'm just a bit upset. I knew this was coming; I suppose I just thought it would not happen so fast... Once he moves in, it'll only be a matter of time before you start looking for your own place..."

Nick couldn't refute her. She carried her glass over to the sofa, sat, and drank another large gulp. "I know." Nick said. Their energy softened.

"I really like living with you."

"I like living with you too." Nick stood at the kitchen counter. Heeta sighed. She knew it was pointless having the conversation. It was done. Stoically, she embraced the reality that life was inserting one its major forks; that this was the beginning of their separation.

"A year?" She asked.

"We haven't discussed the details yet. He's moving-in, not me out."

"Don't do a Fred." She said ignoring his lie.

"Sorry." He walked around the counter and sat beside her. "We said we would start looking at places next summer."

"Thank you for being honest." She was sincere. "I am happy for you – just feel a bit sorry for myself." She smiled her wicked smile, before jumping-up to change her energy. "Right come-on!" She reached-out her hand for Nick to take it. "We have to celebrate. No point fighting the inevitable." Nick stood and followed her lead back to the kitchen, or the worktop at the edge of the living room, which asserted itself as a kitchen contrary to its meagre size and make-up. Heeta reached into the cupboard, moved Nick's bottles of gin to the side, and removed a half-empty bottle of tequila. "Or at least commiserate." She said. "If I'm losing my best friend, it's at least going to be with a bang." Two shot glasses slammed the counter and the unbranded, nasty tequila, a leftover from their housewarming, poured in. "To Nick and Jack." But before either of them lifted the shot glass, Heeta clutched Nick's wrist. "No - that's a rubbish toast."

"To Heeta and Nick." He said, lifting his shot glass and hovering it in the air between them. She was moved. Her delay in taking the shot glass, and the decrease in her wilful enthusiasm demonstrated it.

"To Heeta and Nick." She said affectionately. Their glasses clinked and the liquid tossed into the back of their throats.

"Urghh." They grizzled. "That stuff is nasty."

"Come-on." Nick said. "Let's head into town for a few."

"Deal. But remember, unlike you, I am not a full-blown alcoholic and cannot function at work without a long sleep to wash away the shitfacedness."

"Don't worry. If we head out now, we will have, like, a whole 2 and half hours of drinking, and you can still be in bed for nine-thirty."

"Has Jack clocked how much his man enjoys a drink?"

"Oh, shut-up." Nick said, grabbing his coat and keys from his bedroom. "I've cut back."

Heeta snorted. "Fuck off." She said while putting on her high heel boots.

"I have." He leant down and kissed her forehead as she zipped one.

"What's wrong with you?"

"I'm happy."

"Tosser." She sprang-up, her boots fully zipped. She grabbed her leather coat and began zipping that too.

"I hadn't appreciated how much of a lesbian dominatrix you're becoming."

"I've changed my mind. You can start looking for places at Christmas." The door clicked shut behind them. Autumnal London was on its way. The sky still looked as ocean blue as an industrial port in the peak of summer, but the atmosphere had that refreshing lightness to it; the humidity had gone, thinning the density of pollution in the air. There was promise of crisp evenings to come. Heeta and Nick strolled toward London Bridge, Nick's arm wrapped around her shoulder. They both knew that they would have fewer of these evenings together.

Heeta had already left the apartment by the time Nick had finished in the shower. He decided to make breakfast before getting dressed. The freezer-draw extended, and a blast of icy air blew onto his exposed legs. The bread packet was almost empty – the last but one slice and the crust tipped out. Nick placed them into the toaster, and then filled a glass with tap-water. He drank it and filled another as he waited for the toast. In the nude, he collected his gym bag from the hallway. His most recent packet of steroids was tucked into an empty bottle of shampoo. The lid unscrewed and Nick removed the packet. He emptied the remaining two pills onto his flat palm and swallowed them with more water. Google had eased some of his anxiety to take the pills and having a boyfriend to impress gave him the final little push. The toast popped, and he placed the two pieces onto a used plate to cool while he got ready.

The full-length mirror reflected his increasingly muscular arms, and thicker torso. The steroids had worked as well as Mr. Muscle had promised, and Nick had been going back for more throughout the summer. He examined himself. Each arm flexed, one at a time, and Nick paid close attention to minor fluctuations in the curvature and gradient of the bumps. He twisted each leg, one at a time, and examined the visible throbs, admiring the way they stretched further and wider, week-by-week. His waist twisted so that his bum-cheek curved into the mirror. It was smooth and more spherical than the last time he looked. He noticed a greater elevation between it and his calf glowing beneath. He switched the focus to the other side, exchanging the foot that took the weight of his body, and examined himself there too. He couldn't believe how reticent he had been – the steroids were great.

The pleasure derived from the progress he was making on his body negated some of the drab feelings induced by his daily hangover. After dressing, he smeared butter onto the cooled toast, left, and closed the front door behind him.

On Borough high street, the 186 bus rumbled past. The traffic forced it to continually stop. Nick ended up passing it three times as he repeatedly overtook it on the pavement. The students that knew him treated him no differently in his newly prestigious Assistant Headteacher role. But his teaching hours had significantly reduced and so he found himself knowing fewer students, and having less interaction with them.

His office was spacious. He plonked himself into the twisty comfortable chair and allowed his eyes to rest for a few moments. His sister's white knock-off trainers flashed in his mind's eye. *What the fuck?* He thought, opening his eyes in the same escapist desperation as a nightmare. His palm flattened onto the front of his chest and the pulse of his heart beat faster, much faster, than usual. It rubbed against the equally disturbing throbs of his fingertips. He wondered whether he was having a heart-attack. *I'm 33.* He tried to reassure himself that a heart attack was impossible due to his age. His chest continued to vibrate beneath his palm. *Shit, what the fuck do I do?*

Several kids galloped past the outside of his office, screeching about some interesting thing that had happened. Nick massaged his heart with the palm of his hand, as if he were acknowledging its pain, reassuring it that he was listening; that he would do whatever it needed, as long as it calmed down. *Please.* He begged his body. There didn't seem to be any major changes, perhaps a marginal slowing of its otherwise continued thrashing. Through the narrow slit of glass in his door, he could see the

Deputy Headteacher approaching. *Fuck, she's coming to see why I'm not on meet and greet. Fuck, fuck, fuck.* Her frumpy frame increased in size as she got closer to the window pane. There is no way that Nick would be able to downplay this. He barely had the strength to sit straight.

His feet launched his chair backward and he tipped himself onto the floor. It took everything to not shout out in pain and fear. It was suicidal, not to mention career suicide if she found him hiding behind his desk. He arched his back and hid against the set of drawers, hoping that his feet wouldn't stick out and that the woman wouldn't walk too deeply into his office. A curt knock announced her arrival. The door opened without an opportunity for Nick to grant permission to enter.

"Mr. Du Bois?" Her voice clipped on 'Bois', surprised at his not being where she expected. The light was on, and she noticed his bag on one of the 'patient' chairs, one of the take-a-seat, lets-have-a-chat chairs. It pissed her off. His initial absence had caused her to think that he might be late, but his bag and the sensor-triggered light, prevented that. It led her to conclude that he must have been called to sort something out, which pissed her off even more, because it made her think people were relying and going to him. She snapped the door shut and clacked away. Her frame faded from the little slice of glass.

Nick held his heart in the same manner as before. The throbbing was easing. *Fuck... Fuck.. Fuck.* His inner fucks were decreasing in their intensity, complementing the sync with his slowing heartbeat. He wasn't dying.

More children galloped past his office. Schools and stables have a lot in common. Nick clutched his heart with both hands and pressed harder into the protective layer of skin, as if to both hold it in place, and also reassure that it would not fall out. There was no evidence that his hands were having any impact on the slowing of his beat, but he recognised that the harder he pushed, the more intently he willed his own inner calmness, the more it actually happened.

Then, as if a pick had found the sweet spot in a tricky lock, a gush of air inflated his lungs in one hit. There was no slow pouring down his windpipe: the air seemed to inject directly into his system, and his throat only felt the delayed exhalation of air; by which point, his body relaxed like a junkie topped-up, grateful for having what it needed. It happened as instantly as it started. Nick's hands slid down his chest, separated from one another slightly to rest on his thighs. He remained on the floor for a couple of minutes, listening to his breath like a yoga apprentice. He didn't want to spook away the normality of his once again functioning organs.

He creaked upward as if he were an elderly man afraid of unintentionally assaulting his own weak body. His shins pressed into the blue carpet to support the straightening of his back rising above. His head levelled with the computer screen and his arms leant onto his desk to take some of the weight of his shins. He got onto his feet. *Fucking hell.* He thought.

The door knocked and the Headteacher entered. He closed the door behind him, and sat in one of the 'lets-have-a-chat' chairs, although the dynamics were the wrong way around. The person initiating the 'lets-have-a-chat' didn't sit in the chair.

"How are you doing, Nick?" The Headmaster asked.

"Good." Nick lied, pretending that he hadn't just had some sort of heart seizure.

"What are you working on today?"

Nick had several non-teaching periods this morning, and the truth was that he had planned-on a few of last night's gins leaving his system before he did much of anything. "I've got a bit of marking." He lied. "… And then I was planning on having a look at the data."

"Good." The Head nodded. He left a long enough pause to separate what he was about to say from what had just been said. "Your role is very different now. It can be a strange adjustment.

Teaching fills the day for most staff – there's hardly a spare moment. If they're not marking, they're planning, or preparing for a lesson. You will appreciate this more than me being so fresh out of it. But now you are now in leadership…" His tone became weightier. "You have the space to think deeply about the running of the school. Use it."

The Headteacher stood, and his tone flickered back to its usual heavy lightness as opposed to this heavy, heaviness. "Have a good day, Nick."

"Yes, sir." He left the door open. Nick sank into his chair and held his hands on the keyboard. The screen was blank, but he wanted any passers-by to think he was working. He wanted to express a *What the fuck did that mean?* But he knew what it meant. He needed to prove that he could be proactive. His new position was not about being hand-held; told what to do. He had sold himself as having initiative and an eagerness to drive the school forward, but in reality, he was waiting for orders. He had slipped into bad habits of enjoying the additional time for his own leisure: googling about steroids, reading reviews of new bars and restaurants, scouting property, and analysing house prices. It had been two months, and he hadn't stepped-up. He knew it. *Use it* – the headmaster's efficient, direct phrase lingered, and Nick told himself that he would, but later. Right now, he needed to work-out what the fuck had just happened to his heart.

The computer loaded and *Do steroids cause heart attacks?* punched into the google search bar, letter by letter. But before Nick pressed enter, the words began to disappear. The back-space slammed into the base of the keyboard beneath Nick's finger. He needed to start being more careful, using a work computer to research whether there was a relationship between steroid-use and heart seizures was not clever. He pulled out his phone, and tried to look on his slow connection instead.

A knock on his office door disturbed his search. The phone slid into his pocket. "Sorry, Sir, can I talk to you?" The girl in the doorway asked.

"Shouldn't you be in lesson, Leanne?"

She stood silently, her demeanour haunting. The carpet absorbed into her eyes, and seemed to incapacitate her other faculties. "Leanne?" Nick tried to get her attention, but she was somewhere else. "Leanne?" He tried again and stood after she failed to respond that time too. "Leanne, what's wrong?" he said walking around his desk toward her. His movement stirred some consciousness and she regained some awareness of where she was. "Leanne…" His tone changed. It was no longer a question with an expectation for her to respond. It was now just a statement, a simple acknowledgement of her identity. "Leanne… Leanne, come sit-down." Now it was an instruction. She didn't need to think or respond intellectually, she just needed to follow an order. That was simple. She could do that. She entered his office and sat on the patient-chair where the Head had sat less than five minutes ago.

"Leanne… sit there and take a few minutes to yourself. I'm going to sit at my desk and get on with some work. Talk to me when you feel ready, ok?" His ok wasn't a real question. He didn't expect a reply, not even a nod, but he said it because it acknowledged her agency; that it mattered what she thought and felt, even if that capacity to think and feel was causing her difficulty.

Leanne had been in Nick's class for the last two years. She was a quiet girl. Her clothes were tatty, but never noticeably dirty. Her hair was long and thin – wispy. With his reduced timetable, he no longer taught her, but he knew who she was. He knew that she lacked confidence, that she lived on the estate behind the school in a flat with her mum, who the safeguarding team identified as having 'problems'. These sorts of kids gravitated to Nick. There was something instinctive within that allowed them to smell-out people with the capacity to understand but not try and fix their pain. Nick felt bad for the fact that he was grateful for Leanne's presence: her suffering had taken the seriousness out of his own situation. The significance of his heart seizure faded and became something he shouldn't worry about – some weird reaction, a part of just getting older.

"Sir?" Leanne's instinct kicked-in. She recognised that his thoughts had wondered to himself and that made her feel comfortable. She loosened, breathed a little deeper, and her mind untensed, freeing her to think and process the emotions inherent to thoughts of any serious depth. "My mum is a junkie."

The image of Nick's sister sitting on the back step of his council house re-struck. It felt like God's fingers clicking the world on and off. For a brief moment, reality disappeared. The walls of his office stopped being the boundaries of perception; a vacuous black replaced them, a vacuous black that framed his sister sloping against a crumbling wall. Leanne, again, smelt that Nick was listening to her, but miraculously, without judging or condescending. She sensed that he was processing what she was saying in his own way – relating to her experience, rather than therapizing her. It gave her the security to continue. She didn't want him to do anything. She just wanted to tell someone, someone with the capacity to listen.

"Sir, she's going to die."

Leanne's calm, matter-of-fact tone caused the whites of his eyes to turn a scorched-earth red, a blooded hive of tiny veins multiplied in them. Her words slashed and stabbed at the boundaries behind which he had put his deceased sister. The pain burst through, thick, infectious, spreading down into his gut, quickly. He felt for Leanne. "She might go to prison first, and they'll take me and Donna… I don't want to go."

Nick couldn't speak even if he wanted to. He looked in Leanne's direction but not directly at her. One of his hands folded over the other, and together they rested at his chin.

A helpless silence lingered, that Leanne had become used to, but which Nick resented. He didn't want to feel this shit anymore. He was done with it a long time ago. *Why is she fucking bringing this to me?*

"Please don't say anything sir."

Nick did now stare at Leanne directly. "You know I cannot do that, Leanne. You know I can't!" His voice poured emotion into the room. He was angry at her for asking.

The indifference that she had managed since coming into his office dispersed and she became equally emotional. "Fucking tell them then! Tell them everything so that they can come and take us away!" She was like an inverted rollercoaster, gentle downward inclines went on for ages, and then suddenly shot her up.

She was heartbroken, and so was Nick. Every instinct in his body knew she was right. Social services were more than useless. They harmed families as often as they helped. Donna and Leanne would be taken away, probably moved schools – the one stable thing in their lives. They would become victims of the biggest factor fucking up kids' lives: even more than a drug-addicted parent. The state was shit. Nick knew this, but it was absolutely not something he could say aloud, or even think; in his current position, he was the state.

"I am so sorry, Leanne." He confessed and meant it. She was crying, but his apology soothed and quietened her tears. They continued to roll down her cheek, but the sobs turned silent. She knew deep down that he couldn't keep her secret, and at some level, she knew that the authorities already knew everything about her mum. She was coming to say goodbye to one of the most stable things in her short life. Nick knew it too. He felt sick at the enormous influence he was to this poor girl, who had barely factored into his thoughts – the imbalance was painful. "I'm so sorry, Leanne." His apology meant something different this time. His first apology was for her. *I'm so sorry for you, Leanne – your situation.* This time it was personal. *I'm so sorry, Leanne;* an apology conveying a failure in himself; a failure to speak up and show courage when some twat was being a dick; a failure to demand more when people ignored the bad stuff happening around them; a failure to care and fight about the stuff that mattered. A tear rolled down his own cheek as he made his apology, his confession, to poor Leanne. She nodded and offered a melancholic smile.

"You are a good teacher, Sir. Remember me." She stood and left. Nick wiped away his tear. He did not follow Leanne. He sat back down, and pushed his fingertips into the soft bags beneath his eyes. He rubbed the skin and breathed deeply to regain composure. He was not embarrassed – he was angry, militantly angry, at himself, at his own passivity. He had become a drunk, a voyeur, a watcher. The world was spinning every day, but he was standing still. The same person at the end as he was at the beginning, not in a good way. Yes, he'd bought a house, got a boyfriend – even a promotion – but they were all things that had happened to him. They had chosen him. Heeta had sorted the house; Jack had driven the relationship; the headmaster, the job. Nick lashed and mentally berated himself: *People want you because you don't put up any challenge… you go along with the flow… you're a vessel for them to project and extend themselves into. They don't know you. You don't know you. You don't love anybody.*

"I'm not having it." He said aloud. The chair flew backward as he stood aggressively. It bounced of the wall. *Don't be ridiculous. What are you going to do?*

He stormed across the silent foyer. Lessons had begun, so there was nobody about. Leanne strolled along the History corridor. Nick deliberately went the opposite way. He darted through the double doors leading to English. They slammed into the wall and filled the corridor with a smashing echo. Nick didn't care. He was looking for a fight. He had begun to pop his head into lessons – it was what the leadership team liked to do in his school – but he usually felt awkward… he appreciated how off-putting it was when somebody interrupted his own lessons to flex and peacock their authority. It fucked him off, actually. *Well bollocks.*

He opened the door to Mrs. Peters classroom without knocking as he would usually. He entered without smiling as he would usually; and he walked directly into the main space of the room rather than gently tucking himself away at the side, as he would usually. He had softened his intrusion too many times. He intended to reverse that impression of himself and make his presence known. He stared at the board and frowned at the information it displayed. "Not overly challenging." He said matter-of-factly for the whole class to hear. It wasn't challenging. The work was too easy for over three quarters of the students. "Jonathan Braithwaite is this work challenging you?" Nick asked across the class to a lovely, kind-hearted student. The other children and teacher stopped to stare at Jonathan Braithwaite.

Children are remarkably good at reading energy. The poor boy didn't know what to say: he liked Mrs. Peters and she looked hurt, but he also liked Mr. Du Bois, and he looked ferocious. Nick pressed him for an answer, but the boy was locked into indecision. He did not want to upset Mrs. Peters, but he did not want to piss-off Mr. Du Bois by lying. He looked down at the desk and went with the truth as if he were at confession: "Not really, Sir." Nick shook his head and left the classroom without saying another word. He did not look at Mrs. Peters to shame her. She needed to improve her lessons before seeing him again. He left the door open.

He continued his blitz along the corridor entering each of the classrooms in a similar fashion. He had years of unspoken critique to fire-off in one round. He had become a machine-gun zeal of authority.

"I don't understand what you're being asked to do." He said aloud to Mr. Roger's class. "Tell me what you're supposed to be doing, Sarah Waters." Sarah Waters was a sweet girl, who was born and will die eager to please. She did not know what Mr. Rogers expected her to do, and almost cried at being unable to answer. Nick manipulated the distress caused by her earnest regard for her own personal responsibility. She felt it was her fault when Mr. Rogers and Nick both knew that the instructions were shit because he hadn't thought about the lesson. Nick left the girl upset, and Mr. Roger's feeling a pathetic coward. Nick obviously didn't intend for Sarah Waters to become upset, but he had become a commander in a state of war. There would be casualties in the fight for the greater good. He moved on to another classroom.

"Show me your work!" He said to a boy who regularly disrupted classes throughout the school: Jason Wall. The book twisted around. Nick looked disgusted at the sloppy, uncared for scribbles in his book. "Are you proud?" Nick asked. Jason usually thought nothing of being rude to teachers and even senior leaders if he thought he could get away with it. But he read Nick's energy and calculated that he wouldn't win this time, combined with the fact that he usually liked Mr. Du Bois.

"No." He sulked, resenting that he had to profess standards for himself that he had fallen short of, especially in front of one of the few teachers he thought liked him.

"Mrs. Butters have you contacted Mr. Wall's parents?"

Mrs. Butters flushed. She had barely challenged Jason, let alone rung his parents. "Erm, I was planning on ringing this week."

"Today." Nick snarled while twisting the book back around and pushing it toward the boy. "Higher expectations." He meant the comment for Mrs. Peters, but Jason took it as another comment directed at him. He felt betrayed by Nick's atypical coldness toward him.

"My parents won't care. They don't care about English – they know it's a pile of crap."

Jason changed his approach. Bringing his parents into the equation changed the odds. It was one thing to discipline him, quite another to try it on his family. He didn't care about winning, his family honour was at stake. He would fight no matter the offs of success.

"Your parents won't care that you aren't trying? That you have no aspiration or enough self-worth to push yourself? They don't care about your education; they don't care about you?" Nick's words were harsh and absolute. There was no space for negotiation. Unchallengeable judgement fixed to Jason's parents. Nick distilled Jason Wall's disengagement to the simple fact that his parents didn't care or discipline him. The entire class knew – Nick knew, Mrs. Butters knew – that Nick was insulting them; insinuating that they were trash.

Nick's palms were flat on the desk, either side of the boy's book, and his back arched so that his torso leant forward, enabling his face to amplify into Jason's own. Nick's body language was aggressive and territorial – in playground speak, he was squaring-up.

"No. I didn't think so…" A whiff of coffee came through his otherwise non-smelling breath and landed on Jason's face. The contact was too much, and it was obvious that Nick had been insulting his family – He hadn't been calling the boy's bluff and suggesting that his parents did have greater expectations than he was letting on; he was rubbing into his face that he disapproved of them. He was squaring-up to them too.

Jason knew it and his pride wouldn't allow Nick to go unchallenged. His hand flattened onto his face. The centre of his palm squashed Nick's lips while the bottom of his middle finger pushed against his nose. "Get out of my face you weirdo!" His chair scraped backward. Nick too stepped back, surprised by the physical altercation.

"Get to my office now." Nick said, but the authority in his voice, and the aggression in his body language had dissipated. His conviction had dissipated. His power-kick had dissipated. The words rolled into the classroom. They were hollow, and conveyed a lack of expectation. He didn't expect Jason to do as he said.

"Fuck off! I ain't go anywhere with you, you fucking pervert. Miss, I don't have to go, do I?" Between the Jason's facepalm and the thinning of Nick's authority, Mrs. Butters had stopped hovering behind her desk. She reached-out an arm toward Nick so that her fingertips brushed the edge of his shirt sleeve. Her other arm stretched out toward the boy – her palm faced down and large gaps rested between her open fingers. She epitomised a peacekeeper in her Jesus stance.

"Erm Mr. Du Bois, perhaps Jason should go to the Headmaster's office…?" Nick was dazzled. The image of his deceased sister speaking with Leanne's voice haunted his mind. *You shouldn't have done that.* The ghostly figure repeated. He nodded at Mrs. Butters, not wanting to make the situation worse than it was.

"Yes. You're right. Go to the headmaster's office, now." A little bit of authority returned to his voice.

"But it ain't fair if I get in trouble, Miss. It was his fault. He got right in my face you seen it."

"Jason, pop along now, and we can discuss it later, ok." She said deescalating the situation. The boy grabbed his backpack, and stormed off, more for dramatic effect and the theatre of having the classes' eyes on him, than actual outrage.

"Thank you, Mrs. Butters." Nick said, clutching to the little dignity that he had left. He left the classroom too. He closed the door behind him, this time and walked along the corridor, dazzled. A student came out of the classroom behind him, and shot down the corridor in the opposite direction. Nick meandered to the side staircase leading to the Maths Department, not knowing what to do.

You stupid moron. He thought as his work shoes stumbled from step to step at a glacial pace. *Go to the Head and explain the situation truthfully.* At the top of the staircase, the Deputy Head stood in the doorway. She smiled like Jaws with the girl that had shot down the corridor behind her. The girl had the same vicious smile. He really had been moving slowly.

"Good morning Mr Du Bois. I hear there has been a bit of an incident."

"Yes. I hope the young man has been isolated." Nick said. The smugness of the Deputy Head pushed him to tap into a deeper reservoir of strength that he didn't know he had. The will to fight back and politically manage the situation, pulled him out of his meandering despair – he didn't want to fuck things up. He would sort this. He continued his assault, determining that it was the only way out of his predicament: the boy had hit him but Nick had provoked the situation. He knew that he could cover up his part if he really wanted to – it wasn't like he had a history or reputation for this sort of thing, but he needed to get on top of it now. "It was outrageous behaviour, and we mustn't tolerate that sort of aggression. Have you called his parents?" Nick added before Agnes could respond.

It was enough to wipe away her grin. She was taken aback by not only his confidence, but his audacity to expect her to have made a phone-call. She expected things from staff, and especially staff like Nick. She exploited their conscientious natures. She expected Nick's honesty to make things easy for her. So his counter-expectation: his demand for her support and trust, knocked Agnes off her usual predatory advantage. Their relationship did not work that way. The presumptuousness was a first strike and it pushed her into defence. "Well, I think we need to understand what happened first."

"I'm sure Sabrina already told you: the boy assaulted me by placing his palm on my face and pushing me away. There is never any justification for violence." Nick parroted a cliché, and turned on the staircase to return to the English Department as if there was no more to the matter than what he had said.

"Mr. Du Bois?" She called. She did not want to give the appearance of following or chasing him, so she began trotting down the stairs as if she were heading that way herself.

"Yes?" Nick did not stop descending as he responded. He provided no space for her to easily screw him over. If she wanted to suggest he had done something wrong, she would need to work damn hard and make the accusation out right. He was done with making it easy for her. He was done with being honest, earnest Nick. The feeling of obligation that normally bound him to uncomplicated impartiality was gone. He embraced his power and partiality. His opinion and account of what happened mattered more than the dumb-fuck loudmouth he had provoked. He was the adult. He would control the narrative and ensure the rest of the class wouldn't confuse things.

"I think we need to discuss a few matters, Mr Du Bois." She said.

"I'm busy sorting this at the moment. E-mail me, and we can find time to talk later." He re-entered the corridor and strode toward Mrs. Butters classroom.

"Mr. Du Bois I do not think that is a…" She was unable to finish her sentence as Nick entered the classroom. The girl that had gone to find her lingered at her side and where a moment ago, Agnes had treated her like a valued confidant, she now expressed frustration and irritation at her still being around. "Sabrina, get back to class." She snapped.

Mrs. Butters looked like a walking knife had strolled into her room. Her face drooped and fear melted-down the little composure she had begun to rebuild. "Mr. Du Bois…" But Nick relieved her anxiety by smiling at her with his usual compassionate eyes – he demonstrated that the old Nick was back; that the old Nick had been here the entire time; that there was only the old Nick…

"Thank you for your support Mrs. Butters." Nick announced publicly. She smiled back at him as Agnes arrived in the door frame – the timing was perfect. "Thank you too Year 8. I wanted to apologise for you having to see what happened before. Jason Wall's behaviour will not be tolerated and you – as I – do not deserve to feel unsafe in our own school. Thank you for being so mature and not reacting to his aggressive behaviour despite his repeated disruption to your learning. We are so proud of everything that we have achieved at the school, and we will not allow anybody to ruin that. You are all clearly working very hard with Mrs. Butters, and I've seen the excellent progress that you are making – your test scores are excellent." Nick paused to ensure that he locked eye contact with as many of the children in the class as possible. They drank his enthusiasm and praise. "Please, if Jason's behaviour earlier upset anybody, please pop along to my office or Mrs. Thorn's or Mrs. Butter's." Nick turned to face Agnes and Mrs. Butters, each in turn. He waited for them to smile reassuringly and then waited to ensure the class registered it. He needed to make sure that it came across as them both endorsing him; a united front that would overwrite his earlier weirdness. He turned back to the class to finish his speech. "… and we can have a chat about it. I want everybody to feel safe, and feel proud."

His hands remained open while he spoke, a true politician; his palms faced the class and reinforced the peaceful, benign characterisation he was going for, and achieving. Before leaving, he thanked them once more, and then popped over to Mrs. Butters. He spoke so that the class was unable to hear. "Thanks for your support, Penny. Let's do your lesson observation while Jason is out." He winked and smiled, just about pulling-off supportive. Penny Butters smiled back. She understood what he meant, and the thought of being observed without Jason was appealing – she couldn't take another painful critique from some senior leader telling her how she needed to differentiate better so that the likes of Jason could better access her lessons. She smiled back, sealing their deal. She would downplay Nick's big man charade and focus on Jason's behaviour if asked for a statement.

"Thank you, Mr. Du Bois." She said finding her voice. "Class, let's thank Mr. Du Bois for all his kind words today." Following Mrs. Butter's lead, the class gave Nick a sincere round of applause. Nick felt oddly reassured. He knew the situation was sinister and wrong for so many reasons, but it felt good. And apart from dumb-shit Jason, and Deputy Headteacher, Mrs. Thorn, there didn't seem to be any losers: the class were happy at the thought of Jason not being able to disrupt their lesson for a while; Mrs Butters was happy at a bit of respite and the promise of a good lesson observation; Nick was happy that he wasn't going to be investigated or suspended.

"Apologies for the disruption, Year 8. Remember keep working hard. See you later Mrs. Butters." Nick said leaving the classroom with the Deputy. He clipped the door shut behind them.

Agnes Thorn stormed off without saying a word. She looked like she had swallowed a wasp.

Chapter 14 – No more toxic beliefs

Jason's parents kicked up a stink, but Mrs. Butters and Nick's insistence that there was nothing untoward prevented further investigation.

"Good work, Nick." The Headmaster dropped into his office at the end of the day. He sat back onto the 'lets-have-a-chat chair'. "You know you're doing something right when you get a few complaints."

"A few?"

The Headmaster laughed. "It isn't just the children you've been upsetting."

Nick looked sheepish. He wanted to know who else had complained about him… *Mrs. Peters? Mr. Rogers?* He thought about how rudely he spoke to them.

"Don't worry about it. You can't make an omelette without smashing a few eggs." The Headmaster said. "In fact, I insinuated that it was time for you to start cooking, so like I say, well done, but perhaps think of a few better ways to handle things next time."

"Can I ask who complained?"

"You can ask whatever you like."

"Who complained?"

"I overheard Mr. Rogers ranting to Agnes at lunch." He laughed. "Honestly, don't worry. The lazy prick wouldn't dare come into my office with his entitled bullshit. The man doesn't give a shit, and hasn't for twenty years." The Headmaster pushed the door shut.

Nick was uncomfortable. He wasn't used to this confidence with a superior and wasn't sure where the boundaries lay. The Headmaster read his awkwardness and chuckled.

"Relax, Nick. Have I ever been anything other than straightforward with you?"

Nick nodded immediately, but it was instinctual and overly deferential. He knew he should say something back, something honest, something private – the Head was confiding in him; it was right to mirror that trust, but Nick's stomach felt like steel. He had a protestant distrust of authority, a wariness that wrapped around his bones in the way fat wrapped around other people's.

"Sorry, I'm just really crap at this." Nick flushed as the words came out. He felt like he was on a date.

"Really? I hadn't noticed."

For the first time, Nick eased and cracked a smile.

"You don't have male friends?"

"You're my boss – not a friend."

"That didn't answer my question."

Nick paused, and appreciated that he had responded evasively. The question cycled through his head a couple of times… he had never thought about it. "I suppose not really; not straight ones."

"I think it's more common than you think."

"What? Gay men not having proper male friends…"

"No. Straight men not having friends."

The observation struck Nick as untrue… straight men had loads of friends. They went on stagg parties, played football, drank in pubs or fancy private members clubs. He thought about the huge numbers of people that turned up at his Dad's funeral. He had loads of friends. Straight men have loads of friends.

"You're not convinced."

"Honestly?" Nick asked and the Headmaster nodded. "I'm not. From my experience, straight men are born into belonging. It's easy for them to make friends and share their life with people."

"Wow. Now that's a bold statement."

"You disagree?" Nick asked.

"Experience, has changed my thinking on the matter, so yes, I no longer think that straight men have it as easy as you think, well, the older generations, anyway."

Nick's interest trumped his earlier reticence to engage. The Headmaster's lack of didacticism helped. There was no pressure to agree or accept his viewpoint. It was an open conversation, a chat that seemed to lack an agenda; any nuggets of truth were a bonus, not appropriated wisdom passed from elder to youth on parchment or papyrus. Nick's body language conveyed that he wanted to hear more.

"We all know that suicide rates are way higher in men – three quarters of the recorded deaths each year are men – but I don't want to focus on statistics. Statistics are much better for hiding things. They take away attention from the important stuff beneath them: all the near misses… the rates of anti-depressants… the thousands emptily going through the motions."

Nick was a Mathematician. He knew about the inherent instability and manipulation of statistics, their fickleness and malleability. The simple critique of statistic-use wasn't particularly controversial

"It's the anecdotal stuff that's changed my take. The thousands of boys that have come through the system; the dads, the uncles, the friends, the extended family members, colleagues, drinkers in the pub – the men of real life; there is something unsettled within them that becomes increasingly apparent as they age."

Nick was intrigued again. "What?"

"I've noticed how lonely so many of them become. Desperately alone and lonely." The Headmaster retained his openness. In fact, he spoke in such a way that left so much space that it came across as if he wanted to be disproved, as if he would like nothing more than finding out he had gotten it all wrong. A brief silence exemplified the depressive sentiment to which the Headmaster referred before he continued. "They're surrounded by people. Dogs, children, wives, *mates,* grandchildren, but they've stopped sharing themselves. Listen to their conversations. The substance is thin. There's little talk about who they are – their topics hook onto something immediate… sports… and there's an underlying anxiety about needing to get to the point as if they're in a perpetual court of law." The Head looked around Nick's office and noticing that Nick was still interested, he continued.

"I think they feel that they ought to be getting on with it… of course, failing to acknowledge what "it" is… They expedite life, quicken and rush it. Block out the complexity. There is little appreciation that 'it' will be over someday…" The Head shook his head as he thought about the waste of life he had seen over the years. "And the tragedy is that they seem to think they're doing it for the sake of keeping the peace. They downplay their own thoughts and feelings because they think it'll make things easier; everybody happier; when in reality it just generates resentment, in them and everyone connected to them. They lose the child and the joy within and begin to bemoan it in others – actual children. They eventually stop knowing who they really are; in what man really is. They've done everything right – gone to work, raised their families, played sport, yet there is an empty yearning left beneath it all, a feeling that life has passed them by. An emptiness."

Nick thought about his dad. He responded poetically without any self-consciousness. "… Like they've stopped wanting; like their souls have starved."

The Headmaster radiated a genuine smile – "I knew you knew more than numbers." He stiffened his back, indicating a change in tone. "We aren't just getting kids to pass exams, Nick. This job is a mission, a calling to change the messed-up history of this country and half of civilization. Our real job is to eradicate that toxic belief that human nature is brutish and harmful; that kids need educating to become decent people. It's not only bollocks. It's the crap that justifies unchecked power and let's genuinely selfish pricks get away with murder. People are all sorts of things, but on the whole, what I know for sure, is that the vast majority are not bad. Most children are hopeful and playful – the world chisels that away. We don't need to teach them how to be good; we need to show them that it's possible to balance self-interest and compassion; that one doesn't utterly negate the other. We don't only have day or night. We have both. In fact, we need both. It's our job to help children to keep hold of themselves, to let them safely explore who and what they are; not shape them into our image; not to play God. The world is full of malignant zealots, politicians, big-men-patriarchs trying to fill their heads with propaganda and recruit them into their ideological nonsense. It's our job to show them how to recognise that guff. It's our job to ensure boys turn into men with the ability to make friends; to share their true thoughts and feelings about all aspects of their life, from kinky fetishes and career changes, to gripes about their own children and the understandable desire to spend time away from them. Whatever they feel and think needs bringing to the table."

"So, you have kinky fetishes?" Nick said.

"Quote, 'you're my boss – not my friend', unquote."

"Too far?"

"No, of course not." He said laughing. "I'm proud of my ass-chaps, just don't tell anybody." The Headmaster stood. "I am your boss and sometimes you won't want to hear what I have to say, but I'm your friend too; sometimes you won't want to hear what I have to say in that capacity either…" He left a pause… "Stop taking steroids, Nick. They will give you a heart-attack."

Nick blushed. *How the fuck did he know about the steroids… shit has he checked my browsing History?*

"Nobody bulks up that much over a summer holiday without taking shit." Nick's paranoia eased. "What you do in your own time is none of my business, but you have to ask yourself why you're taking something that is damaging your mind and body, to look good. You're a great guy, Nick, you'll make some bloke very happy and it won't be because of big arms." The Headmaster opened the door, gave a friendly wave, and left.

Chapter 15 – Backlash of perpetual sacrifice

On the walk home, Nick could not stop thinking about his dad. He had barely given much thought to him since the funeral but the Head's brutal account of male loneliness wouldn't shake. Nick had never considered that his dad was lonely. He saw him through what he took to be his mother's eyes: a bit of an uncommitted drunk, a man whose heart wasn't really in it… *It…'* Nick stopped at his own vocabulary. *It…* The word swirled through his mind. It felt exposed like some discovered covert agent. Nick isolated its movement and cracked it open for interrogation. He tried to think without using the pronoun. He tried to think more clearly about his dad's life.

Nick hungered for the vocabulary that would allow him to complete his thoughts. *A man whose heart wasn't really in what? A man whose heart wasn't really in his family? Whose heart wasn't in his children?* The thoughts weren't right… They felt too charged with self-pity… *A man whose heart wasn't really invested in his own life?* Better. *A man whose heart was not fulfilled? A man who stuck around and provided for his family by choice, not feeling? A man whose heart was in a state of perpetual delay, of perpetual sacrifice.*

Like the litter blowing along the edge of the road, an overwhelming wave of sadness swept Nick along Borough high street. Despite the heaviness of the feeling, his body seemed anchorless. His own heart sank under the pity for his father, yet his body drifted like flotsam. For the first time, he felt as if he understood and saw his dad, and the crushing truth that he was gone became real. Somewhere between the Kebab shop and Blue Shi's nightclub, Nick began to mourn.

The smells and sounds of borough market, the vibrancy of the stalls, the office men meeting for a chinwag over posh coffee; the well-groomed, softly spoken men sampling cheeses for their cosmopolitan dinner parties; the yuppy men with long hair, top-buns, and multi-coloured trousers, clinging to their pints of micro-brewery lager; Nick absorbed them. He paid attention to the diversity of these twenty-first century men surrounding him, all clustered into one place and in their own ways, rejecting the traditional roles that society expected. He contrasted their freedom and easy displays of affection, to the brusque solitude and hard edges of the men chain-smoking in the pub-lounges of his childhood. He felt sorry for those men – for his dad; for their stoic, repressed, dutiful existences. He felt for his dad. He felt the pain and the loss of him. He finally felt the sadness, the sinking feeling that he would never be able to walk around Borough market and share this – his life.

A slap on the back nearly made Nick turn and punch the owner of the hand, in the face. "Hey!" Fred said. He was wearing bright pink trousers and converse pumps. "How are you doing?" But before Nick could muster a basic greeting, Fred continued waffling on. "Ryan and I are having a dinner party tonight – you should come! I did mean to text you, but I must have completely forgotten, sorry-not-sorry! Anyway, I need to pick up some cheese. Come-on, you can spare half an hour can't you?" He moved the plastic bag of fresh produce into his other hand so that he could clutch Nick's arm and pull him along toward the cheese stall. "So, how are you and Jack? It's all happened so quickly, but you know when you know, right?"

"Yeah, we're good."

"Bloody hell, Nick. Your arms are twice the size since the last time I saw you… when was it?" Fred seemed to have developed ADHD in his gay liberation. He moved from topic to topic so quickly. "It was a couple of weeks after your dad's funeral wasn't it? How are you doing?" He did actually pause this time, but even the pause came across like a scheduled event… three seconds of sentimental silence, then next question. "How's work? I saw on Facebook that you've had a promotion – congratulations!"

"Look Fred… it's been a bit of a crazy day. I'm going to head off actually. It's great to see you, but I've got a shitting headache, and I need…"

"No problem. Please, I'll give you a call. Go - you go and get some rest." He leant in and kissed Nick on either cheek like a chic Parisian aristocrat. *When the bloody hell did he become so camp?* Nick thought to himself as he began to walk away. But he stopped, and forced himself to turn back, ashamed at his own judgement.

"Fred?"

Fred turned and radiated a smile. "Fred, I'm sorry. I don't have a headache. Have you got time for a quick coffee?"

"Of course." He swept into the little distance that had grown between them and hooked his arm through Nick's. "For you, Nicholas, I've got time for a long coffee."

"I judged you." Nick confessed.

"Oh, don't worry. I judge everybody. It can be fun."

"You've become so confident."

"You mean camp."

"Well, yeah, a bit."

"I know. I'm nervous. I haven't seen you in ages, and well, you know…"

"What?"

"Well, you know… I'm happy…"

Nick laughed. "Your camp because you're happy."

"Absolutely. I just didn't want to rub it in your face… you know, because of your dad…" Nick linked his arm, the way that Fred had done to him a minute ago.

"Well I'm happier for seeing you."

"That's probably one of the nicest things you've said to me."

"I said loads of nice things to you." He said as they began walking.

"Not really…"

"Oh, God. I think I'm becoming less happy again."

Fred half-patted, half-slapped Nick's bulky arm with his grocery bag swinging beneath. "So, really, how are you?" Fred slowed down and left space for Nick to give an honest answer.

"Not great actually. Had a mega-weird day at work, and I think I've just understood who my dad really is…" A gag of emotion pulsed through Nick's throat like vomit attempting to toss itself out.

"Nick?" People around them stopped to stare. Nick's hands clutched his mouth, and it looked like he was trying to stop himself from being sick in the middle of the market. "Nick?" Fred dropped his grocery bag and placed each hand on each of Nick's arms.

"I'm ok." He said beneath the hands covering his mouth." His voice was scratchy.

People continued moving, sensing that the strange man wasn't going to puke. Fred picked up his grocery bag, but kept rubbing Nick's arm with his free hand. "Come-on. Fuck the coffee, let's get a pint." Nick nodded and allowed Fred to wrap his arm over his shoulder and chaperone him along to the Globe pub wedged into the rail arch at the back of the market.

Fred plonked his grocery bag on the bench-seat built into the window, and mumsily settled Nick beside it. "I'll get us a drink."

"Bloody hell – you are happy." Nick said mustering some humour to regain a bit of dignity.

"I'm using Ryan's card – I'm not that happy." Fred replied smiling wickedly and giving Nick a glimpse at his old tight-arsed self. The pub blended old and new. The red fabric of the cushioned seats matched the aged wood of the tables and chairs that created the backbone effect of any traditional pub. It suggested nothing specific, other than a vague notion of Englishness: the core décor wouldn't have been out of place in a pub clinging to a cliff-edge of Cornwall, or an industrial suburb on the outskirts of Manchester. Whereas, the glitzy brass poles shooting upward from the countertop of the bar, and the provocative pieces of art stretching toward the disproportionately high ceilings, complemented the mostly hipster cliental, and undeniably reminded everybody that this pub was at its heart a cosmopolitan watering hole in the centre of London.

A young woman stood at the bar, wearing a jumper that was at least three sizes too large. She wore it for fashion, and it worked. However, the sight took Nick back to his sister. He stared at the woman, but saw Eve. The woman's jovial smile, and bubbly disposition mutilated into a painful frown, eye bags that sank; pupils that looked-up. The woman wore retro trainers that gave the effect of being worn and tatty, but were expensive and designed that way. Nick stared at the way one of the laces drooped onto the floor. He remembered the concrete step on which Eve sloped in her hand-me-down trainers. Her Geordie accent leaked out a breathless "please". She wanted, needed, money. Nick listened to the rustling of somebody else close by, probably his mum, tearing her way through her handbag in pursuit of her purse. A note threw over his hand and landed on the floor between him, his mum and Eve. The screech of his mum's "there" echoed and amplified.

"Over there."

"Oi, stop fucking staring mate. It's weird." A muscular guy with a top-bun, who had been standing beside the woman pushed Nick on the joint of his shoulder blade. He had asked Nick a little more politely – or at least, less aggressively, a couple of times, but Nick had zoned out.

"Hey – hey, what's wrong?" Fred returned with two pints in his hand.

"Your mate is perving on my girlfriend."

"He's gay. So, 100%, he is not perving on your girlfriend."

Fred's comment disarmed the guy. He pulled back, frowned and shook his head. "Is there something wrong with him, then?" Nick looked spaced out.

"His dad had just died." Fred stretched the truth.

"Oh, right. Sorry pal." The beefcake hipster said more to Fred than Nick, who still seemed unfazed with the prospect that he had nearly landed himself in a fight. The guy patted Fred on the side. "Good luck with him, man."

The guy returned to his girlfriend, but they moved to another side of the pub. Fred placed Nick's pint on the table and nudged it toward him. "What was that about? What's going on?"

Nick shrugged. He didn't know what was going on. Fred sat on the chair opposite, but sensing Nick had drifted to a dark place, he moved to sit beside him. He rubbed his knee. "Come-on: it's time to talk. Tell me what's going on? I've never seen you like this… you're worrying me."

Nick swallowed and shook his head. He wanted to speak, but he didn't know what to say. He took his pint and drank a large gulp, hoping it would break his paralysis. "It's not going to make any sense…"

"It doesn't matter. You obviously need to get something of your chest."

"… I'm seeing things…"

Fred tried to contain his reaction, tried to prevent his face from looking like he was sitting next to crazy. He was prepared for an emotional heart-to-heart, not a ghost story.

"See – I told you."

"No. Don't be stupid. I'm listening." Fred found a source of self-discipline and stopped himself from being dismissive. He urged himself to just listen.

"…I keep seeing my sister."

"Brook?"

"No."

Fred didn't understand. "I don't get it, Nick."

"I had another sister."

"Oh, sorry, I didn't realise…" Fred took a gulp of his pint, hoping Nick would elaborate. He thought back to Nick's dad's funeral and remembered the non-vicar mentioning a late daughter. He felt guilty that he hadn't probed further. Nick didn't elaborate, just as he didn't back then, but Fred persisted this time. "…And you're seeing her ghost?"

"No – don't be stupid." Nick snapped… "Let's just forget about it…" They both took a drink. Fred was stumped. He didn't know how to respond to Nick's seeing dead people.

"Have you been taking drugs?" He didn't mean to sound so condescending.

"No." Nick placed his pint with a bit of a slam.

Fred directed his eyes toward Nick's biceps. "Not even a little something to help with those?"

"Fucking hell Fred, steroids don't make you hallucinate."

"Ok, so you have been taking some drugs."

"This was a bad idea. Let's just forget it ok." He downed his pint. Fred watched three quarters of the liquid disappear in a few seconds. The table legs scraped the floor as Nick pushed it away to give him more room to get out.

"Oh, come-on, Nick." Fred said.

"I've got to go and meet my heroin dealer." Nick chided.

Fred swigged his pint, but Nick had gone before he could say anything. The pub door slammed into the brick-wall as he stormed back into the market. His shoulders bashed into oncoming pedestrians, causing them to twist and ricochet out of the way. Anger had erupted within. He was irrationally furious at Fred, at all the stupid dandies flouncing around the market like airheaded princesses. He wanted to fight, a real, tight-fisted visceral fight. He wanted to throw nose-busting, bruise inducing punches. He wanted the world to pay. He forced into an oncoming woman and sent her crashing into the flower stall. The sound of a metal bucket bouncing on the pavement drew the attention of even more people. Many hissed and muttered condemnations. Three ladies rushed to help the woman back onto her feet, while the stall owners tried to salvage several bunches of flowers that had been squashed and bent out of shape. Though nobody followed or challenged Nick directly. His tornado-like advance pressed on.

A small queue for the cash-machine halted his storm. His destructive blitz needed cash. He checked his phone while waiting along the window-front of Tesco-Metro. Jack had sent an essay of a message. *Hey, I wanted to surprise you when you got back to the apartment, but I'm here. For good. I had a job interview this afternoon at this swanky restaurant… and I got it… they want me to start ASAP, and the pub are happy to release me straightaway – they've just taken on a couple of extra staff… can't quite believe it… Anyway, I'm here. Wanted to surprise you when you got home, but am now thinking that you might have something on…? Don't worry – I'll make myself at home ▢ We'll be seeing lots more of each other. See you whenever you get back xx*

By the time Nick had read it through three times, the queue had thinned. He should have felt elated. He didn't. He wanted to go-out, get smashed into oblivion, return to his empty bedroom and pass-out in his double bed alone. There wasn't time or space for Jack. The phone slid back into his pocket and his cash card slid out of his wallet. His middle finger struck the keypad and requested £250. The machine declined the request with a tragic *Out of funds* message. Pay day wasn't until Friday, and his overdraft was already maxed. The additional bottles of gin, packets of steroids, and travelling back and forth to Nuneaton had taken its toll. The cash machine ejected the useless card. Nick's fingers pressed against the smooth edge of another. He didn't pull it out of the wallet immediately. It was the card for the mortgage account that he shared with Heeta. A direct debit transferred money into the account automatically every month, so there was enough for the repayment, and a bit extra that built each month, a pot of reserves for house repairs, bills and other shared expenses. It was very mature. They trusted each other and thought it would be a clean way of handling things. Nick had never taken anything out – that was the idea.

The welcome greeting glittered on the small display screen, and Nick stared at it, knowing that it was completely wrong to put that card into the machine. A woman behind huffed loudly to pressure him to get out of the way. He didn't move. "There are people waiting, you know." She said.

"I fucking know." He snapped, taking the woman by surprise. "I'm just deciding whether to screw over my best-friend, so if you don't fucking mind waiting a couple of fucking minutes." His body had fully turned to face the woman and queue waiting behind her. "I would appreciate it." The woman and the others, averted his gaze. Although she wouldn't say anything else, she continued to purse her lips and maintain a scrunched-up face that conveyed she was still pissed-off.

Fuck it. The card sucked into the machine. *I can transfer the money back into the account at the weekend; she'll never even need to know.* The balance surprised Nick – he knew there would be a healthy amount, but not as much as there was. Nick took as much as the machine would allow, and sarcastically thanked the queue as he left. The woman kissed her teeth, but Nick was done with London Bridge. He was going out-out.

The tube shot him beneath the river and tossed him out of Charing Cross station. Nelson's column welcomed him toward

Trafalgar Square, but he dived into Halfway-to-Heaven before getting there. The underground gay Karaoke bar was packed as usual, Thursday nights especially so.

"Nicholas, darling. It's been too long!"

"I know Simon – it's been a shit-fuck of a week, and I need a large drink." Nick surprised himself with his communicativeness. He usually did sultry and mysterious.

Simon's smile stretched wide. "You've come to the right place, darling." Within an hour, Nick had tossed back at least six gin and tonics, which in that pub meant way more gin than tonic. It must have been at least a half a bottle, because Nick began to feel the effect, and it usually took at least that.

Countless men swam up to Nick through the dense pool of bodies. They wrapped their hands around his new-found muscles and admired his beautifully solid physique. Nick encouraged them. He was done with the introversion and decency. He actively flexed his arms, and lifted his work shirt so that his belly button and snail trail of light hair exposed itself to the drooling men.

Nick requested another drink, and although Simon's husband, Xavier, began making it immediately, he looked uncomfortable. He had no problem with the alcohol in and of itself, he'd supplied Nick before, but he noticed something different within him – the reason for his wanting to drink had changed. Before, he did it to put himself at ease, to loosen himself up; calm himself down; allow himself to relax so that he could mix and enjoy himself. But now, there was a darker force at play. The alcohol was fuelling a more monstrous, destructive impulse. "Perhaps, you want a water, Nicholas?"

"What? No, I'm good with another gin – I'm celebrating."

"Veridad? True? What you celebrating?" He asked.

"Life. Risk. You told me, 'no es life. No es risk, eh?'" Nick imitated his accent, but it came across dismissive and rude. Patronising.

"What are risking?" Xavier asked, ignoring the provocation in his tone.

"My boyfriend is moving in." Two men had their hands on Nick's exposed torso; one was increasingly moving upward toward his nipple, which for now was still covered by his shirt.

"Boyfriend?" One of the men said. "You tease, you."

"We'll see about a boyfriend." The other one said, slipping his hand toward the belt of his trousers, signalling his intention to try and get beneath. Nick laughed, cruelly indifferent to how Jack would feel.

"Hey boys, give space, eh? Five minutes." Xavier said. The men sulked, but they respected Xavier, and so honoured his request.

"What the fuck?" Nick snapped. "We were only having a bit of fun."

"No es fun, Nick. You no feel good. Fun good feeling." He spoke matter-of-factly and Nick resented it. He didn't want a pep talk from some pseudo-father figure attempting to keep him passive and polite, a rule-follower, incapable of putting himself first, and living fully.

"Fuck you. You don't know me. I asked for a drink, not a therapy session. If you don't want to do your job, I'll go somewhere else."

"When you want to talk, I here." Xavier picked-up a dishcloth and squeezed it into a washed glass.

"You're not serving me?"

"No, Nick. No right. I no help you destroy yourself. You want. You go." Xavier dismissively waved his hand at the exit. He did not look at Nick.

"Fine."

The Karaoke singer stopped. He and the other men, stared motionless. The music for Gloria Gainer's *I Will Survive* played with the lyrics muted. Nick walked out the door. Simon followed him.

"Please Nick, darling. Don't go. He didn't mean to upset you. It's just his way." He called from the bottom of the staircase.

"His fucking way with what?"

"Of helping."

"I don't need help. I need a drink! When did the world become obsessed with interfering in everybody else's business? Who the fuck are you? You run some shitty backwater, underground gay bar with a husband that I've barely seen you speak to. Go and play some more pop music, you sad pathetic man, and then get another face-lift to hide your patheticness." Nick did not stick around to see the hurt he had inflicted. Simon watched him fly out of the main doors on the ground floor.

The air struck his face. *Bring it on.* Nick bashed into tourists and pedestrians. Middle-class women tutted as he barged their shoulders and knocked their handbags out of his way. Suits and older men shouted "Watch-it" at him. Younger men saw him coming and moved.

He bobbed from bar to bar in Soho, buying horrendously expensive rounds for everybody and anybody on their shared card. He was paralytic drunk before dark, knocking back shots and mixing drinks as if he were at an all you can eat buffet. Nick wasn't used to being drunk in this way. Alcohol had become part of his life; a staple that he lived with. Its power to effect dizzying, destabilising manic depressiveness was now a rare occurrence. To Nick, it had become a habitual way of blurring and fading reality, not make it spin, dance and energise chaotically.

He became gregarious. He flirted with attractive men, told jokes to groups of people he'd only just met (and bought drinks). He was the life and soul of the party. Then he would crash, offend his new friends, and move onto another bar to repeat the process. The debit card of their shared account sliced through card machine after card machine as freeloaders drank away his and Heeta's savings.

By the fifth circle of friends, he was bored. Mid-way through telling the same joke he had used with another group, he stopped. The group stared in amazement at their eccentrically generous friend. They thought he had paused for dramatic effect. Nick walked away without explanation. He left the bar. They lingered in silence, wondering what the theatrical chap was up to. They stood waiting for the big reveal as if they were in a West-End show. Nick had plodded half-way along Old Compton Street before they accepted he wasn't coming back. They shrugged and enjoyed the expensive cocktails he (and Heeta) had bought them.

A strong smell of cannabis wafted as Nick drifted into a side street. The cobbled pavement appeared to dance beneath his feet. Two men with long, wavy hair toked a joint that continually passed between them. Nick wasn't into it. He's smoked it a few times, but it wasn't his thing. It made him shit. He stumbled along and made the wise decision to abstain from asking them for some.

Nick re-joined the main labyrinth of streets and wound his way into Soho square. The air thinned and the crowds of drinking picnickers mostly dispersed. A few camp men with bald heads congregated around a bench. They were more of a mess than Nick. They were dancing like hippies on acid, with cartons of cranberry juice wavering and spilling in their hands. Nick drifted through their little party. One of the men hooked his arm around Nick's neck and passed him his carton. Nick sipped from it and handed the cartoon back to the man, who had begun to twirl. One of the other men sang incoherent mumble jumble, more of a drunken slur than a song, and not overly loud. But to Nick, the volume amplified unnaturally. It scratched and hurt his ears. He swept away from their weird, spaced out groupie and wandered onto an empty area of grass. He dropped his exhausted body and fell flat as if God had switched his off button. Pink strips of cloud stretched across the sky, but Nick's eyes clamped shut. The world turned off as the drink, the LSD from the juice, and the exhaustion from his day combined and became too much.

Denser blocks of black cloud forced away the pink, and covered what little blue remained. Night invaded the sky above Nick's sleeping body. The few drinkers left in the park packed up and left - the group on LSD had already spiralled away. Wretched, homeless addicts swept in. A trio pointed at Nick, then crept over to poke and prod his stomach. They were checking to see whether he was as unconscious as he looked. Their dirty finger nails and unwashed hands padded his trousers. They slipped into his pockets and removed his wallet and mobile. The £250 from the cash machine slid into the darkness of their own pockets. The cards and wallet itself were worthless. They tossed them onto his stomach.

Their snake like wrists slithered down his forearms to check for a watch. They tore at his sleeves and took it. Their hungry eyes moved to his shoes. They untied a lace and wedged one off. His cheap white sock fell to the grass. They began on his other shoe. They were like rats: if given the time, they would eat his flesh after removing everything of value.

A husky Spanish voice bellowed from one of the park gates and the homeless addicts scuttled back into the shadows from which they came, as quickly as they emerged. Xavier stomped over. He reached down to examine whether Nick was ok. Despite looking like one of the wretched thieves, he wasn't hurt. Xavier gently slapped his cheeks and called his name. He was flat out.

Xavier forced his arms beneath Nick's body and scooped him into a lift. Nick's legs flapped over one of Xavier's arms and his feet flopped to the side. One foot had an untied lace that bounced through the air while the other foot bobbed along shoeless. He looked like a vulnerable baby narrowly saved after being ravished by wolves, but he was as heavy as a 6-foot basketball player. Xavier would not be able to carry him for long.

As they paraded along Old Compton Street, they looked like something out of a movie: Nick's head tilted into Xavier's bosom while Xavier, headstrong, willed and literally carried Nick onward like some hero retrieving his fellow from a battlefield. People in restaurants and bars stopped. Waiters stopped taking orders. Yuppies stopped drinking their prosecco; gays stopped sipping their cocktails. Smokers' cigarettes burned that little bit longer. The street absorbed this odd, epic scene – Nick unaware of it all.

Xavier stopped at the church tucked into the street opposite The Village. He lumbered through the gate and laid Nick onto a small patch of grass. His muscles ached and almost spasmed. He was used to carrying heavy crates – he'd run bars for most of his life. But Nick was heavier than two stacks of Budweiser or a barrel of Guinness. He sat on the grass beside Nick, to regain his strength.

People stared through the aggressive railings that separated the church grounds from Soho's party pavements. They were intrigued, but as tends to happen in large cities, not enough to intervene or get involved. They toddled on and within a few minutes, Nick and Xavier went unnoticed. Their Game-of-Thrones come Lady-Godiva-like parade along Old Compton Street reduced to legend. *Remember that old bloke carrying the unconscious beaten-up boy through Soho?* The event already exaggerated.

Nick began to splutter. Xavier twisted in the hope that he was waking-up, but Nick's coughing lips had no bearing on his clamped eyes. He was out. Xavier braced himself for the second stint. He needed to cross Shaftsbury Avenue, negotiate China town, and then he could break in Leicester Square. He had never been more grateful for London's oases, its little green square parks.

"Bloody hell." Xavier said as he heaved Nick into the air and set-off. Luckily the traffic was atrocious outside the Les Miserable theatre and so he was able to swerve between taxis and diplomatic limousines, without having to stop. It was a good job, because Xavier's arms were giving way. Nick was close to ending-up on the pavement of the West End. People stared with much greater alarm outside of Soho: *What's he doing with that poor boy? Is he a pervert-psychopath? Has he killed him? Is he performing some voodoo ritual?*

Nobody challenged or interfered though. In fact, people moved out of the way, for which Xavier was glad. It made the walk a little less burdensome. The stint between the church and Leicester Square was shorter than the stint between Soho Square and the church, but Xavier's arms experienced twice as much pain.

He dropped Nick onto the grass less delicately. His muscles didn't have the energy for the luxury of a soft land. "Mierda." He said to himself. People stared more unashamedly through the less territorial iron fence ringing the park inside Leicester Square. But again, within a few minutes, they lost interest. Nick was out of Xavier's arms. He was just a drunk laying flat on the grass – his exotic, intriguing status nosedived. He became a simple druggie-drunk of no interest.

"Estas perdido…" Xavier said like a man talking to a coma-patient. "Pero, no durara." He leant his hand on his shin and patted it gently. "Pero, no durara." He repeated: *It won't last.*

"Ooomf!" He heaved him back into his arms and made the short stint back to his bar. Xavier called down the staircase for help. A guy, close to the door, heard. He peered around and saw Xavier at the top of the stairs holding an unconscious young man in his arms. He screamed into the Karaoke bar and Simon rushed out, with a small army behind him. They began trampling up the steps, but Simon stopped mid-way and scorned them for following.

"No. No. Back down!" He waved his arms dismissively toward the bar, gesturing that they should be given space. The men sulked back into the bar upset that they would miss-out on the drama. "Oh my God. What happened?" Simon asked Xavier before immediately speaking at Nick's unconscious face. "Oh, you poor darling."

"No serious. Drunk!" Xavier snapped. He wasn't annoyed. He was in pain: his arms felt like they were going to drop off. He needed his husband to open the door to their flat above the bar so he could lay Nick down. His eyes bulged out to express his pain.

"Oh sorry, darling." Simon said to his husband. He rushed past. Keys jangled in his hand. His fingers sifted through to find the one to their flat. It scrambled into the lock. Simon pushed their door open and dived in so that he could hold it from the inside. Xavier passed through and began the tortuous ascent up the staircase.

"Mierda!" He shouted over Nick's twitching face. Nick's eyelids flittered, but he remained out.

Chapter 16 – Facing the music

Yellow and green checked wallpaper gave the effect of waking-up in a benign grandparent's house. No style, but complete love. The warming drone of morning London hummed outside. Nick's eyelids peeled open, and the room imprinted itself on him. His body was weak. He had no idea where he was and although he knew that he ought to care, he didn't. He lacked the strength and motivation to move. The place seemed nice. The bed was warm. Life could wait. Cleaning-up his mess could wait. Heeta and Jack's panic could wait. *Oh fuck.*

His hand rubbed his forehead and shaded his eyes. The memory of what he had done returned. *Shit.* A deeper despair crept into his stomach as he concluded that he must have gone home with some man. He couldn't remember anything after a couple of guys smoking weed in a side street. *The place doesn't look like it belongs to a dope-smoker.* Nick paid greater attention to the room. He became aware that he was in a single bed; that his head was pressed against a single pillow and that there didn't seem to be an imprint of anybody else's head. The duvet smelt fresh, much fresher than he did. *Where the fuck am I?*

The serenity of the room, its yellow and green pastel colour scheme and gentle figurines began to freak him out. A kinky black and red double bed with a load of leather underwear would have at least allowed him to work out he'd gone home with a sex addict – not his usual thing, but not beyond belief given that he was shit-faced in soho. This was weird though. *Have I been kidnapped by some Kenneth Williams Misery freak?* Panic struck. Then, the realisation that his phone was missing intensified the panic. *Work.* His heart thumped. He whipped the duvet off and ran toward the door in his boxer shorts. He expected it to be locked, and so yanked the handle. The door flew open and smashed into the wall creating an almighty bang. Nick scrambled for his trousers and T-shirt. With them scrunched in his hands, he ran onto the corridor, but the house was not the horror story his paranoia would have him believe. Doors were open everywhere – the place felt light and easy – relaxed. Ahead of him was a kitchen with a circular round table covered in a homely tablecloth. Xavier had a piece of toast in one hand and a cup of tea in the other. He twisted his head and saw Nick standing in the hallway holding his bundle of clothes.

"Bathroom is on left door. Toothbrush on top cupboard. You can have." His toast crunched.

Nick felt mortified. He went into the bathroom without acknowledging Xavier. *Fuck I wouldn't have slept with him surely?* He climbed into his trousers, slid into his shirt and threw water into his face. He looked as wretched as he felt. Brushing his teeth at least, gave some comfort. As the bristles took away the scum clinging to his teeth, he told himself that all mess can be cleaned. He slurped water from little pools of it cupped into his hands repeatedly, and then willed himself to face the music.

He opened the door and heard the song of a beautiful Spanish guitar player radiating from the kitchen. Bare foot, he entered.

"Hello darling." Simon said pouring boiling water into the teapot. *Fucking hell – I didn't sleep with them both, did I?*

Xavier kept his head in the newspaper as he said hello. Nick took a chair without being asked to sit. He assumed they were past formalities.

"How's your head darling?" Simon asked, placing a plate of toast on the table in front of Nick.

"He should apologise first, Simon."

"Xavier, enough. The boy doesn't need a lecture."

"Si! He no need a lecture. He need to apologise."

"Sorry." Nick said out of instinct. He didn't know what he was sorry about, but he felt it nonetheless. He knew there must be something. "I'm really sorry..." He repeated. His voice was earnest.

"Very hurtful things you say to Simon. We hear. We listen. But important you say sorry."

"He just did, Xav. Give him a break."

"He no knows what for." Xavier put his paper down and looked at Nick. "You speak very nasty to Simon. Very hurtful. You remember?"

The memory of Simon standing at the bottom of the stairs in Halfway-to-Heaven thickened; the word pathetic spat-out of Nick's mouth and rolled down the staircase to smack Simon in his plastic-surgeon face. Nick nodded ashamed at the memory.

"No need for feel shame - that about you. Feel sorry. This is about Simon's feeling."

"I'm sorry Simon. I shouldn't have said those things. I was…"

"Darling I know. You don't need to apologise."

"Es no veridad! It is important Simon for Nick to feel sorry."

"And he has. Enough now."

Xavier eased his assault.

"I am sorry Simon. I didn't…"

"Darling, no more. Please?"

The Spanish guitar poured from the radio and filled the silence. Simon rubbed Nick's back affectionately and nudged the tub of butter toward his plate. He then left the two of them alone in the kitchen. The rest of the song played out. The simplicity of the strings was beautiful.

"You are lost." Xavier said, controlling his English. "You will not find yourself in a bottle of gin or angry at world."

"I know."

"You listen now." Xavier interrupted him with an authority that conveyed he shouldn't speak. "You are also not lost. You know who you is, but you are run away. Why?"

Nick saw his sister at the table opposite. She sat in the spare seat and held her hands together. More girlish and innocent than her usual desperate appearance on the step. Nick didn't react to her. He allowed her to sit. They sat together, the three of them. Nick glanced at her a couple of times in the silence Xavier provided. Her eyes remained locked on him. Each time he looked up, he met them, and for longer than the time before. Xavier sat patiently as Nick transitioned from an inward posture where his eyes sat on his lap, to a bold stare ahead. Xavier watched his eyes lock onto the empty chair at their table.

"What you see?" Xavier expected Nick to answer now.

"My sister."

"What she say?" Xavier did not flinch but continued to expect Nick to tell him the truth.

"Nothing." His sister stared at him.

"What you say?"

Nick broke his gaze to look at Xavier, surprised by his question. He repeated himself. "If she no speak, what you say her?" Fear stung Nick like a queen bee. Royal venom seemed to rush through his gut and make his legs weak and his head light. The idea of speaking to it felt repulsive. Nick was afraid of looking back at her. He looked like a little boy trapped in a situation where he was desperate to, but intent on not, crying. His lips waivered and his airflow became chaotic. Breathes didn't go deep enough in and so he hyperventilated. He couldn't speak to her.

"What is wrong with you?" Nick snapped at Xavier. He knew she was watching him; them. Xavier didn't flinch. He remained patient and unfazed, mirroring none of Nick's emotion. "Why are you encouraging this?" Again, Xavier displayed no reaction. He sat, heavy and present. He listened intently. But he did not allow Nick to run away by turning the situation into a ridiculous heated argument that distracted them from the important issue. That trapped feeling returned. Nick stood to inject and reclaim power. It didn't work. Xavier and his sister looked upward to him, which made his helplessness feel amplified – broadcast. He fell back into his seat and without anywhere to run, met his sister's gaze.

"What do you want?" He asked.

She stared at him in her usual silence.

"What do you want!?". Ten years of indifference escalated from acknowledgement to impassioned fury within a sentence as his civil request mutated into a ferocious demand. Rage missiled across the table. Ten, twenty-years of repressed emotion, of pain, of hatred, of love fired across. The plate of toast, cutlery and butter flew onto the floor as Nick swept it all away. The smash did not faze Xavier. He remained in his heavy, calm posture. He did not react. Nick breathed deeply. His palms pushed into the displaced tablecloth. "What do you want?" His voice reduced to a plea.

Xavier stretched his arm and laid it on Nick's shoulder. His sister shifted her eyes to observe the spot where Xavier's hand touched his shoulder. Nick's eyes filled with tears and several droplets broke through. They trickled down his cheek as he watched the subtlest flicker of life return to Eve's eyes. He watched her desire the hand resting on his shoulder; he saw a deeper need in his sister: the human need for love that went beyond the junkie's need of a fix.

With tears rolling down his face, he acknowledged his deceased sister. He properly looked at her and allowed her to look at him. He stopped keeping her at bay, and the flicker of humanity in her eyes caught fire. Like a tinder box, her entire face ignited. Flames chewed her hair and warmed her burning lips. A burnt orange shrouded her cheeks. She was completely ablaze, but beneath it she was smiling. For the first time since they were children, Nick watched his sister smile.

The light and heat from the flame wrapped itself around Nick too. The kitchen faded and the table disappeared. The illumination spun and squeezed Nick and his sister together. He felt her inside him. Her heart where his heart was. Her eyes where his eyes were. Her feet and hands in his.

Then like that divine flick of a switch, she was gone. The fire was gone. The kitchen was back with the cutlery and broken plate scattered over the floor. Xavier sat on his chair at the table, his arm still resting on Nick's. They were back as they were. Nick looked at Xavier. "She's gone." And she was.

He rubbed Nick's shoulder and smiled. "No more running."

The sun blossomed over London and Nick strolled along the embankment to his apartment. Xavier and Simon had filled him in with last night's events. Xavier told Nick about how Simon had pleaded to go out searching for Nick after his blowout at the bar: he knew there was something deeply wrong. Xavier told Nick about his bumbling along Old Compton Street asking people if they'd seen someone of his description and the stories they told him about the gregarious man that had been buying strangers expensive drinks.

He knew he had a lot to fix. Jack would be worried sick. Heeta would need talking down from murdering him once she found out how much of their shared account he'd blown, and work would need reassuring that he hadn't died. But none of it fazed him. The ghost of his sister stuck in his mind had left. She was gone; no longer locked as a prisoner. His mind was no longer exhausted with the maintenance of her incarceration. It was indescribably liberating. His mind felt like it had discovered new rooms – new wings – that it didn't know existed. Space for life and memories that he didn't have before. Space for people.

He had lost his keys as well as his phone and wallet, so it was lucky that Jack was home. The bell rang and he rushed to open the door. He leapt from the doorway and hugged Nick.

"I'm so sorry." Nick said.

"I'm just glad you're safe." Jack squeezed his arms tighter around Nick's shoulders.

"We thought something might have happened."

"It did."

Panic appeared on Jack's face.

"Let's go inside and I'll explain." The Edwardian door shut.

After showering, Nick explained everything. Jack listened intently and didn't question the surreal description of his sister bursting into flames. He knew it was the mind's way of dealing with trauma. Nick accepting the psychological damage caused by the sad truth of his sister's short and painful life. Jack listened and Nick loved him for it. He knew that he loved him.

"Where's Heeta?"

"At work…"

"What's wrong?" Nick sensed Jack's shift in tone.

"Look. I think it's better that you talk to her. Your friend Fred messaged to say he was worried and told her about seeing you at the market. So we had a sense you were on one… but then she had notifications about a load of card payments and a cash withdrawal on a shared account… let's put it this way, she became less worried at that point… just that, well you know, she seemed to think you were on a bender…"

"Which I was…"

"I'm sure she'll understand when you explain…"

Nick knew she would understand but he also knew that she would rip his head off first. It wasn't the first time a friend had screwed her over and things were never quite the same between her and Fred after that incident.

"You should call her."

Nick nodded. "I will – but I better get to work first." Jack kissed him and they said goodbye.

"I'll text Heeta and tell her that you're alive." Jack said in the hallway as Nick tied the laces of a pair of dark trainers. He only owned one pair of work shoes, and one had disappeared last night. Simon had lent him a pair of white trainers to walk home in. Even though his own darker trainers were more comfortable, he was mortified at the thought of having to turn up to work four hours late and without proper shoes.

"Thank you." He kissed Jack once more and left. It was what it was. He and school would have to get over it.

Police cars were parked on the school site. Nick rushed along the pathway as if arriving a couple of minutes faster would make a difference. The receptionist looked alarmed as Nick entered.

"What's happened?"

"One of the Year-9 girls has committed suicide. Apparently, her mother overdosed and she didn't want social services to take her and her sister away, so…"

"Leanne?"

"Yes."

Nick dropped onto one of the waiting chairs and covered his mouth. "Where's Donna?" He said against the skin of his palm.

"With social services."

Tears streamed down his cheeks. Oceans of tears. He was silent, barely breathing. "How did it happen?" He said eventually.

The receptionist was disturbed by Nick's reaction. It was sad, but it wasn't as if Nick was a family member. She gestured to a colleague for them to get someone, while she provided more information. "Jason Wall was at home. He was playing music loudly from the flat next door – his parents were at work… Leanne pleaded with him to turn it down, but he wouldn't. He kept shouting 'your mum's a junkie' through the wall and turned the music up. The poor girl was out of her mind. She obviously couldn't take it anymore. She tried to phone the police – the poor darling, but just couldn't say anything. Apparently, she left the phone dangling, took the needle beside her mum, and injected herself. Donna was left with both of their dead bodies sprawled across the living room floor.

Nick's ache gushed out and his agonising sob filled the reception lobby. The delayed mourning for his own sister and father merged with the death of Leanne, and the barbaric pain brewing in Donna. He screamed. His insides burnt and contorted. His body recoiled. It was agony. Visceral. Tortuous. The receptionists stared in horror. The police officers and the Headteacher rushed down in panic at the sound.

Nick was sobbing. Snot ran into his hands. The Head took his arm and gently chaperoned him into a meeting room. "Nick? Nick?" He repeated his name several more times, but Nick was inconsolable. He couldn't breathe through the sobs. A decade of delayed sadness frothed out of his nose. He was a complete mess. The Head rubbed his back and held his palm flat as several people approached the door.

"It's my fault."

"No. It isn't."

"It is – she came to me yesterday…" The Head removed several tissues from the box on the small coffee table. He passed them to Nick, who used them to absorb the snot and tears mixed into his hands. "She came and told me her mum was going to die."

"Nick, the authorities knew her mum had problems. This isn't your fault. What's happened? Where have you been?"

Nick had prepared himself to say there had been a family emergency, but it seemed too disingenuous given the situation. "I…" He didn't know where to begin.

The Head stopped rubbing his back, sensing that Nick had calmed. He continued to pass fresh tissues.

"I'm sorry… I… My sister died of an overdose too." He changed the topic to try and explain his current emotional state. The Head nodded, but remained silent and present as Xavier had done earlier that morning. Nick regained composure and felt a flush of embarrassment, but he also recognised that the situation had escalated too much to hide in that embarrassment. He needed to tell the truth, for better or worse. He needed to tell the truth and allow his life to move in accordance with that truth.

"Jason should never have been suspended. It was my fault. I provoked him."

"Nick, we don't need to bring that up."

"Yes, we do. It was my fault he was suspended! It wasn't right. I pushed him. I was childish, offended his family to shame him. Then, covered it up. And now she's dead."

"Nick, nobody is perfect. You don't need to bring up Jason's suspension. It will make things more awkward than they need to be."

"I can't do it anymore. I don't want to do it anymore."

"You're emotional."

"No. I'm done."

"Done?"

Nick met his stare for the first time since entering the room. He had wiped his tears away, but his cheeks were still damp. "With teaching. I'm done. I don't want to be part of the problem any longer."

The Head stiffened.

"It's broken. It needs to change." Nick hardened too.

The Head disliked his comment. It felt reckless and out of proportion, but that wasn't what irritated him. It was Nick's calm, measured voice. He was no longer emotional. Well, he was emotional, but his mother's rationality glowed behind it. He felt deeply, but he thought even deeper. He wasn't speaking from impulse or rage, but a core sensibility that was stronger than even the most devasting emotion. He spoke from heart-throbbing truth. He seemed to disregard the Head's accomplishments and suggest that he was part of some larger problem. "You realise what you're saying?" The Head said. His voice was less compassionate.

Nick nodded. "I can't do it anymore. It's not right for me."

"It's not right to help kids try and make something of themselves? It's not right to give them structure and direction. To give them a future?" Disappointment and anger charged his tone. He believed in Nick.

"That's not what I'm saying..."

"I don't know anything of what you're saying. I think you're being overly impulsive. Throwing your future away in one heated moment. Change doesn't happen just because you want it to. Don't throw everything away."

"You told me this job would involve challenging superiors."

"You're taking my comments out of context. Quitting isn't challenging; it's giving up. Tell me: what are we doing that is so wrong?"

"Leanne is dead."

"And it's sad and tragic." He paused to show he meant what he said, but that he also meant what he was about to say. "But we aren't her parents. We cannot resolve all drug addiction and family dysfunction overnight, and sometimes ever. It's naïve and unfair to suggest otherwise. You have to look at the big picture – the progress we're making overall. The difference we're making… look at how many kids are leaving more qualified and equipped for the world. It's slow but we're moving in the right direction. Leanne is a tragic situation, not something you make a life-changing decision on."

"It's not good enough. They deserve more than a GCSE that is of no value to anybody outside of the state. Something is wrong. I know it – I can feel it in my bones."

"The system isn't perfect. You know I agree that students deserve better, but that won't happen from criticising from the side-lines, irrespective of what your bones tell you."

"It's not good enough. The direction is all wrong. We're shaping them rather than letting them be."

"Oh, come on Nick. Be an adult."

"It's true. Leanne is the tip of the ice-berg."

"Not the fucking ice-berg argument." The Head was losing his temper. "We're not in an A-Level Politics class. This is reality. The world is complicated, and we do what we can. The world is in a far better state than it's ever been because we're practical."

"It's not." Nick responded. He was coldly certain of what he said. "It's a story. Something is broken and nobody is acknowledging it. You might want to spend your life bandaging wounds, but I'm not you. I'm not interested in joining a doomed mission; teaching kids to suck it up. The adults need to be adults, and stop it. Stop this charade of a mission. There is no mission. There is no need for reform. Civilisation to attain; targets to hit. Only children to comfort and accept for who they are."

The Head was furious. He felt deceived and disappointed in Nick's naivety and lack of vision. He viewed himself as a force for good. He woke-up and worked hard to move kids forward. The sense of progress motivated him. Nick was undermining a lifetime of work and accomplishment. He was the good guy and he felt flanked by his own soldier.

"You're not a bad man." Nick said, sensing the Head's fury and feeling of treachery. The authority was reversing among them. Nick began to speak as the superior. "I'm not condemning you and the profession, outright."

"Aren't you?" A sarcastic, bitter edge shaped the Head's tone.

"No." Nick said. "You're doing your best and Heads like you have made things less worse, but the outside world isn't a danger, and even you haven't accepted that. You're still scaring children; attempting to protect them from reality."

The Head's rage eased despite Nick's accusation. He appreciated and could deal with his directness. He remained silent to encourage Nick to continue.

"Change won't come from within… there're too many people that can't see beyond the paperwork and statistics. In your heart, you know it. And too many children are hiding as a result; attending because they have to, not because they feel that they belong. They're enduring and complying…" Nick slowed his speech. He wiped the dampness of his cheek even though his tears had stopped. "They're children." His voice was a plea. "They are human children. We need to bend to that. Not assume they are enemies in need of taming and controlling."

"It's a bit romantic Nick. We do our best to make the curriculum engaging, but we can't please everybody all the time, and classes do need discipline."

"I'm not so sure anymore. The need for discipline seems more of a giant reg flag – a sign of a fuck-up. The more interesting question is why children become so irritable and disengaged. What's caused them to pull-away? What went wrong with Jason Wall; when did he begin to hate school and see us as the enemy? Answering that isn't romantic. It's our duty."

"We don't always have the resources for that level of personalised…"

"And until people demand it, there never will be." Nick was releasing a lifetime of restrained anger at the state; he was telling the authorities what they did not want to hear. He was rejecting the hand that fed him – rejecting the security that kept him. "I don't want a bit of extra funding that comes with strings, the expectation of improved exam scores, a few more kids bent into line… I'm done with making the best of a bad situation."

The Head felt dejected yet also consoled. The truth of Nick's ferocious condemnation of the state chipped away some of his own moral certainty. He stopped feeling the good guy so absolutely. However, there was an equal sense that he was doing some good for Nick. Even if he didn't agree with everything that Nick was saying, he knew that it was doing him some good.

"There is less room for open conversation – like what we're doing." The Head conceded to show Nick that he was listening. "I get things have become a bit too systematised, and that not all children respond well to that; that some kids thoughts are messier, a bit random and chaotic. I get it. But these systems are easing workload overall, giving teachers more space for those that need it."

"I don't think so." Nick said. "I think teachers are increasingly unable to handle unscripted interaction."

The Head shrugged to suggest it was up for debate. "Then help us to improve things Nick. That's why you're in leadership."

Nick shook his head. "You told me once that I'd need an ego to go further. I tried, but it isn't me. I can't do it. I feel a fraud: I can smell the bullshit on myself."

The Head smiled. It was the first point which he truly conceded with an open heart. Being egotistical really didn't suit Nick. He agreed.

"It may be naïve, but I think the only way I can make a difference is by being honest. And from your own words, I can't do that without an ego… If I stay, I'll end up that annoying old fart in the staffroom room bemoaning every aspect of the job, characterising every leadership decision as some dictatorial edict on the road to tyranny…"

The Head smiled. Nick was winning him over. Maybe teaching wasn't for Nick. He listened like so many of the little boys and girls that had listened so eagerly to him.

"I can't bring myself to care about uniform; about starter tasks; about neatness of exercise books, routines, homework – GCSEs…" The heat had cooled within Nick, leaving him to speak more honestly about himself rather than argue about the future of teaching. "For the interview I tried to answer why I wanted the job: I came up with this pompous MBA nonsense about having a *thrill for resolution*…" Nick laughed, his cheeks still wet from his tears. "… When I should have just said the truth: I care and see kids. I see their pain; their fears; their hopes; their anxieties; their heroin-addict mums; their depressed fathers… their need to be loved; their need to belong; their desire to be good at something. I see it all… it's not a choice… just something that happens… I get it from my mum… I wanted the job because I'm good at it… because it's safe… because it's something that doesn't scare or challenge me…"

The Head understood where Nick was going, and he was increasingly convinced, but still wasn't sure quitting was right. "Nick think of what you could be throwing away… are you sure about this?"

Tears trickled down his cheek again as he thought of Leanne. He was sure. The tears answered for him. He wiped his nose by brushing the snot onto his hand and in turn, his shirt.

"Leanne deserved someone that wanted her. She deserved space to talk about who she is, where she's from without fear of social services taking her away, or Mrs. Safeguarding reporting her to some agency. She deserved the space to express her pain, her experiences; without teachers killing her work with red pen; diluting and reducing her self-expression with a sticker. She never had that. She was petrified every day she came to this school, and we couldn't help her. We taught her to hide. To bury that shame so deep so that no authority could smell and investigate it. It's time for me to let go; to stop trying to fix something that I can't fix."

"You're not speaking about Leanne, are you?"

Nick wiped his nose again with his sleeve. The Head, like Nick, saw people too. He saw Nick for the first time. He saw why he had been teaching. He had been compensating for the loss of his sister as a subversive force within the system. The Head's heart went out to Nick. He listened without any challenge.

"She was petrified of whether her mum would be alive when she got home…" Nick continued to speak about Leanne, but they both knew he had moved to talk about Eve. "She was petrified by the cold foster home that she visited, a precaution, a just-in-case… yet she learnt not to say a thing. She learnt the true meaning of what the authorities meant when they insistently told her to "talk to them." She knew it meant tell them everything is fine so that they could leave her alone. She knew it was a deal. Her silence for their lack of interference. She learnt quickly what authority was about. That fake motherly kitchen was a stern example to warn her to keep her mouth shut; it was a threat. It showed her what would happen if she didn't behave; if she didn't keep quiet. She would be taken. She would be put there. She learnt to shut up. We encouraged her to shut up. I encouraged her to shut up when she needed to speak."

"You need to go Nick." The Head changed his tone as a police officer knocked on the window.

"What?"

"You need to go. I don't want you getting involved in all of this. I'm going to tell them that you've had a family tragedy. That your upset isn't anything to do with Leanne. If you want to quit, do it on your own terms – not because of Jason Wall and Leanne. I don't mean to be harsh…" The Head held his palm up to the window where the police officer stood to halt and refuse his entry. He knew it would only work for another thirty seconds or so. Nick's inconsolable outburst was too suspicious given the circumstances. Half of the school was gossiping. "I mean it Nick. I'm not so out of touch as you think. If you have any respect for me. Promise me that you will not mention anything. The grief of your father has hit you and it's just become too much, so I'm sending you home, ok? Ok?"

Nick nodded. "Ok."

"I don't mean to sound conspiratorial, but you deserve this Nick – I believe in you. Not all police, and not all teachers are the same. You know this. Leanne didn't have nobody. She had you. She spoke to you. You didn't break her trust. You showed her that trust still exists and that was something. But believe me, they will not understand. Do you hear me?"

The Head twisted and saw the police officer becoming impatient at the window.

"You didn't do anything wrong, Nick – not legally. You did what you thought was best by that poor girl and if there were more people in this world like you, it would probably be a better place. But do not say anything. This will ruin you. You might want to leave and in fact, I give you my blessing. I think you need to do something that challenges you; something that scares you to the bone and makes you feel alive." He smiled, genuinely. "You are a special man that has a lot more to give to the world. But do not let this follow you. Go on your own terms. Don't get yourself messed-up in disciplinary proceedings and nasty media hunts for some dumb failure to disclose an incident on some stupid form. You know and I know that under any other circumstance, you would get a slap on the wrist, but I cannot protect you on this one. A girl is dead, and people need somebody to blame... somebody alive. Things will get twisted, and you will be in that firing line. You don't deserve that."

The police officer barged into the room with the Jaws-like Deputy stood behind. He was unwilling to wait any longer. But before he spoke, the Head jumped into action.

"Excuse me officer. I'm aware that there is an extremely serious incident, but I still have a school and a staff to look after. My assistant Headteacher's father recently died. We were having a private moment if you don't mind."

"My apologies." The officer withdrew immediately and the smirk on the Deputy's face disappeared. He closed the door to return a bit of privacy.

"There is only so long I can justify this degree of emotion on your father's bereavement before it looks funny." The Head had Nick's best interest at heart. He spoke candidly out of need, not harshness.

Nick nodded. "Thank you." They stood together, and the Head took Nick's hands into his. He squeezed them tight.

"Go and make a difference Nick. Go do something that you love; something that *your* family will be proud of. Live a life so full that Eve and Leanne would be proud. Have no regrets."

PART 5

BEYOND THE MONSTER

Chapter 17 – Five years later, Nick's song

Three champagne flutes clinked to celebrate three toasts. Heeta announced the first. "To Jack, congratulations on your first rave review." Jack's smile radiated. His eyes dipped toward the table, but Heeta's hand cupped his chin to ensure he couldn't escape the praise. "We are so proud of you." Jack had trained as a chef, and he had worked hard over the years to become the head chef at a fancy Soho restaurant. They sipped the champagne.

The flutes clinked again. This time led by Jack. "To Mrs. Patel, Headteacher and all-round badass." In her third year as Head of Department, Heeta led her students to another fantastic set of results, enabling her to join the leadership team at her school. In that position, she helped to transform the south London comprehensive dump into a high performing, proud School of the Arts. Her students outshone the grammar school kids, shipped to the outskirts of the city. Heeta's school became a beacon to the thousands of urban kids and school leaders. She inspired them to celebrate their own voices and identity; she was making kid's talents matter; she believed in them; believed that they could become accomplished members of a dynamic, creative world. She powered from Assistant to Deputy over the five years, and at 38 became one of the country's youngest Headteachers. "To Mrs. Patel!" Her wife, Miranda said – the waitress from the restaurant. The three of them sipped again.

Miranda then raised the flute to initiate one final toast. "To Nick and his beautiful voice."

"To Nick." Heeta repeated.

"To my darling Nick." Jack's flute clinked theirs.

The waitress removed their dessert plates and a collective round of applause erupted across the tables throughout the restaurant-come-theatre. The velvet curtains drew back, and Nick walked onto stage with his musicians. Fred carried the guitar he was about to play.

"Thank you everybody." Nick said into the applause that still electrified the room. No matter how many times he had performed on stage, the hairs on the back of his neck never failed to rise, nor emotion fill his eyes. He never cried, but sentiment swirled and poured out of his hazel orbs – the orbs that Sasha had once lost herself in. They now opened for everybody. The audience continued clapping and cheering. Only his singing would ease them. He gave Fred a glance and he began strumming his guitar. The violinists followed and beautiful music swept the room.

"This one is a dedicated to my mum and late sister; to Evelyn and Eve!" Nick shouted joyfully into the mic and then began singing… *"I'm better with you."*

Acknowledgements

Those that know me will appreciate some of the personal experiences that have gone into this story. It is a work of fiction, but hopefully fiction full of truth. I am grateful to the people that may identify with aspects of the characters and reiterate to them, that the story is told out of love and pride.

Thank you so much to the people in my life that have boldly stood against the harmful legacy of shame; those who have helped me to let go of my own shame. There are too many people to name, but especial thanks to my friends Carmel and Rajiv; Emma-Jo and Ben; and of course, my husband Arron and pooch Max.

More from Mark James Birkett:

Finding Fred – March 2021

What About Nick? – July 2021

Containing Brook – Coming November 2021

Please leave a review

If you have enjoyed this story, please leave a review. The number of reviews a book accumulates has a direct impact on how it sells, so just leaving a review, no matter how short, helps make it possible for me to continue to write.

Here's a link to Mark's books on Amazon. Please click on 'ratings' and then 'write a customer review'.

https://www.amazon.co.uk/Finding-Fred-Mark-James-Birkett/dp/183844890X/ref=tmm_pap_swatch_0?_encoding=UTF8&qid=1616585907&sr=8-1